EINSTEIN

by

Miles Gibson

First Published in Great Britain in 2004
by The Do-Not Press Ltd
16 The Woodlands, London SE13 6TY

British Library Cataloguing in Publication Data
A catalogue record for this book is available from
the British Library.

B-format paperback: ISBN 1-904-316-39-5
Casebound edition: ISBN 1-904-316-36-0

1 3 5 7 9 10 8 6 4 2

Printed and bound in Great Britain

www.thedonotpress.com

FOR SUSAN. THANK YOU.

'De god wat made shark must be one dam Ingin'
Herman Melville

1.

Charlie Nelson was watching TV when the stranger appeared on the roof. It was a cold night in late September and the streets were shining with rain. All day the wind had roared through the dirty city, snatching at rags and hamburger wrappers, newspapers, beer cans, plastic bottles, sucking them into the shimmering sky where they sailed like flocks of fabulous birds. Handbills swarmed over Piccadilly. A flight of empty cardboard boxes turned and tumbled over the river. After the wind came the rain, exploding from clouds the colour of gravy, drowning the city in darkness.

Charlie was slumped in his favourite armchair watching a woman in a cocktail dress flirting with a dancing pig. The pig wore spats and a jaunty topper. They were singing in praise of a microwave dinner. They were singing, laughing, dancing in circles. This tasty microwave miracle was an Instant Gourmet™ Pork Surprise. It would certainly be a surprise for the pig in the jaunty topper.

Charlie yawned. It was hot and crowded in the room. The walls were loaded with books and pictures, pencil sketches, watercolours in cheap gilt frames. Beneath the window a large pine chest supported trays of dusty houseplants, pots of exhausted cactuses, twists of ivy, a faded myrtle in a china bowl.

Beside Charlie's chair a bag of peanuts spilled on a varnished coffee table. Beneath the table an old dog moaned and snuffled in a troubled sleep. His whiskers twitched and he paddled his paws. The dog was called Einstein. He must have been dreaming of Instant Gourmet™ microwave dinners.

Einstein

Charlie didn't know that a stranger had landed on the roof. In a few hours the intruder would be stepping through the shower curtains like the Jolly Green Giant and Charlie would be screaming and his entire life would be rushing before his eyes. But now he was eating salted peanuts and watching a woman dance with a pig while Einstein snored and the rain came hissing against the window.

2.

At midnight Einstein woke up and cracked his head against the table, spilling peanuts over the floor.

'It's raining,' Charlie said, as he watched the dog trot towards the door. 'Can't you wait until morning?'

Einstein grinned and scratched the carpet. He looked like a child's drawing of a dog: a square body and a cone for a head, his tail a dash and his nose a squiggle. His coat was white, his ears and feet black, one eye was green and one eye was yellow. He wore the cordial expression of the violently insane. He was a small mongrel with a loaded bladder.

'You've got to stop drinking at night,' Charlie grumbled as he struggled into his overcoat.

It was cold in the passage. The walls gave out a damp, sour smell. Above their heads a small bulb flickered in a chipped glass shade. He locked the apartment and followed the dog down six flights of stairs to the windswept street.

At the entrance to the building they paused, breathless, bracing themselves against the freezing darkness. 'You've got three minutes,' Charlie shivered. 'Three minutes or you stay here till morning.'

Einstein growled, hesitated for a moment, and then he was running forward, his ears flying like flags, the rain on his back like a saddle of sequins. He scampered to the corner of the street and cocked his leg against a sack of rubbish.

Charlie huddled miserably in the doorway. And then he spotted the old man. He was dressed in nothing but pyjamas and a pair of swollen slippers. The rain sprayed from his face. Water

11

spurted from his sleeves. He was standing alone in the middle of the street, his head thrown back and his mad eyes fixed on the rooftops. He looked wild. He looked crazy. He looked like he'd just seen a flying saucer. He was smiling, smiling, and his face was shining with a bright, unholy light.

'Did you see it?' he shouted, when he caught sight of Charlie. He staggered forward, stopped and turned his face to the sky.

'What happened?' Charlie said, from the safety of the door-way. He peered up and down the empty street. There was nothing but rain and the rumble of drains.

'There!' the old man shrieked. 'There!' He raised his fist and stabbed with a bony finger at heaven. He began to laugh.

Charlie squinted into the sky, hidden by a curtain of sodium light. He shook his head and shrugged. What? What had happened? But the old man wouldn't wait for him. He was splashing away down the street, shouting and laughing into the rain.

Charlie caught Einstein, took him back to the safety of the apartment and dropped him into his basket. It was twenty minutes past midnight. The dog sneezed and grinned.

'Sleep!' Charlie said.

Einstein shook himself and turned three circles before he settled into the basket. Steam curled from the top of his head. His wet coat leaked a comforting stink.

When the little dog had made himself comfortable, Charlie snapped out the light, pulled off his shoes and shuffled into his bedroom. The room was warm and dark and familiar. There was an oak wardrobe against one wall, a chest of drawers and a small chair. An alarm clock chattered under the chair. The mattress farted when he climbed into bed. He lay beneath the blankets and blinked at the ceiling, waiting for sleep to press down on him.

At two o'clock in the morning he started to dream. He dreamed he'd been carried away from the room and was shrinking into the sunlit past. He dreamed he was back with his mother and father, in a house behind a privet hedge. He was three or four years old, sitting on the carpet in the shadow of his mother's skirt. His arms were wrapped around her knees and his head was buried in her petticoats. He could hear his father in the room and smell the barber's cologne as it wafted from his clothes. His father was shouting and clacking his dentures.

Charlie groaned and rolled his head in the pillow.

3.

The dog grunted and cocked his ears. It was three o'clock, cold in the room and rain still hissing against the window. He sat up in his basket and shivered. Something had shaken him from his sleep, teased his whiskers and dragged its fingernails down his spine.

He leaned forward, hung his head from the broken edge of the basket and watched the floor for the scampering shadows of mice and beetles. Nothing moved. He snuffled suspiciously at the air. Nothing. For some time he sat in his basket, perplexed, swinging his head from side to side, trawling the darkness with his nose.

And then, through the comforting household smells, came a strange and unfamiliar odour. It was the most sublime smell of wet earth, warm goat leather, soft cow dung, sweating horses, a rich and pungent flavour that seemed to gather around him like smoke. He slobbered and slapped his snout with his tongue. He was hypnotised with delight.

He scrambled from his basket, padded quickly across the room and followed his nose into the hall. The trail evaporated. He was left with nothing but the stale smell of carpet. He sat down, astonished, and looked around him. Released so abruptly from his trance the dog felt confused and frightened. He listened to the distant rain, the creak of the furniture, the tapping of his own heart and the trumpeting of Charlie's breath as it penetrated the bedroom door.

The thought of Charlie gave him courage. The stump of his tail began to quiver. He sprang to his feet and conducted a jaunty patrol of the hall, snapping and growling at ghosts. There was

14

nothing here to threaten him but the cooling scent of his own dreams.

And then, very gently, a doorknob turned and the bathroom door swung open. Einstein snarled and sprang back in surprise. A shaft of sunlight spilled into the hall like the memory of some distant summer. It was warm and fragrant and sparkled with pollen. The light carried with it a concentration of tantalising odours, grain sacks, warm hay, salt air and cedar, the sprayed scent of the wild fox, the soiled sand of the rabbit hole.

Einstein crouched against the floor. But now he was trembling with pleasure. He dipped his snout into the light and sucked at the smells that tormented him. He mewed. He whimpered. He crawled on his belly into the source of the miracle.

And the door clicked shut behind him.

4.

Charlie woke up in a sweat.

The blanket was wrapped around his neck and his face was stuffed in the pillow. He struggled to stretch out his arms like a man drowning in glue, twisted and turned until the pillow fell to the floor and his head flopped down against the mattress.

He opened his eyes, no longer asleep and not yet awake, trying to make sense of his surroundings. He rubbed his face and yawned. His tongue felt swollen and his throat burned. He needed a glass of water.

He gathered the blanket from the bed and threw it around himself like a shawl. It was past five o'clock and the rain had dwindled into a drizzle. He groped his way across the room and lurched towards the kitchen trailing the blanket behind him.

The kitchen was cold. A blind at the narrow window concealed a view of a dirty brick wall. Beneath the window stood a small sink with a cluttered draining board. The room was filled by a stove, a fridge, a set of painted chipboard cupboards and a table surrounded by scuffed wooden chairs. The table still bore the remains of breakfast. The fridge groaned and shivered, its shelves arthritic with ice. Beyond the window the gutters were dripping.

Charlie switched on the light and screwed up his eyes against the glare. When he reached the sink he rummaged on the draining board for a cup, filling it, drinking greedily, gasping for breath. Oh, that was good. The cold water hurt his teeth and burned against the back of his throat.

He was wiping his chin with the back of his hand when he paused, shivered and frowned at the window. He had a strange sensation that something, somewhere, was watching him. He glanced back towards the door, half-expecting to find Einstein peeping at him with a stupid grin on his face. But the doorway was empty. He stared down at his feet, prepared for bogeymen grabbing his ankles. So many bogeymen in his childhood, hiding in cupboards and laundry baskets, waiting to make their lunge at him. Monsters mostly disguised as shadows. But the floor was bare.

And then he saw them!

As he turned to retrace his steps he glanced across the room and saw the ghosts of his mother and father sitting together at the table, holding hands and staring at him with sad, exhausted eyes.

His mother was wearing the same, old-fashioned summer frock printed with tiny posies of flowers. Her hair was caked with dust and her petticoats were torn. One of her shoes was missing.

His father was wearing a Sunday suit, a starched shirt and a black silk tie. The celluloid collar had broken loose and the tie was cutting his neck. He looked stiff and uncomfortable, sitting there trying to flex his feet in a heavy pair of brogues, as if he'd been called from his barber's shop and forced to dress up for the haunting in someone else's clothes. He gave off the scent of brilliantine, tobacco and stale cologne.

'Hello, Charlie,' the barber said. 'Fancy finding you here tonight.' He didn't sound surprised.

Charlie felt his legs start to buckle and he clutched at the draining board for support. This wasn't happening. It couldn't be true. He clenched his jaw and grinned in horror. He opened his mouth to scream but nothing ballooned from his throat.

'He looks thin,' his mother said, shaking her dusty head. She sighed, raised one hand and absently touched her shoulder straps, as if crossing herself in private devotion.

17

'He looks fine,' the barber said softly. His eyes were red and rheumy. A dewdrop hung from the tip of his nose.

'You didn't look after him.'

'I gave him everything!' the barber said indignantly.

'He hasn't been eating properly,' his mother insisted.

'Eating? Hah! When I was alive he wouldn't stop eating. It wasn't natural the way he put away his food,' his father said. 'He never looked healthy. He was never a picture of heath.'

'He would never take enough fresh air,' his mother sighed.

'A head full of high-falutin' notions,' his father snorted. 'That was his trouble.'

'Look at the state of this kitchen,' his mother said, shaking her head as she stared around the room.

'What's wrong with it?' his father said, looking puzzled.

'It's filthy!' his mother complained. 'He should have been married. Why isn't he married? He needs a wife to look after him.'

Her voice sounded very distant and faint, no more than a whisper in Charlie's ear. He stared down at her naked foot and saw the bracelet of bruises where a child's hand had clutched so desperately at her ankle. She was so much younger than he remembered.

'Is this a dream?' he whispered. He was pressed against the wall. His legs were shaking. The room was spinning around him.

'Yes,' the barber said softly. 'Yes, son, it's only a dream.'

'Go back to bed,' his mother said. 'You'll catch cold.'

Charlie nodded and heard his teeth chatter. He had to sleep-walk as far as the bed and dream his way back to safety. He was dreaming. He had to wake up in the sunlit world. He was out of the kitchen now and lurching across the narrow hall. He had often walked in his sleep as a child, crawling from the warmth of his mother's bed with his hair in spikes and his eyes closed, stumbling into the wardrobe door, waking suddenly from the dream, shouting at himself in the moonlit mirrors. And his mother had gathered him into her arms and settled him back to rest.

He stopped and flinched as if something had smacked his face. He jerked back his head. The blanket slipped from his shoulders and fell in folds around his feet. He stood naked, trembling, his mouth open and his eyes blinking in terror. There was uproar in the bedroom!

The bulb in the ceiling was flashing and swinging wildly on its flex. The alarm clock rang as it skittered in circles under the chair. Charlie ran forward. Beneath the swirling light he saw the ghost of his father standing beside the ruined bed. The old man was standing with his arms outstretched and his Sunday suit on fire. Smoke rolled from his collar and sleeves and poured through the cracks in his blazing shoes. Flames filled his ears and shot from his melting fingertips. The silk tie shrank to a necklace of sparks. His shirt was crumbling to cinders.

As Charlie watched, the bonfire turned to his son and his mouth snapped open in a smouldering grin. His tongue was a lick of yellow flame. Black smoke squirted between his teeth. 'Save me, Charlie!' he bellowed. 'Save me!' He staggered forward, scorching footprints into the carpet.

Charlie screamed.

5.

He ran from the room, trapped his toes in the tangled blanket and sent himself sprawling over the carpet. He rolled sideways, struck his elbow against the wall, shouted, stood up, fell down, scuttled away on his hands and knees and reached the safety of the bathroom.

He closed the door by falling on it and managed to turn the key in the lock. Then he pressed his face against the door and listened, stupid with fright, for sounds of the burning barber. He could hear nothing but the murmur of walls, a ticking floorboard, the soft thumping of his veins, the whispering silence. He turned on the light and stared at himself in the mirror. The bathroom was small and spartan: a porcelain basin, a cupboard, the curtains drawn against the shower. The face in the mirror was white, the mouth slack with shock and exposing the teeth, the eyes shrunk into their sockets. The hair stood out from the skull like tufts of dirty wet wool.

Charlie gripped the edge of the basin and studied his face for a long time, frowning and shaking his head. What was wrong with him? Is this what it meant to be insane? Did your dreams slither out through your ears like worms? Did you lose your way in a maze filled with ghosts?

He found a comb and pulled it slowly through his hair. The nightmare began to evaporate. He was bruised and cold and exhausted. He raised a hand to his face and tried to control the trembling fingers. In a few moments he would unlock the door, feeling foolish, and tiptoe back to bed. The room would be empty, his ghosts transmogrified into shadows. He would collect his blanket and pillow and settle back to sleep. It was late. In a couple of hours Einstein would come to disturb him, scratching, demanding breakfast.

He shivered and managed to smile at the mirror.

The shower curtains blew apart and the bathroom seemed to explode. Charlie was hit by a great gust of air that threw him back against the wall. A cake of soap struck him hard in the chest. A toothbrush shot past his face and stuck like a dagger in the door. The cupboard collapsed, a bottle of mouthwash started to boil, aspirins were bouncing like hailstones. Charlie moaned and pulled himself into a ball, closed his eyes and covered his head with his hands. Above him the lightbulb melted and sagged into strings of shining sugar.

And then, through the curtains, came the stranger. He was wearing an armoured flying suit and carried a pistol in his hand. His skin was green and his eyes were lumps of burning coal. He stood, tall as a titan, filling the room with a choking, phosphorescent light.

Charlie opened his eyes and screamed. He turned and clawed at the door, desperately trying to find the lock. His knuckles knocked out the key and sent it spinning across the floor. He fell back, kicking out with his legs, sweeping the floor with his outstretched hands.

'Freeze, monkey-man, and you won't get hurt!' the stranger roared. His voice was huge and rolled like thunder. He tightened his fist on the pistol.

'Don't hurt me! Don't hurt me!' Charlie sobbed. 'I'm not wearing any pyjamas!'

The stranger shot him in the head.

6.

When Charlie woke up he was stretched naked on the floor of his living room with his arms folded neatly over his chest. He felt immensely cheerful and was grinning vacantly at the ceiling. His body seemed to be melting away and he couldn't work his arms and legs.

He lay on the carpet and he thought: I'm dead and I never knew what hit me and there's nothing left for me now but to wait here until my spirit leaves the carcass and floats away to heaven. And then he thought: or perhaps I'm not dead but dreaming still and soon I'll wake up and there'll be sunlight at the bedroom window and all the ghosts will have gone with the night and the horror will have vanished. And then, after a long time, he managed to raise his hand to his face and feel for the wound.

His fingers fumbled for his mouth, searched for his nose and counted his eyes. There was nothing missing. He brushed his hand against his brow and burst a wobbling bubble of blood. There! The wound was a tiny puncture mark placed neatly in the centre of his forehead by a high velocity sedative gun. The pellet had dissolved on impact and filled him with enough anaesthetic to make him feel he could float though walls.

While his fingers probed the bruise he sensed something moving across the room, saw a shadow spreading over the ceiling. He rolled his head and grinned to find the monster looming over him. He no longer had the wit to feel alarmed or the strength to protect himself. He lay on the floor and stared up at his assailant and his jaw remained locked in a ghastly grin.

The creature stared back with its curious, glowing eyes. Its face was very narrow and seemed almost human beneath the huge green pumpkin skull. But its mouth protruded like a beak and it had the ears of a goblin, very small and sharply pointed, marbled with fine, black veins. It was a freak, a devil, a terrible travesty of a man.

It stared down at Charlie and hooked the pistol to its flying suit. The suit was made from articulated armour plate, like the scales of some prehistoric fish. The feet were clad in metal boots but the hands were sheathed in tight, transparent gloves. Surgeons' gloves. Torturers' hands. Charlie tried counting the fingers and thumbs.

'It's time to wake up, monkey-man!' the monster bellowed and gave Charlie some encouragement by jabbing at him with a boot.

Charlie moaned, crawled as far as his old armchair and managed to hoist himself aboard. 'There's money in the bedroom,' he croaked. 'It's not much. It's all I have. Take it. Take all of it. But please don't shoot me again.' He was grinning and wagging his head in horror. He tried to curl up in a ball, pulling his knees against his chest and clasping the top of his head in his hands in an attitude of surrender.

The stranger looked astonished. The fingers tightened on the pistol butt. 'I've come for the dog.'

He was a Deep Time Mariner from a giant solar system on the edge of the Cyclops Cluster. This was his first mission to one of the planet's cities and he was almost as frightened as Charlie. He'd been told that monkey-men were the most dangerous species in all the chartered galaxies. Charlie certainly didn't look dangerous but when you were six long light years from home you couldn't afford to take any chances.

'What?' Charlie groaned. He looked at the intruder and quickly turned his eyes away, for despite the powerful sedative he felt repelled by the creature's appearance.

Einstein

'The dog,' the Mariner said. He turned and pointed in the direction of Einstein who was lurking beneath the window. The dog cocked one ear and growled.

'What's wrong with the dog?'

'He has to come with me.'

'Fine,' Charlie said. 'He's not mine. That dog doesn't belong to me. I mean, I didn't steal him.' He was confused. He'd adopted Einstein years ago when he'd found him running wild in his garden. The brute had been starving. 'He was lost,' Charlie said. 'I didn't do him any harm. I gave him something to eat and then I couldn't get rid of him. Take him if you want. Take anything.'

The Mariner paused and wiped his hand over the huge and shining skull. 'It's not that easy, monkey-man,' he rumbled. He glared at Einstein who cringed away and pretended to hunt for crumbs in the carpet.

'Yes,' Charlie said eagerly. 'He looks nasty. But that's just his usual expression. He's housetrained and he won't bite.'

'He won't come with me,' the Mariner complained. 'He says he wants to stay here with you.'

'Einstein? He'll go anywhere for a slice of liver sausage,' Charlie said. He closed his eyes and moaned. He wanted to sleep. He wanted to fall to the floor and sleep.

'You talk to him!' the Mariner shouted impatiently. 'Tell him I have to take him away and then we can leave you here in peace.'

'Talk to him?' Charlie mumbled. 'Talk to him? Dogs don't talk'

'That's because nobody ever asked them an intelligent question,' Einstein said.

7.

'No!' Charlie shouted. 'I don't believe this is happening!' He'd had enough. He was going to finish this nightmare in bed. He launched himself from the chair and fell in a heap on the carpet. The drug was still working its way through his system.

'Why don't you stop moaning and get dressed?' the dog growled in disgust. 'You're like a skinned rabbit. It's disgusting. You're making us both look ridiculous.'

Charlie managed to pick himself up and hobble into the bedroom. As he wrestled with his clothes he looked around for the ashes of his father but the old man had vanished. Charlie wasn't surprised. He struggled to pull on his pants and forced an entry into a sweater, wrenching it over his head and punching his way through the twisted sleeves.

By the time he'd returned to the living room he had broken into a cold sweat and the floor was swaying beneath him. He found the dog perched on the table, licking peanuts from the bowl. The monster had wedged his massive frame into Charlie's armchair. He sat there brooding, his head thrust forward, his hands splayed across his knees.

'Do you think I've damaged him?' the Mariner asked, as they watched Charlie stagger across the room.

'No,' Einstein said. 'They're born fighters.'

'Do they bite?'

'Soft teeth but a positively poisonous mouth,' Einstein slobbered, trying to lick salt from his snout. 'It's their diet. They'll eat almost anything. You wouldn't believe it.'

'What's happening?' Charlie pleaded.

25

Einstein

'We're in big trouble,' Einstein told him.

'What have I done?'

'You've just encountered a Deep Time Mariner.'

The Mariner leaned forward and stared into Charlie's frightened face. 'Prepare yourself for some bad news, monkey-man!' he bellowed. 'It's the end of the world!'

He paused for dramatic effect, expecting Charlie to fall down in a faint or lash out in a sudden explosion of panic. But the stupid animal just stood there, with his mouth open and a string of saliva on his chin. So he grabbed him by the throat and lifted him into the air.

'We came here on a rescue mission but now it's impossible!' he thundered. His eyes glowed like lanterns, burning with some wild and terrible despair. His fingers tightened on Charlie's throat. ' What have you done to the place? How could you make such a mess of it? So much damage! So many innocent victims! We're too late, too late... '

Charlie honked and paddled his feet. His face was turning black. The Mariner hissed in disgust and dropped him to the floor. Einstein threw back his head and let out a mournful howl.

'The end of the world?' Charlie wheezed. He turned and crawled to the window, pushing his head through the threadbare curtains, staring down on the grey, deserted street. And he thought, so this is how it ends – not with a bang but with silence after the sudden, killing rain. Clouds of acid ten thousand feet deep suffocating the sleeping cities. This is how it ends – not with fire and brimstone but with a pale and failing sunlight, the dawn fading into twilight, the twilight sinking into night. The planet a vast ball of bones and hair, rubber sheets and plastic shoes, wrapped in the ice of perpetual winter, spinning away through the dark, eternity of space.

It couldn't be true! It couldn't be happening here, on this dismal autumn morning, without warning, without the collapse of authority, revolution and the threat of war.

He turned on the TV, punching buttons, searching for news but found sex and shopping on every channel. A smiling man in a turtleneck was demonstrating a power drill by making holes in a block of concrete. A woman sitting in a bath was searching between her legs for the soap.

'The end of the world?' Charlie whispered. He was still stupid with sleep. He shook his head, desperately trying to clear his brain.

The Deep Time Mariner nodded.

'The end of everything?'

'Everything.'

'How long have we got?' Charlie whispered. His voice sounded very far away, a faint echo from a locked room.

'How should I know?' the Mariner said impatiently. 'You think I can forecast the future? Today. Tomorrow. Next week. Next year. Who cares? As soon as we've completed our task it's farewell, goodbye, goodnight, the end.'

'I don't know,' Charlie said. 'I don't know. I need time to think.' He looked forlornly around the room, blinking, wiping his palms against his sweater, as if waiting for the furniture to offer instructions.

'It's too late,' the Mariner said.

'But I can't just walk out!' Charlie protested. 'I still don't believe this is happening. And why should I trust you? I don't even know where you want to take me.'

'I'm not taking you anywhere, monkey-man!' the Mariner roared, prising himself from the chair. 'I came for the dog!'

'But you can't leave me here!' Charlie wailed. 'What will become of me? What will happen?'

'You'll die,' the Deep Time Mariner said.

27

8.

'I'm hungry!' Einstein said. He chased a peanut over the table and watched it drop to the floor.

'Shut up!' Charlie snapped.

But the Mariner bent to the dog and scratched him gently between the ears. 'What do you fancy?' he asked. As he touched Einstein, the monster's expression seemed to change. He smiled. His face was flushed with a beautiful green phosphorescence.

'Well, since you ask, I think I could manage the remains of that roast chicken chilling in the fridge,' Einstein said hopefully, sneaking a guilty glance at Charlie. 'A morsel or two.'

'That's mine!' Charlie protested. 'He can't have that. He always has a bowl of Spillers for breakfast.'

'You think I can live on hard tack and water?' Einstein complained.

'And your Mr Bully Boy™ Choice Cut Meaty Chunks and Rabbit Gravy Dinner,' Charlie reminded him.

'No wonder I have such problems with my bowels,' Einstein said lugubriously.

'I never heard you complain before,' Charlie said. 'I thought you liked Mr Bully Boy™ Meaty Chunks.'

'Have you ever eaten a bowl of compressed sheeps' lung?'

'Give him the chicken!' the Mariner commanded.

So Charlie led them into the kitchen, took the chicken from the fridge and reluctantly placed it on the floor.

The little dog whimpered with pleasure, snatched up the bird in his fangs and dragged it into a corner. He was drooling. He couldn't believe his good luck.

While Einstein tore at the chicken the Deep Time Mariner tried to explain to Charlie what was happening in the world and why he needed to take Einstein away. He told him that the Mariners had constructed a flying ark, roughly the size of Australia, and now the ark was moored behind Mars. He told him that the purpose of the ark was to contain all the listed life forms on Earth and transport them to another blue planet on the far side of the Cyclops Cluster. The ark had been designed like a giant seedpod and each seed was a bubble of oxygen large enough to hold a forest. Some of these chambers had been planted with tropical jungles, some had been chilled to polar conditions and some had been flooded with salt water to accommodate fish and marine mammals.

For the past forty years the Mariners had been coming to Earth and collecting their precious living cargo. It was dangerous and depressing work. Many species were already lost. Many plants had already vanished. The rescue operation would soon be abandoned and the ark would begin her long voyage home. He told him that he couldn't predict the future of the planet but frankly he didn't fancy its changes. And when the Mariner had finished explaining these things and Einstein had nearly finished the chicken, Charlie still didn't understand.

'Why?' Charlie said. 'What are you planning to do with all these creatures? I don't understand why you want them.'

'The Deep Time General Council marked the planet as a red alert disaster zone nearly a hundred years ago,' the Deep Time Mariner said, watching Einstein crack chicken bones. 'It's the talk of the Cyclops Cluster. I'm surprised you haven't heard the news.'

'You mean we're going to die?' Charlie blinked. He had an uncomfortable notion that he might be talking to an angel, sent by God to warn mankind of future perils. A flood. An earthquake. A threat of war. When the vision was complete and the angel departed he'd be obliged to broadcast the message. Nobody would believe him. He'd get into all kinds of trouble. At the very least he'd have to buy himself a bible and read the Book of Revelations. He'd become a Jehovah's Witness, with a sour smile and a damp handshake, banging on strangers' doors. Have you heard the good news? You're going to Hell and this time God isn't going to save you! The ship is sinking and we've burnt the lifeboats! No. It wasn't fair. He wouldn't do it.

'Everything will perish,' the Mariner said. 'There's no doubt about that. You're living in the time of the last great plague.' He picked up a carton of milk, squeezed it open and held it under his nose. The smell seemed to intrigue him. He dipped a finger into the milk and licked it clean with a flick of his long black tongue.

'There's a plague? What sort of plague?' Charlie ventured. *For behold, tomorrow this time I will cause it to rain a hail mixed with fire, very grievous, sayeth the Lord, such as hath not been in Egypt since the foundation thereof even until now. And if the hail doth not finish thee off then taste the waters of the river for they are grown bitter and runneth over with blood and I shall fill thine house with frogs and thine women with lice and thine barns with flies and thine fields with locusts and thine faces with boils breaking forth with blains such as hath not been in Egypt since the foundation thereof even until now. And that's just for starters.*

'How can you ask such a stupid question?' the Mariner roared. 'Open your eyes and look around. Six billion monkey-men. You're the plague. You're the pestilence. And it's too late for cheap remedies. A hundred years ago there might have been some glimmer of hope. But now...' He paused, peering down at the greasy-gobbed mongrel. 'My instructions are to take the dog.'

'Screw the dog!' Charlie shouted. 'What about me? What about the women and children? You can't leave all mankind to perish!'

'It's Armageddon for you, monkey-man. The slaughterhouse. The knackers' yard. You've done enough damage for one solar system. You should have stayed in the trees.'

'But we must be worth more than the beasts,' Charlie insisted. Armageddon! The Witnesses' favourite forecast. Serpents with seven heads and dancing with the whores of Babylon. 'You can't leave us here to die.'

'Why?'

'We're brothers,' Charlie said desperately, trying to forget that he was talking to a thing from outer space with a head like a giant marrow. 'Two superior civilisations greeting each other across the vast darkness of space. Men have dreamed of this moment since the dawn of time. We share a common destiny. Together we can conquer the stars.'

'Don't flatter yourself,' the Mariner said.

'We must seem primitive to you...' Charlie agreed.

'You are primitive!' Einstein chortled. 'You've no sense of smell, you're virtually deaf and you can't even lick your balls.'

'But look what we've already achieved,' Charlie protested. 'Art and science. Law and order.'

'Defoliants and striped toothpaste. Nylon shirts and Odor-eaters™. Leg wax. Nostril trimmers. Low fat milk. Ronald McDonald™,' Einstein added helpfully.

'Shut up!' Charlie hissed at him. 'We're God's chosen children. We came down from the trees and built great cities in the wilderness. We created civilisation.'

'That was your first big mistake!' the Mariner shouted. You weren't designed to leave your trees. You weren't supposed to build roads and drive to Shoppers Paradise.™ You mutilated the land!'

'Progress,' Charlie argued. 'We were making progress.'

'No! You should have been sitting in your trees, sucking fruit and admiring the view. As soon as you hit the ground there was trouble. You were frightened of other creatures and fear made you want to conquer them. You went blundering into the forest to hunt the wolf and the giant elk, the antelope and the pig. You ate their flesh. You wrapped yourselves in their skins and wore their teeth as necklaces.'

'The world was young,' Charlie said. 'We were learning by our mistakes.'

'You learned nothing! You became an infestation!' the Deep Time Mariner roared.

'It wasn't my fault!'

'You burned the forests and grasslands, poisoned the rivers and lakes. You butchered the blue whale and the red wolf, the mountain gorilla and the timid forest rhinoceros. You murdered the moa and the great auk, the painted vulture and the laughing owl. You exterminated the tarpan and the pig-footed bandicoot. You turned the dodo into navy rations and the quagga into grainbags. You ruled the planet with terror. Open your eyes and look around, monkey-man. Look at the waste and the ruin. This is the end of your world!'

The Mariner strode across the kitchen, wrenched open the blind from the narrow window and stared, in surprise, at a dirty brick wall.

9.

This was not the first time that the Deep Time Mariners had made contact with the monkey-men. In 1985 a Mariner had been sent down to the South American forests on an important fishing trip. He had orders to collect two hundred different species of fish together with samples of water from the Amazon and her tributaries. Many of these species were unknown to the inhabitants of the planet – one beautiful fish, a spiny mud dweller, carried an oil in its marvellous liver that could cure several kinds of cancer. The Mariners were fond of fish and anxious to save them before the waters were poisoned and spoiled by invading hordes of monkey-men with their sprawling towns and industries.

It was a routine flight from Mars but the Mariner had encountered problems trying to navigate his small craft through the discarded junkyard scraps that hurtle around the planet.

As he made his descent, a three-inch bolt from an abandoned Soviet satellite struck his starboard bow and burned a hole through the radiation shield. The ship corkscrewed for several dangerous plunging seconds before the computers seized control. The Mariner escaped injury but the collision altered his angle of descent and sent him skittering through the outskirts of Chicago.

On a deserted road, at ten o'clock that night, Joe E Flyshacker was driving home from a late meeting with the men from Amazing Snacks™. Joe was an advertising executive working in one of Chicago's most famous advertising agencies and was responsible for the launch of a new kind of canned milk shake called *Squelch!* The laboratories at Amazing Snacks™ had spent a fortune developing *Squelch!* in several exciting true fruit flavours but something had gone wrong. Nobody wanted to drink it. The advertising hadn't worked. Joe E Flyshacker was taking the blame.

He was driving home, worrying about losing the *Squelch!* account and the state of his stomach and the size of his mortgage, when he saw a light on a bend in the road. It was a clear night and the light seemed suspended, like a brilliant ball of green gas a few feet above the ground.

At that moment the car engine went dead, sparks shot from his fingertips, the rubber melted on the soles of his shoes and he could only sit, helpless, watching in horror as something that looked like the Jolly Green Giant stepped through the light and approached him.

The Deep Time Mariner asked him for directions as far as the coast of Venezuela and told him the world was going to end. He told him something about the ark and the spreading plague of monkey-men. He sounded very apologetic. Joe couldn't remember exactly when he had fainted but when he woke up he was sprawled on the empty road, it was past midnight and he was alone and shaking with cold.

After this encounter, Joe E Flyshacker experienced a spiritual awakening. He quit his job and left his wife and mortgage. He bought a one-way ticket to Central East Africa and found himself work in a famine relief operation. He wanted to do something about all the misery and suffering in the world. He wanted to do what he could to help before it was too late. He couldn't explain it. His family thought he'd been nobbled by Moonies. They wanted him to go home for treatment.

When he reached Somalia he sent letters back to his wife, enclosing some snapshots of starving children, and tried to describe the situation. She sent a letter out to him, enclosing a newspaper clipping that featured a story about their son who had taken a hunting rifle, driven to the local liquor store, shot the owner and stolen a six-pack of beer. The newspaper didn't blame the boy. They called him the victim of a broken home and a father who had neglected him and gone crazy with a Jesus cult. There was a photograph of his son in handcuffs, wearing battle fatigues.

Joe stopped writing letters and stayed in Africa. During a drought in Ethiopia he was sent to organise a food drop on a makeshift landing strip at a refugee camp cut from the thorn scrub three hundred miles east of nowhere. There were twelve thousand men, women and children in this camp and they had nothing left to eat but the sand. Joe set up the radio and established his position with the airport in Addis Ababa where emergency foreign aid was being loaded into an ancient British Hercules. For several days a violent dust storm prevented the aircraft making its delivery. When the transporter finally found the landing strip Joe and the rest of the team ran from their tents to watch the Hercules make its approach.

The big-bellied bird made a circle and swooped and her precious bundles of blankets and food seemed to spurt from her body like long strings of turds, bouncing and rolling into the dust. A great shout went up from the camp. As Joe stood there on the edge of the strip he knew that he had finally done something he could feel proud about and that his wretched life had not been wasted. He danced in the sand and began to laugh. He waved and clapped his hands. And twenty yards from where he was standing a bale exploded hitting the ground and a drum of *Squelch!* knocked his head off.

Since Charlie Nelson was only the second of his species to have stumbled into the path of the Mariners, it was obvious they had gone to great lengths to avoid contact with monkey-men. Yet, despite this, there were thirty million Americans convinced they had encountered alien life forms. Their experiences ranged from sightings of flying kitchenware to serious abductions involving flights to other planets and nasty moments with anal probes. Why a distant civilisation should want to construct an ambitious space programme to travel a billion miles with the sole intention of sticking a probe up the arse of a farmer in Kansas was a question no one asked.

The American Government had already laid plans to receive extraterrestrial visitors on the lawns of the White House, an idea encouraged by Hollywood. As the Pentagon saw it, America was the most powerful nation on Earth, the US President was the most important man on Earth, and it was natural that any alien embarked upon an official visit would want to shake his paw at a press conference on the lawns of the White House.

The Mariners saw it differently. If they had judged a civilisation according to its share of the world's gross domestic product and levels of morbid obesity, they would certainly have spoken to Washington. If the Mariners had felt obliged to make contact with the largest military force on the planet they would have landed in China. If the Mariners had needed to discuss poverty and disillusionment they might have chosen any outpost of the old Soviet Empire. But the Mariners viewed the inhabitants of Earth from a galactic perspective.

It had been decided, should circumstances require them to make contact as a last resort, that the Mariners would announce themselves in the Congo Basin. The rain forest, by this time, barely covered six per cent of the planet's surface but remained a vital refuge for half the known species of plants and beasts. The South American forests were being bulldozed, the forests of South East Asia were burning. The Dzanga-Sangha rain forest in Central Africa had now become the most significant place on Earth for visitors from another galaxy.

The Americans were waiting for a sign in the sky, but the Baka pygmies would be the first nation on the planet to receive the Deep Time Mariners. The Baka nation had the smallest share of the Earth's wealth and no morbid obesity. But they knew everything there was to know about hornbills, parrots and pangolins.

10.

Charlie fell into a chair and he looked at the Mariner and he looked at the dog and still he could not accept the truth of it and he began to argue and plead for more time and the chance to have a few words with God until the Mariner grew tired of him and felt obliged to set him straight and tell him the history of Earth.

'In the beginning,' the Mariner said, 'the world was shrouded in silence and its lands were barren and its waters were without life; and then the Mariners came from a faraway world and filled the oceans with worms.'

'Worms?' Charlie said.

'Worms,' the Deep Time Mariner said. 'Silver worms, ribbon worms, feather worms and thistleheads. Star worms, flatworms, pin worms and yellow threads. The worms twisted and danced in the warm seas and turned the water to soup. And then Mariners scattered the seed of the vast forest. And when the forest had grown, they filled the branches of the forest with flying insects bright as meteor showers. The bristling dragonfly, the jewelled wasp and the luminous painted moth.'

'And then?' Charlie said.

'And then,' the Deep Time Mariner said, 'nothing happened for a long time. When my brothers returned to Earth they came in a ship in the shape of a giant eggbox and carried with them all manner of birds' eggs, fish eggs and the eggs of the thunder lizards.'

'Dinosaurs,' Einstein said helpfully. 'They were the Brachiosaurus, Camarasaurus, Tyrannosaurus and Diploducus. Wonderful dragons the colours of rainbows.'

'And what happened to them?' Charlie asked.

'The squirrels ate them,' the Mariner said.

'The squirrels ate the dinosaurs?'

'These were the stories our fathers told. After the lizards there came many small and curious creatures and among their number were the squirrels and rats. They ran on tiptoe through the undergrowth and they slew the dragons by stealing their eggs. This was the first great calamity on Earth. The birds took their nests to the spiny trees and the fish spewed their eggs in the fathomless deep, but the lizards tried to build their empire in sand and their hopes were turned into omelette.'

'And the rest of it,' Charlie said. 'Everything that jumps and crawls and bleats and barks. The whole damned menagerie. You mean everything came from outer space?'

'What did you expect, you anaemic anthropoid!' the Mariner roared. 'We're not magicians. Is that what you think? You suppose we can cruise through the galaxies, snapping our fingers at empty planets, turning dust into elephants?'

'But where did you find all these animals?' Charlie demanded stubbornly. He needed an answer to everything. 'How did it all begin and where does it end?'

'They were rescued from planets across the universe, from the wobbling satellites of Argos Major to the dwindling Spider Star constellation, from the planets of Betelgeuse to the moons of Andromeda.'

'And how did life reach those planets?' Charlie asked.

The monster sighed and tried to explain. 'The life on those planets was planted by the ancestors of the Deep Time Mariners from life on other planets and those planets were first planted from other planets planted by the ancestors of the ancestors and so on forever until time folds back upon itself and stretches into the future and the universe becomes a single loop of light spinning in a web of darkness.'

'But what about the Big Bang?' Charlie asked him, bewildered.

'The big what?'

'The universe started with a bang. Before the bang there was nothing. There was no universe, no time, nothing.'

'Who told you that?'

'I saw it on the Discovery Channel.'

'And that's your idea of a good creation myth, is it?'

'So are there other planets like Earth?' Charlie asked, wondering now how many creation myths the lizard might have encountered on his epic voyage around the stars.

'There are 100,000 million planets in this galaxy alone and 100,000 million galaxies in the known universe. There are stars bigger than your entire solar system. There are stars no bigger than walnuts. And, yes, there are many planets like Earth but none so small and beautiful and none with such monkey-men.'

'But if we came from the stars,' Charlie said, 'where do we really belong?'

'In the trees with the rest of your kind,' the Mariner said. 'You are the second great calamity on Earth.'

Charlie fell silent. He felt frightened and absurdly small, as if his world were collapsing around him, the past and the future rushing together, shrinking him into a grain of stardust. What were ten thousand years of human history? No more than the distance God could spit. And what had become of God in this lonely infinity of stars? Charlie wanted the planets to be a painted ceiling suspended on strings above the Earth. He wanted the Earth to be a shallow bowl balanced on the shell of a turtle and the turtle to be held in the hands of an ape and the ape to be sitting on the knee of an angel. He wanted God in Heaven and the Devil in Hell.

Charlie turned again to the Mariner but the visitor had lost interest in him and was roaming about the kitchen, pulling open cupboards and examining food on the shelves. Everything seemed to fascinate him. He spent a long time reading labels, squeezing cans of fruit salad and peering into jars of yellow pickle. For a while he forgot about Charlie.

Einstein stopped cracking bones, licked his nose and went over to comfort his master. He tried to leap onto the chair but lost his balance, caught his claws in Charlie's sweater and fell, twisting, to the floor.

'You should have seen your face when he came through the shower curtains!' he grinned, sitting up and wiping his whiskers on Charlie's knees. 'You nearly wet yourself!'

'Where were you?' Charlie hissed. 'Why didn't you warn me? You're supposed to be a dog!'

'Barking and running around in circles wouldn't have made any difference,' Einstein said. He belched and slapped at the air with his tongue. 'Anyway, he didn't mean you any harm. He came here on important business. He came for me.'

Charlie reached down and gently pulled the old dog's ears. 'Why don't you go with him?'

'Is that what you want?'

'No. But you're free to go where you please.'

'It's not that easy,' Einstein said. 'When your tribe came down from the trees the dogs were your only friends. We went hunting with you and helped you find shelter and guarded you from the night terrors. You were so helpless. We were always plucking you from the water or digging you from the snow or sniffing you out of the bog. We taught you to dig for roots, sleep in caves and swim in the rivers. When you built your first villages we guarded your fires, worked in your fields and patrolled your graveyards and temples. And in helping you, we became outcasts from the wilderness and when you destroyed the wilderness we had only ourselves to blame. So I can't leave you. I'm a dog. I have to stay until the end.'

Einstein

'What's going to happen?' Charlie whispered, watching the Deep Time Mariner try to puzzle out a box of cornflakes. The monster frowned at the box, sniffed it, squeezed it, held it up against his face and gave it a shake to make the cornflakes rattle.

'Don't worry,' Einstein said. 'He'll be gone as soon as he's tired of looking around.'

'And that's the end of it?'

'That's the end of everything,' Einstein said sadly.

'No.' Charlie shook his head. 'He's just trying to frighten me. Why should I listen to him?'

'He's a Mariner,' Einstein said.

'But if the world was really going to end they'd do something about it,' Charlie said.

'Who?'

'The authorities. The government,' Charlie said. 'You think they'd lose control? They'd never risk losing control. Would they? No. The principal purpose of government is to remain in power. Why should they let the planet drift into chaos?'

'Whatever happens they'll think of something,' Einstein chortled. 'You can depend on them.'

'You wait,' Charlie said. 'They'll have plans. They'll have the answer.' He was looking at the dog but he was talking to himself and he knew that he didn't believe it.

'But what would happen,' Einstein said, 'if they have the answer to the wrong question?'

'It wouldn't make any sense!' Charlie said fiercely. 'They're paid to have all the answers. They've even planned out the future. If there's a disaster, if there's a threat of nuclear war, they'll spring into action with emergency control centres, stores of medical equipment and deep underground bunkers.'

'Where is the nearest bunker? Einstein asked. 'It might be time to conduct an orderly retreat.'

'Well, they don't have bunkers for everyone. Obviously. They'll be needed for selected members of government, military leaders, important men of destiny.'

'So we're supposed to protect ourselves by hiding under the chairs?' Einstein asked in disgust.

'I'm not saying it's a satisfactory state of affairs. But when the time comes, the survivors will emerge from their bunkers to make peace and rebuild the world.'

'They'll get the lights working again, the trains running, the chimney pots replaced,' Einstein grinned, cocking a leg and scratching an ear.

'That's the idea,' Charlie scowled.

'You can't crush the human spirit,' Einstein said.

'Civilisation will rise from the ashes,' Charlie said.

'What will they use to rebuild this brave new world?' Einstein inquired, after a moment's reflection.

'How do you mean?'

'Well, imagine the worst has happened,' Einstein said. 'After a long time, when the air has cleared and the fire storms have finally blown themselves out, these underground bunkers will unlock themselves and hatch old men. Presidents and generals. Economists and town planners. Architects and industrialists. What do you think will be left for this army of choice little despots?'

'They'll start again.'

'But they can't start again.'

'Why?'

'They've already squandered the planet's resources. They've stripped the Earth of its timber. They've burned the reserves of coal and gas. They've clawed out the iron and copper, bauxite and phosphates, tin, lead, chrome, nickel, zinc and tungsten. They won't have the raw materials. It's already too late. If they blow themselves into the Stone Age, that's where they'll have to remain.'

'How do you know all this?' Charlie demanded.

'You're not the only one who watches a lot of television,' Einstein said.

The Mariner grew impatient, tore the box apart in his hands and sprayed the kitchen with cornflakes.

11.

Charlie might have been comforted to know there were hundreds of organisations dedicated to Doomsday. But none of them had the power to evacuate cities, maintain essential services, construct mass graves or direct survivors to underground bunkers. They were more concerned with their own salvation through spells, incantations and prayer. They wanted to see the planet burn because God was going to make them fireproof. Some of them would inherit the cinders while others believed they'd be flown as far as paradise in a fleet of chauffeur-driven spacecraft. Since they had so much to gain from the forthcoming global misery, they'd become obsessed with picking the date of the world's destruction.

The Jehovah's Witnesses had announced the end of time, the day of wrath, the fire and flood, finger of God, return of Christ and a football team of Old Testament prophets as far back as 1874, after Charlie Russell had announced he'd been hearing voices – he thought they were angels telling him that Jesus would return wrapped in a Cloak of Invisibility. When the world failed to end in 1914 the faithful pinned their hopes to 1918, 1925, 1940 and 1975. They were still counting.

The Children of God had braced themselves for the Battle of Armageddon in the August of 1993. August is a wicked month. Nice try but no cigar.

The Daughters of Nostradamus had expected the God of Terror riding a starship disguised as a comet in 1999 or 2000. The pyramids were astral beacons built to guide him down to Earth. When he failed to make an appearance, they settled for 2062 or possibly 2242. They kept looking wistfully into the heavens.

Einstein

When he arrived they expected handsome rewards for suffering the years of ridicule. They'd survive the reign of terror and be given special, secret powers. Amazing strength. X-ray vision. Anything they wanted. Their every wish would be granted.

Members of the New Revelation Church had been promised that the death of non-members by giant hailstones and the resurrection of the dead would take place on a Saturday. They hadn't been told which Saturday but it certainly made the weekends exciting.

The flock of the Early Apocalyptics who thought they were reincarnations of Christian martyrs from Ancient Rome, predicted that the New Jerusalem would be carried down from Heaven on a huge cloud of brimstone during a lunar eclipse in the winter of 2002 or the spring of 2003. Once the city had landed a thousand angels would march through the gates, blowing trumpets and killing the wicked with magic swords. The faithful would be spared and blessed with eternal life. They'd never grow old. They'd never need to work again.

The Church of the Righteous Living had told its congregation that God would blast the wicked with bolts of lightning. The Heavens shall pass away and the Elements will melt with a fervent heat. It would happen when they least expected it, so they sang hymns in rubber shoes.

Converts to the Star Church of Tampa, who'd been told they were really visitors from a number of distant planets, had been expecting to leave the Earth for another galaxy in 1987, 1991, 1993 and 1999. The transport would be a nuclear starship and they were told to assemble in the church with a packed lunch for the journey. Every time it happened they gave away their furniture.

The German composer Karlheinz Stockhausen, who thought he'd been possessed by an alien spirit from Sirius, was alone in having no date for the apocalypse. But he was writing the music for it.

Everyone waited for something to happen. But all these doomsday prophets had made the same mistake – they were looking to an egocentric God whose sole concern was the genuflection of one particular kind of primate. It had never occurred to them that any superior force in heaven might be more concerned with the welfare of the okapi or plight of the flying opossum.

12.

'It's time we were gone,' the Mariner said, turning to Einstein. He tried to bend down and scoop up the dog in his arms.

The dog yelped and scrambled under Charlie's chair. 'It's my duty to stay with my master,' he growled.

'Is that your final word?'

'Yes.'

'You want to die here with your monkey-man?' the Mariner roared. 'I don't understand it. Can you imagine what this does to my paperwork? We go to all this trouble to save your species, and you want to die with your monkey-man? What's wrong with you dogs?' He snorted and shook his great head. He looked baffled and angry.

'You'll find another dog,' Charlie said, impressed by Einstein's loyalty. 'The city is teeming with dogs.'

'He can hardly wander the streets, hooting and banging a feeding bowl,' Einstein said.

'Don't you understand?' the Mariner thundered. 'It has to be this dog. Those are my instructions. This operation has already been planned down to the smallest particular. Can you imagine the organisation required to evacuate a planet? I can't ignore my instructions – if I get it wrong they'll have me collecting swamp flies and fleas.'

Charlie looked down at Einstein and surveyed the dog from the tip of his quivering nose to the end of his dusty tail. 'He's only a mongrel.'

'I may look like a mongrel to you,' Einstein said, in a very superior tone of voice, 'but my ancestors mixed with kings and emperors. They came from the courts of China and the forest kingdoms of Africa, they played in the harems of Persia and battled with bears in the snows of Russia.'

'You're a mongrel.'

'Dogs are very proud of their mixed blood,' Einstein said.

'This dog holds the entire history of his kind,' the Deep Time Mariner said. 'He's an important animal. If he won't come with me we'll be obliged to strike dogs from the list.' He stepped back, crunching cornflakes under his boots. 'It's probably not important. We have the wolves and coyotes, foxes and jackals. I've always felt the domestic dog was something of an aberration… ' He seemed to lose interest in the debate and started checking the buckles and clasps on his spacesuit.

Wait! Einstein thought. I can only abide by this rule if he makes the same judgement against the common alley cat. That venomous, flea-bitten bag of bones! That fur-wrapped parcel of piss and wind! That saucer-eyed killing machine! That miserable mouser! That grizzling grimalkin! Would the cat be borne aloft in the arms of the Mariners? The universe could not tolerate the cat without the dog!

'Is that it?' Charlie asked anxiously. 'Are you leaving?' He wondered how the monster would make his escape. Would he spread his arms and fly from the window? Would he wrap himself in the shower curtains and vanish in flames and smoke? Would he open the door and hurry downstairs, rushing like a vampire through the shadows, trying to shield his face from the dawn? Charlie didn't want him to leave, but he didn't know how to stop him.

'I've no time to waste,' the Mariner said.

'What will happen now?' Charlie demanded.

'Anything could happen,' the Mariner said, strolling cheerfully from the kitchen. 'The forests will shrink, the oceans will stink, the deserts will spread and you'll starve. You'll murder for a scrap of potato, wage war for a field of rice.'

He walked slowly through the apartment, touching the furniture, peering at the paintings on the walls, lingering like a departing tourist, bidding farewell to exotic sights. He was so tall that the top of his head clipped the lampshades, making them shudder and throw out dust. In the living room he paused by the window, dipped a hand in his flying suit and pulled out something that looked remarkably like an old-fashioned pocketwatch. He flipped open the lid with his thumb and studied the intricate hieroglyphics.

'What do we have to do?' Charlie pleaded. 'I'm scared. I don't understand what we have to do to help ourselves!' Everyone knew that something was wrong. The air was poisoned. The oceans were dead. The world's great cities were in decline. There were millions starving to death. They made TV shows about them. Hollywood stars were flown to Africa and photographed blessing pot-bellied babies. Everything was changing so fast. It was out of control.

'I'd be scared if I were a monkey-man,' the Deep Time Mariner said. 'You're losing one species every twelve minutes.' He glanced down at his pocketwatch. 'Ten minutes. You're losing one species every ten minutes. It's like walking around with a stick of dynamite lodged up your arse. In a few years, if the planet survives, there'll be nothing left here but monkey-men, cockroaches, rats... '

'And dogs?' Einstein asked hopefully.

'They'll eat you!' the Deep Time Mariner said.

'But you can't... you can't leave us here to die!' Charlie cried. He was standing in the court of eternal justice, pleading for mercy on behalf of mankind. But he didn't have the knowledge to argue their cause. What did they want beyond survival? What did they want beyond control of the world and domination of heaven?

'You don't understand, monkey-man. It's far too late. You should have read the signs.'

'You could help us find another home,' Charlie begged. 'Take us to another planet. We could start again.'

'You're joking,' the Mariner said, staring at him with astonishment. 'Is he joking?' he asked Einstein.

'No,' Einstein whispered. He looked ashamed of Charlie. He swung his head away and pretended to study the stains on the wall.

'Don't leave me here alone,' Charlie said. He was quite convinced that once his visitor had left the lights would go out all over the world.

'You won't be alone,' the Mariner said. 'There'll be six or seven billion of you kissing the world goodbye.'

'And I'll be here,' Einstein said, a little annoyed to find that his sacrifice was not providing Charlie with comfort. 'We'll go together.'

'No!' Charlie shouted. 'I need more time to prepare myself. I'm not ready to die.'

'You were warned,' the Deep Time Mariner said. 'You were warned many times. You should have prepared yourself for the worst.'

He was most surprised by Charlie's despair. He'd been told that monkey-men were the most destructive force in the universe. He had seen the evidence all around him. They were cruel and stupid and violent. They were butchers. They were criminals. He couldn't afford to let them escape to infest another planet. He had his instructions. But when he looked at Charlie he also had his doubts. How could this ridiculous animal have established such a reign of terror? They should have broken their necks when they first fell from their trees.

'It's not his fault,' Einstein argued. 'Why pick on him? What

51

could he do to save the world? Look at him. His life has just been one damned thing after another.'

'He doesn't look very dangerous,' the Deep Time Mariner agreed.

'Dangerous?' Einstein hooted. 'He's nothing but a danger to himself. Why, if it weren't for me, he'd probably have killed himself years ago. He's an accident waiting to happen.'

The Mariner paused and considered Charlie for a few moments. 'What have you done with your time that makes you so special? Why should you alone be spared the fate of your species?'

'There must be something,' Charlie said, catching the faintest glimmer of hope.

'Are you worth saving?'

'Yes,' Charlie said, without hesitation. 'Yes.'

'And if you came with me,' the Deep Time Mariner said, 'I suppose you'd bring the dog?'

'Don't worry about him,' Charlie said, not daring to catch the little dog's eye. 'He'd follow me through Hell if I asked him.'

'Then show me,' the Mariner said. 'Show me something you've done with your life that made a difference to the world.'

'What?'

'He doesn't understand,' Einstein said.

'Are you sure he's not soft in the head?'

'They're really rather primitive.'

'Make him show me something of his miserable past,' the Mariner instructed. 'We'll go back there and look around.'

'Are you crazy?' Charlie shouted as he struggled to follow the conversation. 'It's gone. Lost forever. No one can go back again. If we knew the secret of calling up the past we might not have destroyed the future.' He snuffled and wiped his nose on his sleeve.

'You're wrong,' the Mariner said. 'I was here when you summoned the dead. You spoke to your mother and father.'

'Was it you?' Charlie said. He stopped moaning and stared in surprise at the Mariner. 'What did you do to me?'

'You were dreaming. I picked your brains.'

'Why?'

'I couldn't resist the temptation and, besides, I wanted to know how you worked. It's a simple trick but more than you'd understand.' He bent very low over Charlie and breathed on him. 'Now show me the rest of your life. Close your eyes and dream yourself into the past.'

'And then what happens?'

'I'll watch,' the Mariner said.

'But how?' Charlie asked suspiciously. 'I don't understand.'

'You're just a monkey-man – I don't expect you to understand more than a fraction of what's happening here!' the Mariner hissed impatiently. 'Close your eyes. I don't have time to argue with you.'

'I don't know where to begin...' Charlie stammered.

'Tell him about your mother and father,' Einstein said. 'Begin at the beginning.'

13.

So Charlie began to tell the Mariner about his father, the barber, and tried to describe the shop with its large revolving leather chair and window of engraved glass. As a young man the barber had lived in the attic over the shop and when he wasn't cutting hair he was drinking Guinness with his friends. He was tall and slow with heavy hands and ears sprouting tufts of coarse, grey hair. He wore a dainty Errol Flynn moustache and a lot of scented brilliantine.

The shop was in Church Street, on a corner of the Edgware Road. On Saturdays a market ran the length of the street, turning it into a shantytown of wooden crates and canvas stalls.

You could find anything in this market. There were pineapples fresh from the Ivory Coast and turnips wrapped in Normandy mud. There were perfumes from Arabia, blankets from Bolivia and towers of white, enamel bowls from beyond the Great Wall of China. Between the cabbages and yams, beneath loops of sausages and pyramids of cheese, there were fat men with shining eyes hawking goldfish, gloves and cut throat razors. Brown men with gold teeth stood on boxes selling soap and ivory buttons. Old women, mad as gargoyles, sat scowling over heaps of dead men's shoes. There were rolls of carpet, bundles of spoons, fireworks, firewood, candlesticks, walking sticks, mothballs and glass eyes.

Between the stalls, young men with crafty fingers prowled the pavements picking pockets. Where the market met the Edgware Road a few girls with nothing to offer but themselves beckoned strangers into doorways, leading the lonely into danger with crooked smiles and promises of paradise.

Charlie's father had often been tempted to spend his profits on these painted poppets. But he never found the courage to talk to them. Eventually he married the daughter of a grocer. Her name was Geraldine, a local beauty with tight curls and a bright Max Factor face. He was fifty years old and it was time for him to be married. She drove him from the attic above the shop and settled him into a yellow brick house set back from the street by a privet hedge.

Charlie was born in a bad winter. The first few years of his life had been spent in his mother's bed, curled beneath the sheets in the hot and suffocating darkness. The barber slept in another room, for fear of disturbing the child, and Geraldine would never again let him press home his affections. He continued to admire her from a distance but he knew that he couldn't win her away from the child that snored between her breasts. He retired with his cronies to suckle on stout.

The woman, for her part, rarely left the bed and never left the child alone. They ate together and bathed together and on the few afternoons that she spent standing upright, dressed and working in the kitchen, Geraldine would lift up her skirts and push him under her petticoats where he'd cling to her ankles in silence.

When he finally learned to walk, he only walked behind his mother, following her footsteps, stopping when she stopped or trapping his toes beneath her heels. He was a small moon caught in a dangerously narrow orbit. He spoke rarely and only to echo his mother's words, repeating the questions she directed at him and then waiting for her to give him an answer.

'The boy's an idiot!' the barber grumbled.

'He's a mother's boy,' Geraldine said.

This peculiar state of affairs lasted until a week after Charlie's fifth birthday when a nasty twist of fate prised the mother and child apart.

Einstein

It was a brilliant summer's morning and Geraldine was hanging fresh curtains at the bedroom window. She was balanced on a chair, her arms full of floral print, while Charlie stood beneath, eclipsed in the gloom of her petticoats and clinging miserably to her feet.

He was a large child and already finding it difficult to fit snugly into his mother's shape at night. He was uncomfortable under her skirt. The petticoats were hot and peppery with perfume. They tickled his nose and irritated his eyes. There was not enough room to breathe. He clung to her feet and tried to stifle the sneeze that had seized his throat. He buried his face in her legs. He screwed up his eyes. He held his breath. He tried everything he knew to swallow the dust in his nose and mouth. But nothing worked.

The sneeze, trapped under her skirt, roared wetly up through the darkness and threw his mother into a fright. She kicked out her legs, fell from the chair and sailed through the open window. She left young Charlie blinking in the sudden daylight and holding a warm but empty shoe.

Geraldine's death broke the old barber's heart. He pickled himself with brandy and brooded. He tried not to blame the boy but the shoe haunted him. After the funeral he stalked Charlie for days in a stubborn attempt to remove the fragment of mother from child. But Charlie clung to the shoe and screamed.

When Charlie was finally packed off to school he managed to take his mother's shoe with him. The scent of the worn leather was a balm to his troubled spirit and a comfort through the cold dormitory nights. It became a secret article of worship.

Every child had a smuggled household god. A small boy named Carver had brought a necklace of amber beads that he wore beneath his pyjamas. A boy called Snitcher carried a biscuit tin secured with a piece of frayed ribbon. The tin contained an old toothbrush with bent bristles, a belt buckle and a stump of lipstick. He would arrange these objects beneath his pillow before he could settle down to sleep. At night when the doors were locked and the lights went out, this miserable tribe of pygmies would rummage and mutter for hours in the dark as they prayed to their curious fetishes.

As the years passed the deities took many different disguises. Carver traded his necklace for several dog-eared copies of *Stiffy*, a magazine so dangerous that its pictures were rumoured to strike you blind if you dared to look at them in daylight. Snitcher emptied his biscuit tin and began to collect pictures of Elvis Presley. Blue Hawaii. Viva Las Vegas. But Charlie never gave up his shoe.

It was a fancy high-heeled slipper, a narrow purse of blue leather balanced on a curving spike, and its power grew more potent as Charlie grew older. In the end it seemed to hold such fascination that it might have been Mary Magdalene's sandal or contained the shrivelled foot of the Buddha.

Carver, who would grow up to work in a deep pan pizza restaurant and steal scraps of food and poison his wife with cont-aminated sausage meat, wanted to buy the shoe with a special Christmas edition of *Stiffy* starring a nympho in see-through scanties playing in winter wonderland. She's the sort who'd eat you for breakfast! Look at the size of her baloneys!

Snitcher, who would grow up to be an instant coffee million-aire and live in Florida and wear women's clothes and die of a heart attack because of bad harvests in Central America, offered to trade his wristwatch and a signed photo of Elvis in concert. Take the watch. It cost a fortune. Luminous means it's radioac-tive. Every night it glows in the dark.

But Charlie could not be tempted.

He was happy enough at school. He learned to smoke and swim and to swear in foreign languages. After two years in the carpentry class he managed to finish a pipe rack which he sent to his father who trod on it. He was slow at sport and stunned by mathematics but found that he loved to draw and paint.

For a few precious hours each week he would sit in the art room, hunched over sheets of coarse grey paper, coaxing his hand to obey his eye. Nothing gave him so much pleasure as the smell of pencil shavings, the crumble of charcoal under his fingers, the taste of a paintbrush in his mouth. While he worked he found himself absorbed in daydreams, carried into a secret world secure as the shelter of petticoats. There was nothing to harm him. There was nothing to fear.

When he woke from the reverie and looked around, it surprised him that others found the work so difficult. Carver, who could draw nude women with all the dexterity of an aboriginal cave painter, was defeated by a flower or bowl of fruit. Snitcher managed nothing but cartoon portraits of Elvis Presley. They were both amazed by Charlie's gift. He could draw anything. He was a genius. It seemed to them that he had mastered a baffling conjuring trick and they made him perform it endlessly. They made him doodle on walls, desks and the backs of their hands. One boy asked for a spider tattoo, red and blue ink on the side of his neck. Charlie was always willing to perform his simple magic. And yet, no matter how closely they followed his hands, they could never discover how it was done.

Charlie's only enemy was the art master. His name was Figgins. He was as short and dirty as a winter's day. He had the hands of a butcher and a dreadfully withered leg. He hobbled through the world, clacking his cane against the floor and beating on desks with his fist. He loathed boys almost as much as he hated artists. The Impressionists were blind. The Cubists were mad. The Abstractionists were criminals. They were all faggot wops and crazy dagoes.

The function of art was to glorify the struggles of man. Art was colossal. Art was the marble of war memorials, the tombs of generals, heroic statues of cavalrymen. Art was the epic canvas depicting battles and great processions. Art was the regimental silver, the marching band, the triumphal arch. There was also church art and the function of church art was to glorify the terror of God. Flood, fire and pestilence. Art had a duty to serve its purpose with cold precision and discipline.

Figgins had wanted to be a soldier but the army had refused him. He thought of himself as a crippled fighting machine. He took Soldier of Fortune magazine and owned a collection of replica guns. He could recite from memory all the major battles of the Second World War together with the casualty figures, dead and wounded, for the Allied and Axis forces. He had a wardrobe of mothballed uniforms, a box of medals and a genuine silver Schutzstaffel dagger. But while he dreamed of running with mercenaries through blood-spattered African villages, he wasted his life counting pencils and smacking the ears of nut-brained boys.

He lurked in a corner of the room, watching the class with his dark mad eyes. He was proud of any boy who could prove he possessed no natural talent, had doubts about those who were willing to learn and felt deeply suspicious of Charlie Nelson.

He was appalled by the boy's enthusiasm. It wasn't natural to sit in a room sketching little bunches of flowers when you could be in the gymnasium banging another boy's brains to pulp with a pair of decent boxing gloves. It was wrong. It was frankly effeminate. He did everything he knew to ridicule and discourage the child. But Charlie never surrendered. He wanted to be a painter.

14.

While Charlie thought of these distant schooldays he slipped imperceptibly into a trance and without even knowing how it had happened or thinking it anything out of the ordinary, found he was back in the evil-smelling art room, a small boy sitting at an ink stained desk, drawing a vase of wilted flowers.

Carver was sitting close to him, scribbling fantastic diagrams of women's reproductive organs on little scraps of paper to be passed among his smirking friends.

Snitcher was at the back of the room. He had just completed an Elvis Presley and was sitting peacefully picking his nose.

Figgins was propped against a window, reading the back pages of *Combat & Survival*. For the last few minutes he'd been deep in thought, considering the purchase of a genuine, military surplus, tactical assault vest with trauma pouch and pistol holster. But there were so many temptations. He couldn't decide between the vest and a pair of police issue high-speed handcuffs. He knew he was a danger to himself but he had the drive and ambition to be a danger to others. He smiled as he turned the pages.

He looked even more terrible than Charlie remembered him, a humpbacked dwarf wearing a heavy tweed suit and mirror-polished army boots. As Charlie worked on his drawing he heard the master hobble towards him until he was leaning over the desk.

'What's wrong with you?' he snarled at Charlie. 'When are you going to pull yourself together, you pathetic ponce?' He wrenched the pencil from Charlie's grasp and broke it between his hairy fingers. 'What do you think you're going to do when you leave school? Do you think you'll be drawing flowers for a living?'

'Yes, sir,' Charlie said nervously.

Figgins nodded and paused for thought, tapping his cane against his leg. 'Have you ever met an artist?' he inquired, in a kindly confidential manner.

'No, sir.'

'Well let me tell you something about them,' Figgins said, puffing out his chest like a mad old turkey cock and looking around the room. 'Artists are generally froggies, dagoes, spicks and wops,' he announced to the class. 'They're artists because they're sodomites. Pacifists and pansies. They have no regard for authority. They have no discipline. They have no backbone. They're beatniks. They cheat and steal and interfere with one another.'

Carver tried to suppress a snigger but Figgins heard him spluttering and gave him such a smack in the face that the boy was knocked from his chair and fell on the floor in a flurry of lewd confetti.

'And do you know what we do with an artist when we find one in the army?' Figgins said, returning to Charlie. 'Do you know what we do with a fairy when we catch one?'

'No, sir,' Charlie said.

'We bend him over a chair and shove a broom up his windward passage. It's a fine old army tradition. Do I make myself understood?'

'Yes, sir.'

And why do we shove a broom up his arse, my winsome little friend? Any notions? Any idea?'

'No, sir.'

'Because it's the only way to reach his brains,' Figgins roared. And as the class erupted into great shouts of laughter, he screwed up Charlie's drawing, tossed it to the floor and flicked it away with his cane.

Einstein

Charlie woke up in a sweat, moaning and shaking his head. 'What happened?' he said, staring wildly around the room. 'What have you done to me?'

'You were back at school,' Einstein growled, with his ears pressed flat against his skull.

'Is he finished?' the Mariner roared. 'Is that it?'

'No!' Einstein said. 'Give him time. He's still trying to get the hang of it. Concentrate,' he said, turning back to Charlie. 'Concentrate and close your eyes.'

So Charlie closed his eyes and covered his face with his hands and this time he was back in the barber's shop and his father was alive again and he could smell the soap and the brilliantine and feel the sunlight through the window.

The old man was standing by the revolving leather chair, staring down on a customer. His arms were raised against his chest. He held a pair of scissors in his hand. His shirt was darned at the elbow. There were snippets of hair on his shoes.

A young man stood in the shop. A young man with freckles and a dazed expression on his face. He was standing forlornly in a corner, holding a long-handled broom. It was Charlie.

'I can see myself!' he gasped. 'I can see myself in the barber's shop.'

'You're sweeping the floor,' the Deep Time Mariner complained. He sounded disappointed.

'Can you see it?' Charlie whispered.

'Everything,' the Mariner said. 'Everything but the dog.'

'It's long ago. I wasn't born,' Einstein said.

The three of them were silent for a moment, gazing down into Charlie's past as the years began melting away.

15.

A wasp was banging against the window. The barber snapped at the air with his scissors. Charlie leaned on his broom. The little shop was hot and cramped and Charlie was feeling bored. When the barber had been told that his son displayed an artistic bent he had promptly pulled him from school and set him to work in the shop. He'd half-expected to find the boy wearing green mascara and clutching a plastic handbag. Nothing would have surprised him.

Charlie was disappointed but he tried to learn the barber's craft. He swept the floor, boiled brushes, strapped razors and helped mix the bottles of sweet cologne. He was made to shave chins, trim whiskers and watch his father at work with the scissors.

His father cut hair like a gardener hacking at nettles. He slashed impatiently at the roots and raked through the stubble. The customers were left looking startled, their skulls chafed and their ears full of melting brilliantine.

When Charlie arrived business was bad. Nobody wanted a prison haircut. Young men walked the London streets, hairy as Bible Land prophets, rings on their fingers, bells on their toes, their beards wreathed in fragrant ganja smoke.

'Lunatics!' the barber would bark as he watched the world strutting past the window. 'Look at the state of them!'

'That's the fashion,' Charlie said wistfully, gently stroking his own savaged scalp.

'Fashion?' the barber shouted, snapping his scissors. 'You half-baked potato! I've been cutting hair since before you were born. Don't talk to me about fashion.'

Einstein

'Styles must have changed in all that time,' Charlie said, rather doubtfully. He looked around the walls at the faded pictures of Douglas Fairbanks and the dirty display for Blue Gillette blades. The word Durex in red neon tubing fizzled and crackled over the door.

'Styles?' the barber growled. 'Don't talk to me about styles. I learned my trade with the Hollywood Correspondence School of Electro Massage and Grooming. I've got a diploma. It cost me eight guineas. I'm qualified to nurture the scalps of the stars.'

'Ivor Novello had a lovely head of hair,' the man in the chair said. He was an old street trader called Dancing Perkins. His head poked through the nylon sheet like a large and poisonous fruit.

'That's right!' the barber said.

'Rudolph Valentino.'

'There's another!' the barber agreed. 'He kept himself immaculate. Ronald Colman. Clark Gable. There was never a hair out of place. They were always jumping out of express trains or being shipwrecked or fighting the heathen hordes. But they were always most particular about their personal grooming.'

'And Fred Astaire,' Perkins added. 'He was another dapper gent.' He winked at Charlie in the mirror.

'Fred Astaire had a wig,' the barber growled. 'He used to dance with a blasted wig.'

'I thought that was Ginger Rogers,' Perkins cackled.

The barber grabbed the scruff of his neck and began to attack his head with the clippers.

'There are two kinds of haircut,' he said, with the absolute conviction of a man with a diploma.

'Short and very short,' Perkins said.

Charlie didn't like to argue with them. Regular customers, loyal for more than forty years, continued to come and sit in the chair. They were glad that nothing had changed. It gave them comfort. It made them feel secure. They had watched themselves growing old in these mirrors. Some of these men had so little hair on their heads they only required a hot towel and polish.

The barber taught Charlie everything he knew and found that his son was quick to learn the tricks of the trade. He was happy enough to have him working in the shop, but while they shared the house he began to find that the boy was a source of irritation. Charlie was quiet and clean and spent the evenings in his room. He was no trouble. But the barber had to stop drinking and shouting at shadows and remember to wear his teeth at breakfast. He was too old to break bad habits. It made him feel crusty and constipated. So after a while he suggested that Charlie might like to live in the attic over the shop.

'I've been thinking,' he announced one afternoon when Charlie was on his hands and knees trying to clear the washbasin pipes. 'You shouldn't be living with an old man at your time of life.'

'You need me to look after you,' Charlie said, hooking a wet plug of hair from the drain.

'It's not healthy,' the barber said, wrinkling his nose and wrapping the stinking mess in a copy of Sporting Life. 'You need a little place of your own where you can play your jungle music and entertain your lady friends.' He grinned at the thought and jerked his thumb at the ceiling.

'I don't play music,' Charlie said, surprised by his father's concern for his comfort.

'And you don't have any lady friends,' the barber said darkly. 'That's why you need a place of your own.'

'But you need someone to cook for you,' Charlie argued. 'You can't live on pork pies and Guinness.'

'It's never done me any harm!' the barber said impatiently. 'Forget about me. It's time you looked after yourself.'

65

Einstein

The attic was large and draughty and divided into tiny rooms with the help of plasterboard walls. There was a sitting room with a chest of drawers and a bed that folded into a sofa; there was a kitchen with a table and stove and even a little bathroom, tucked away beneath the eaves. The windows had a view of the sky trapped between rooftops and chimneys. At night Charlie could sit on the bed that served as a sofa, drink hot soup and look at the moon.

'It will need cleaning,' the barber said mournfully. 'It hasn't been touched in years.' He gazed at a shelf of empty bottles, their shoulders white and hairy with dust, and sighed to remember those faraway days when he was young and glad to be living.

'I could paint it,' Charlie suggested, tapping his knuckles against the plasterboard walls.

'That's the spirit,' the barber said, turning away and painfully treading downstairs. 'You're supposed to be good with a paint-brush.'

Charlie smiled and said nothing.

He loved the freedom of the attic and tried to turn it into a studio. He painted the walls white and the floorboards green. He painted the ceiling a summer blue and used the stains in the plaster as clouds. He searched the market for scraps of wood and constructed a crude kind of easel.

At weekends he haunted the Tate Gallery, looking and learning and hoping, in vain, to meet other painters. He bought postcards and prints and studied the masters. He tried to imitate Gauguin, Lautrec, Matisse and Picasso, but everything he copied was transformed by the primitive energy from his swift untutored hands. His work was vigorous, fresh and swirling with life.

In the solitude of the attic he created his own fantastic world in brilliant surges of colour. He had embarked on the grand adventure and nothing could stop him. One day, when he had mastered his art and saved a little money, he would pack his paintbox and set out to explore the world.

His father didn't question how he spent his time and never felt tempted to visit the attic. Charlie was down every morning to open the shop and served as a watchman at night and that was enough for the barber. The boy had been the curse of his life and he was glad to be rid of him.

Charlie never returned to the house behind the privet hedge. The barber died alone in its kitchen. He cremated himself one night by forgetting to watch a frying pan. The pan exploded. He laughed in surprise as beautiful blossoms of fire wobbled from the ceiling and petals cascaded over the walls. He was so drunk that he lost his feet in the smoke, lay down on the floor and went to sleep with his head in the flames.

His ashes were sent to Geraldine at Golders Green Cemetery and Charlie was left in the painted attic above a run-down barber's shop.

16.

It was several weeks before Charlie discovered the final remains of his father. They were hidden in a small yellow cupboard at the back of the shop. The cupboard had been sealed shut by many coats of paint and the collapse of its rotting hinges. Charlie broke it open with a butter knife.

On the shelves he found a forgotten stash of rusting King Gillette blades, a roll of styptic pencils, a flat red tin of Elastoplast, a bundle of *Skirt Lifter* magazines, an unframed photograph of Geraldine and a military issue handgun.

The *Skirt Lifter* magazines were black and white catalogues of portly women in corsets, stockings and garter belts. They had been obtained for the barber's personal comforts during his lonely bachelor days and when he had grown tired of them, he'd offered their frazzled pages for his customers' amusement while they waited their turn in the chair.

Calling all Men! A hundred gorgeous views of gals. Artists models. No two alike. Every one guaranteed a study. Sent in plain cover. Your money back if not satisfied.

Attention! Restore energy, defeat bad health, with the famous Vitabrace iodised jock strap and body-belt, the perfect support for men of all ages. Prevents rupture and varicose strain.

Victimised by nerves? Dr Niblett's Sedative gives prompt relief. Every bottle with full instructions. Booklet sent free.

The women in *Skirt Lifter* were the ancestors of the girls in *Stiffy*. By the time Charlie uncovered them some of the women were already dead and the rest were so old they'd adopted waterproof underwear.

The photograph of Geraldine had been taken by her father with a Kodak Instamatic and showed his favourite daughter as a young woman posed proudly in the grocery shop. She was wearing a starched apron and standing before a pyramid of canned pineapple chunks in heavy syrup. Her face was frozen into a smile. A pencil was stuck in her tight curly hair. She was eighteen years old and had no idea she would marry a barber and fall to her death from a bedroom window. At the time of the photograph she thought she would marry Burt Reynolds, bless him with children and live forever.

The handgun was a small .380 Beretta automatic presented to the angry barber by one of his customers after a series of minor thefts in which nothing much had been stolen but soap, brushes and boxes of condoms. The barber had fully intended to use the gun to defend his property against any future intruders. But the thieves had failed to return and the weapon had been forgotten.

Charlie added his mother's shoe to these curious relics and kept them in a metal cashbox stashed under the bed.

17.

'Is that it?' the Mariner said. He yawned a vast reptilian yawn exposing the back of his bright blue throat.

It was hard to believe that these peculiar primates had continued preening and grooming themselves while all around them the world was dying. What had gone wrong in their big, soft brains?

Charlie woke up from his dream and groaned. He blinked at the light and wiped his face in his hands. As he recovered he sensed something move among the trays of dusty plants he kept on the chest beneath the window. He glanced furtively in that direction, half-afraid of what he might find staring back at him.

The cactuses, which an hour ago had been no more than shrivelled brown thumbs, had swollen and stretched and cracked their pots! They gurgled and rattled their quills. Some of them now were as big as marrows, pushing and heaving against each other, their tops crowned with trumpets of painted flowers.

'What's happening here?' he whispered in amazement. 'Everything is going mad!'

'It's my fault,' the Deep Time Mariner said, inspecting this outbreak of undergrowth. He looked rather pleased with himself. 'I can't help it. Plants seem to like me.' Charlie took a step towards the window. The myrtle shattered its china bowl and burst into masses of perfume flowers. The ivy began to unravel and clamber across the curtains.

'What do you think of his story?' Einstein demanded anxiously, running up and down the room, trying to attract their attention. 'Didn't it make you want to weep? Didn't it squeeze your heart?'

'Frankly, I'm not impressed,' the Mariner said, bending down to bury his face in the myrtle flowers. He appeared to suck up the scent of the bloom, drew back his head and sighed.

'There's more!' Charlie protested. 'That was nothing. We haven't scratched the surface.'

'I think I've seen enough,' the Mariner said, turning away from the window. 'I came for the dog on an errand of mercy. There's nothing to be gained by watching you stroll down memory lane.'

'But you've seen nothing!' Einstein complained. 'Nothing. He was groping in the dark until I came into his life. He was less than a slithy tove when I became his guardian. A rath. A mimsy borogrove.' He snarled and snapped at the ivy as it curled surreptitiously under his legs.

'I can speak for myself,' Charlie said, scowling down at the angry mongrel. 'It might mean nothing to you,' he said to the Mariner, 'but I had my hopes and ambitions like everyone else. I was going to be an artist. My life was going to make a difference. I was going to change the world.'

'There was nothing wrong with the world until you fell out of your tree,' the Mariner said, shaking his head. 'I'm disappointed. You'd be of greater interest if you were more typical of your species.'

'Typical?' Charlie hooted. 'I'm as regular as clockwork. I'm a positive model of average ineptitude. I've wasted my time, crushed my own spirit, squandered my talents, done everything that can be done to encourage disappointment and self-disgust. That's typical. What's missing?'

'Everything!' the Mariner growled. 'You're a poor advertisement.'

'What did you expect to find?'

'If you were a textbook primate I'd have found you astride

your mate,' the Mariner said. 'You'd be grinding your teeth and squirting your seed in every direction. I might have escaped detection if you'd been bent to your buttock business.'

Six billion monkey-men swarming over this tiny planet like maggots infesting a corpse. How had such a catastrophe happened? He had heard that the males were always on heat and the females were always in season. And he knew they had bred at alarming rates, despite the fact that their world was no longer fit to inhabit. They continued to breed in flood and famine as if they dwelt in a land of plenty. They were mad. No doubt about it. But if he could learn the reasons for this madness he might have an answer to the tragedy.

'I'm as normal as the next man,' Charlie said indignantly. It hadn't been easy living alone, deprived of a woman's comfort.

'You're all freaks,' the armour-plated lizard murmured.

'I once had a wife,' Charlie said.

'She was a rough and randy piece of work,' Einstein interrupted, 'but all the same, it can't be denied, she gave him a champion litter.'

'A litter?' the Mariner said. 'Is that right?' His curiosity seemed to stir again.

'You want babies?' Einstein the seasoned slave trader said, cracking a wet and whiskery grin. 'He had babies. Certainly. Dozens of them. Shouting and steaming and puddling corners.'

'You're exaggerating.'

'Strike me dead – every word is true,' Einstein said. 'He had a house stuffed with babies. The carpets crawled with them. There were so many brats you couldn't count them.'

'What happened?' the Mariner asked suspiciously. 'Did he eat them?'

'That's another story,' Einstein said.

'I'm not to blame for what happened,' Charlie began.

'Shut up and sit down, noodle-brain!' the faithful scamp snarled. 'Can't you see that I'm trying to help you?'

'Close your eyes and concentrate,' the Mariner ordered, turning again to Charlie. 'Show me what happened...'

18.

Charlie closed his eyes again and now they saw a stranger in the attic, sitting on the sofa that served as a bed, staring at a pile of Charlie's paintings. He was a fat man in a dark suit and a fancy satin waistcoat. He was fat, there was no doubt about it. He was supremely fat. He was dangerously corpulent. He had a stupendous belly and a head that was pillowed on many chins. And yet, despite his size, this man held an air of sombre elegance. His hair was silver. His teeth were a most expensive blend of porcelain and gold. His hands, which were very dainty, were embellished with blue tattoos, as fine as copper engravings. His name was Harry Prampolini.

Harry was from a circus family. His parents had been famous jugglers but he had chosen to work with freaks. He had exhibited mermaids, wild men from Borneo, dogs with feathers and pickled human babies with wings. But the shows were no longer popular. The modern world was filled with freaks. Farmers found them mewing in lambing sheds. Midwives pulled them from screaming mothers. Trawlermen came home with their nets torn by fish with human heads. It was an age of monsters. He could see a time when everyone would have a hairy baby with flippers or keep a legless kitten rolling around on a rubber cushion.

He had abandoned all the old fairground traditions. He had cut himself loose from his family and friends. He was a man in search of adventure and fresh business opportunities.

Charlie had first encountered Fat Harry when the showman had ventured in from the street, sat down and ordered a shave.

While he was in the chair he had tried to sell Charlie a two-headed sheep. She was a good-natured sheep, very friendly, and living with a travelling circus that was going bankrupt in the outskirts of London. He was trying to save her from slaughter by finding her another home.

'What would I do with a two-headed sheep?' Charlie grinned. He liked this man with his strange talk and illustrated hands.

'She'll be no trouble,' Fat Harry said. 'She's grown so old she does nothing but sleep. You could put her in your window. A two-headed sheep is a big attraction. You could give her a wash and shampoo, shave a slogan into her fleece.'

When Charlie couldn't be persuaded to buy the sheep he offered him a shooting gallery. A dozen rifles and a gizmo that balances coloured balls on jumping jets of water. When that failed he offered him a helter-skelter. Guaranteed a hundred years old. A museum piece. A collectors' item. Finally he set out to sell Charlie a Chuck Wagon business.

The Chuck Wagon was a Bluebird trailer equipped with a hotdog machine. It carried gas bottles and a water tank on the roof. The walls unfolded to make counters and windbreaks. The windbreaks were painted with pictures of palm trees and dolphins jumping in sapphire seas. Fat Harry carried a photograph of the Chuck Wagon in his wallet. He claimed you could make a fortune selling boiled franks in soft steamed rolls.

'Everyone loves a hotdog,' he wheezed. 'It's the smell. You hold a dog in your fist, smother it with onion and ketchup and it smells like every circus between here and Marrakech.'

'It sounds good,' Charlie said.

'It is good,' Fat Harry agreed. 'A man takes one bite from a hotdog and he remembers the world when he was young and he thinks about the penny arcade and the Big Dipper and the Ferris wheel. He remembers the goat-faced woman and the India-rubber man. He remembers the fire-eater and belly dancer, the sword-swallower and stilt-walker. He remembers all the long,

75

starlit summer nights when he was tall and trembling with love for the beautiful girls who were sawn in half and smothered by snakes and shot from the mouths of smoking cannons. When a man eats a hotdog he's biting into his own memories.'

But Charlie shook his head.

'I don't want to sell hotdogs for the rest of my life,' he said as he ran the blade around the fat man's chins.

'It's an honest trade,' Harry snorted, finding insult where none was intended. 'It's no worse than being a barber.'

'I want to be a painter,' Charlie tried to explain. 'I want to travel and paint the memories of my journey. I don't want another trade.'

'You want to see something of the world,' Fat Harry suggested. He understood. He had been to Moscow and Vienna, Kathmandu and Casablanca. He relaxed and closed his eyes.

'Yes.'

'You'd better get out and do it fast,' Harry warned.

'Why?'

'I heard that Disney™ want to buy the planet and turn it into a leisure park. One day you'll wake up and find them charging admission whenever you leave your own front door. When you walk down the street you'll have to shake hands with Mickey Mouse™ or some other cartoon character.'

'I've got plans,' Charlie said confidently. 'I'm not staying here forever. Do you want me to trim your ears?'

'No,' Harry said. 'Do you have any cologne?'

'Royal Prussian or Sweet Lime?'

'Bay Rum,' Harry said. He stirred and opened his eyes, staring at the paintings around the walls.

They were a collection of small landscapes, brilliant tangles of colour and movement, emerald lakes, chrome yellow mountains, vermilion fields under cobalt skies. Charlie had hung them in the shop because the attic walls had long since been covered. He had paintings stacked in the little kitchen and paintings stashed beneath the bed.

At first Charlie had felt shy about putting his work on public view but none of his customers gave it a glance. Fat Harry had been the first person to have noticed his paintings and taken the trouble to study them.

'Is this your work?' he said at last, as Charlie splashed him with the sour dregs from an empty flask of Bay Rum cologne.

'Yes,' Charlie said, wiping his hands on a towel.

'It's all very bright,' Harry declared, squinting through a keyhole of dainty blue fingers.

Charlie looked shocked. He stepped back from the chair and stared around the shop, as if looking at the paintings for the first time.

'People like a cheerful view,' Harry said. He meant it as a compliment. He cocked his head at Charlie and grinned.

'Would you like one?' Charlie said hopefully. 'Choose one that takes your fancy. I've got hundreds.'

'Is that right?'

Charlie nodded.

'How much do they cost?'

'I don't know...' Charlie stammered. 'I've never thought about it. How much do you think they cost?' As far as he had been concerned paintings were either worthless or priceless, nasty daubs or masterpieces. Something happened to artists, something he didn't yet understand, that catapulted some of them from obscurity into the world's great museums and galleries. This transformation was sudden and violent. Between neglect and adulation there was only darkness.

'You need a manager,' Harry frowned. 'Someone to help you sell your work.' Paintings or hotdogs, it was all the same to him.

He was looking for the big opportunity. The chance to make some money.

'Do you really suppose that people will buy them?' Charlie asked, begging for admiration.

'I'm surprised you're not famous. I'm shocked you're waiting to be discovered,' Fat Harry said. 'We should go into business together. You paint 'em and I'll sell 'em.'

Fat Harry knew that a good artist must also be a showman and the best showmen were accomplished artists. When the circus retired to its winter quarters it was Harry who had always stayed with the show, repairing the hoardings and carousel horses. Paint and varnish. Spit and polish. Appearances were everything.

He had painted the mural for his own freak show, a huge canvas depicting a mermaid, a cannibal, a cockatrice and a two-headed sheep. And behind this extravagant painting, in the gloom of the narrow circus tent, the freaks themselves were triumphs of Fat Harry's art. He had made the mermaid with his own hands. She was a porcelain doll with glass eyes and graveyard hair, stitched by her hips to the tail of a fish, afloat in a murky tank of broth, embellished with sequins and shells. The cannibal was a large ape, purchased from a taxidermist, shaved and sporting a bone through its nose. It wore handcuffs and a startled expression. The cockatrice was a skeleton made from rabbit and chicken bones. The sheep alone was a work of Nature and failed to look in the least convincing, slumped in her crate like a scrag-end of carpet, matted with dung and straw.

Fat Harry became a daily customer at the shop and while he sat in the chair for his shave he told Charlie about his plan. It was simple. They would change the course of their lives by entering into a partnership. Charlie would paint in the attic and Harry the brilliant showman would sell all the work downstairs in the shop. They would throw out the barber's chair and basin, the pictures of Douglas Fairbanks and the sizzling Durex sign. They would redecorate, strip the walls, polish the floorboards, install a proper system of lighting and call it the Church Street Gallery.

Harry would need a new set of clothes and he'd stay in the attic until they'd made enough money to move him.

'You'll find me no trouble,' he promised Charlie. 'I've done a lot of sharing. I know how to keep myself to myself. We used to travel six in a trailer and that included a bearded lady and a highly flatulent dancing bear. You'll find me a tolerable companion. And I don't care where you give me quarters just so long as the sheets are clean and there's always plenty of piping hot water.'

If Charlie had been a few years older he would have known not to trust strangers who turn up on the doorstep and promise to make your fortune by spending your savings. He would have known that nobody makes big money, working at home, no experience required. But Charlie was an innocent and as a result he prospered.

19.

'I thought we were going to study the monkey-man's mating habits,' the Mariner complained, turning to Einstein.

'You have to be patient,' the dog explained. 'Monkey-men need time for their courtship. But trust me, once they've found their mate they go at it like sewing machines.'

Charlie wiped his face and peered around him. These excursions into the past left him feeling sick and exhausted.

'He closed my shop!' an angry voice cried from the far side of the room. Charlie turned in alarm to find the ghost of his father treading his way through the wall. 'That damned whippersnapper destroyed my business! He squandered a lifetime's hard work and devotion!'

'The business sank without trace. There weren't any customers,' Charlie said, no longer surprised to find himself talking to phantoms, but greatly relieved that the spook was no longer spouting smoke.

'There were plenty of customers when I had the business,' the ghost of the barber retorted. 'Plenty of customers. Regulars. Most of them were my friends.' He wagged his decrepit head and the dewdrop quivered and flew from the tip of his nose.

'That was the problem,' Charlie said gently. 'The last time I saw your friends they were at your funeral.'

'Did Dancing Perkins pay his respects?' the barber asked. 'Did you have beer and sandwiches? Was it a good affair?'

'Perkins and Parsons,' Charlie said, to please him. 'And they hadn't spoken for fifteen years.'

'Did Stonker Wilson go to the service?'

'Stonker Wilson, Trust Me Davis, Filthy Frank and Tony the Turk. Everyone came to say goodbye.'

'So what happened to them?' the barber demanded, sticking out his chest and scowling at Charlie. 'Did the shock of my death make their hair fall out? You want me to believe that as soon as I'm gone nobody needs another haircut? You never wanted to make a success of your life. That's the truth of it. You never had the application. I could tell by the way you held your scissors. You had too many nancy notions. I blame your poor mother. If she hadn't met with her accident you would never have gone to that blasted school.'

'It was my own idea to become a painter.'

'And who gave you all these other ideas?' the barber demanded. 'Who said you were so special you had permission to throw away a lifetime's hard work, turn against your own family, waste my savings and close the shop? Who told you? I'll tell you who told you. It was that fat spiv in the fancy waistcoat.'

'It was a business arrangement.'

'Business arrangement my arse! It was vandalism. I worked all my life to leave something behind me. I slaved every hour the good Lord gave me to give you some security. And what happens? As soon as I'm in my grave you give it all away to the first fat spiv who walks through the door and spins you a hard luck story.'

'It was an investment. Harry knew about the world. He gave me an opportunity to make something of my life.'

'Hah! What did you know about him? Nothing. A jumped-up gippo with a few airs and graces. He could have slit your throat for sixpence,' the poor barber raved, wagging his head so violently that his teeth began to rattle.

'I don't have the time to listen to all this nonsense!' the Deep Time Mariner roared, making a lunge at the startled dog. Einstein yelped and scuttled for cover.

Einstein

'You keep out of it!' the ghost snapped. He glared indignantly up at the giant and flared his nostrils in contempt. 'Blasted foreigners! You come over here with your boogie-woogie, taking our jobs and stealing our women by teaching 'em your smutty dances and you think you own the place…' He stopped. His voice trailed away. He had started to disappear again. He raised one hand as if he were waving goodbye.

'Leave him alone,' the Mariner said, as Charlie reached out to his fading father. 'Tell me the rest of your story.'

So Charlie closed his eyes again and sank back into his dream.

20.

After the grand opening at which a few market traders, a lion tamer and a troupe of Russian acrobats consumed a huge quantity of cheese and wine, nothing seemed to happen for a long time.

Charlie worked hard in the studio but whenever he ventured downstairs he found Fat Harry standing alone, staring at the gallery walls. He began to have doubts in his own talents as a painter and in Fat Harry's skills as a salesman. The showman remained optimistic but Charlie was tempted to burn his paintings and search for work in one of the local hairdressing shops. The brave new enterprise seemed set for failure.

And then, one evening, Fat Harry announced that he'd sold everything. Charlie was in the little kitchen chopping onions for soup when Harry broke the news.

'Everything?' he gasped as he chopped the end of his thumb into the pile of onion rings.

'The entire collection,' Harry grinned. 'The works. Two hundred landscapes. Cash on delivery.' He was dressed in a pink silk suit and a pair of crocodile shoes. He thought they made him look artistic.

'Have we got two hundred paintings?' Charlie said, sweating with pain and excitement.

'No,' Harry admitted. 'We're going to need another twenty landscapes by the end of the month.'

'But I can't...' Charlie protested.

'Nothing fancy,' Fat Harry said helpfully. 'Make 'em small ones with plenty of sky. That should do the trick.'

'But who bought them?' Charlie demanded, sucking blood and onion juice and peering nervously at the wound.

Fat Harry closed one eye and stared at the ceiling. He whistled. He raised a finger and tapped his nose. 'A very big collector,' he said.

'Who?'

'A very influential man,' Harry whispered, glancing around as if there were microphones everywhere. 'You've got to laugh. He doesn't want me to mention his name for reasons of security.'

'And how much is he willing to pay?' Charlie asked him.

'£50,000,' Harry said. He sounded almost apologetic. 'I had to give him a discount.'

This was more money than Charlie could imagine. It was a fortune. It was £250 a painting. He was rich beyond his wildest dreams. Who could afford to make such a purchase and who would take the risk with a young and unknown artist? He burned with curiosity. But whenever he asked about the mysterious benefactor, Fat Harry would only tap his nose and smile a secret smile.

When Charlie eventually discovered the name of his patron he was very discouraged. It was not, as he had dared to hope, the curator of a big museum. He had not been discovered by an influential critic nor yet an eccentric foreign collector who wanted to hoard him in a cellar.

His name was Joe Persil. He was the founder and chairman of The Haughty Hamburger Restaurant™ chain who'd been shopping for pictures to hang on his restaurant walls. Charlie's paintings were bright, cheerful and appetising. They were also, as Fat Harry had carefully explained, original, handcrafted works of art. Joe Persil didn't know much about paintings but he liked the idea of owning two hundred works of art. It had style. It had class. Every Haughty Hamburger™ was an original work of art, according to the advertising. Joe Persil wrote the advertising. The Haughty Hamburger Hefty Half-Pounder™ was a beauty, a classic, a masterpiece. He owned forty restaurants in prime locations. He was going to hang five paintings in every one of them.

'I'm an artist!' Charlie raged, as he struggled to complete the order. 'I'm not a machine. I can't paint landscapes on demand.' He glowered at a cornfield burning with poppies, scrubbed at the canvas with his brush, reducing the harvest to mud.

'You've never painted anything but landscapes,' Fat Harry argued. 'That's your gimmick. You always produce the same painting. People like that. It makes them feel secure.'

'I don't want them to feel secure!' Charlie shouted.

'I don't get it,' Harry said. He was baffled by Charlie's reluctance to work at the easel. This was their big opportunity. This was everything they wanted. What was wrong with him?

'It's not the sort of success I had planned,' Charlie said.

'It doesn't come in fifty seven varieties!' Harry shouted.

'I don't want to have my work hanging in hamburger joints,' Charlie finally confessed.

'Are you crazy?' Harry gasped. He looked amazed. He clapped his hands against his ears to shield himself against such nonsense. 'You have to go to the people. And where are the people? They're not storming the National Gallery, they're fighting for cheeseburgers. You think Picasso was famous? He's nothing compared to Ronald McDonald™. Nothing. I'm giving you the chance to have your work seen and admired by millions and millions of people.'

'But they're not interested in my paintings,' Charlie said. 'They're interested in how much pickle do they get with their half-pounders and how thick is the milk shake and should they try the fried fruit pie.'

'Give 'em a chance,' Harry said.

'I can't do it,' Charlie complained. 'I made a mistake. I thought it would be different.'

'Think of the money,' Harry said. 'That should help stir your creative juices.'

He couldn't understand Charlie's attitude. Fat Harry's ambition was simple. He had reduced the meaning of life to a shopping list. A large house in St Johns Wood with a Spanish porch and security gates, a fancy German car with tinted glass and white leather seats, a gold Rolex with diamond strap, a glass of champagne and a Cuban cigar. He wanted to make money and spend it on rich living to show the world that he'd earned big money and knew how to spend it. People had always told him that money can't buy happiness. But they were wrong. This was going to make Harry very, very happy. He meant no harm. He wanted Charlie to share the riches and taste the pleasures of life. It was a partnership. He was selling for both of them.

The deal with Joe Persil was just the beginning. He had plans to build a business empire. He dreamed of owning factories where a thousand paintings a month could be turned out for the walls of restaurants and hotel chains, offices and shopping precincts. Soothing pictures of lakes, sunsets and fishing boats. The kind of picture you'd give your mother. Bright, cheerful canvases depicting lovely scenes from Nature. And every picture guaranteed a genuine, hand-painted work of art. Charlie, rewarded for his patience, would have students to work on the pictures while the master strolled from easel to easel, signing his name with a long sable brush.

He was full of bright ideas.

21.

Charlie did his best to oblige Fat Harry, but after a series of fishing boats at sunset for the Salty Seadog Biscuit™ Company and the thirty views of poppyfields for a string of Popular Funeral™ Parlours, he'd had enough of fame and fortune. The money was good, he couldn't deny it, but he wanted more from his work and his life.

Fat Harry was away on a business trip with samples of Charlie's most popular views. He was hawking his way across the country, hoping to persuade sausage kings and pork pie barons that Charlie should paint their factories.

'Imagine! Your own factory, beautifully painted in oils by an international artist and presented in an elegant, gilded frame of tropical hardwood veneers, ready for you to hang with pride in your boardroom or management suite. In the tradition of the European aristocrats who commissioned the greatest artists of their day to commemorate their houses and gardens now you can transform your factory into a sumptuous work of art that will be the envy of your colleagues and competitors!'

Fat Harry was on the road for a month and Charlie was supposed to divide his time between the attic and the gallery. But he had no desire to work. He spent all day in the gallery, sitting at the corner desk, staring out of the window. A few visitors strayed through the door. They paced around the shop as if measuring the floor and then quickly returned to the street. They never spoke and they never stopped to study the paintings but merely glanced over them, like people searching a grocer's shelves. Whatever it was they wanted, the Church Street Gallery didn't stock it.

Einstein

And then, one morning, Baxter Pangloss swept through the door and into Charlie's life. She was a tall girl, perfectly starved, with a pale and beautiful face hidden by curtains of coarse black hair. She was wearing a leopard skin coat, very old and faded, workman's boots and a straw hat. The leopards had been shot a century before by a party of tourists in British India. The skins had been sent to a Bombay tailor. He hadn't made a very good coat – there were bullet burns in the collar and sleeve. The boots had been borrowed from a building site near the Charing Cross Road. The hat had been made in the West Country Workshops for the Blind.

Her name was Baxter because her father had wanted a son and he was a stubborn man who didn't like to be contradicted. Baxter had managed to contradict him only twice in her life. 1. She had insisted on remaining a girl. 2. She had refused to pursue her education at a finishing school in Switzerland and enrolled, instead, at a dismal London college of art.

Charlie watched her walk from canvas to canvas, frowning, snorting, wrinkling her nose. Fat Harry had hung a set of landscapes. French Vineyard in High Summer. Spanish Harbour at Dawn. Storm Clouds of Portugal. Picturesque views in lurid colours. Baxter Pangloss wasn't impressed.

When she had finished her tour of inspection she marched briskly towards the corner desk, her boots crunching on the polished pine floor. She clasped a portfolio under her arm.

'This is good,' she said, tugging savagely at the ribbons and pulling open the marbled boards to reveal a pile of drawings. There was something in her voice, Charlie thought, that suggested everything else in the room had just been condemned as bad.

He took a peek at the first drawing. It was a meticulous examination of a decomposing haddock.

'Why do you hang this rubbish?' Baxter complained, glaring into a painfully bright Sun Sinking on an Alpine Meadow that flared like a firework on the wall, creating a halo above Charlie's head.

'It's very popular,' Charlie said, trying to absorb the insult without looking up from her drawings. He'd been told so often by Harry that he was a popular genius, the common man's artist friend, he'd almost come to believe it was true.

'I'm not surprised that it's popular,' Baxter snorted. 'It's dreadful!'

'What's wrong with it?' Charlie demanded impatiently, frowning as he glanced around the gallery.

'It's puerile,' Baxter said, flicking the hair from her lovely face. 'What are you advertising, the Greek Islands or cheap flights to Spain? It looks like an exhibition of giant holiday postcards.' She was certainly beautiful but, oh, she could be cruel!

'They are giant postcards,' Charlie said. That was the secret of his success. Whenever he'd tried to paint his surroundings Fat Harry had refused to hang the work. People wanted romance. They wanted to be carried away to exotic scenes in foreign lands. They wanted to look at a painting and dream. They wouldn't buy pictures of London attics. So Charlie had been presented with a shoebox full of postcards and told to work his way around the world.

'I just don't get it,' Baxter said, shaking her head. 'It's crazy.' She looked flummoxed.

'It's simple!' Charlie growled, trying to smother his irritation but raising his voice to a shout. 'Nobody is going to buy a pencil drawing of a decomposing trout!'

'It's a haddock.'

'I don't care if it's smoked wild salmon!' Charlie said. He slammed shut the portfolio and leaned back in his chair, folding his arms against his chest as if locking himself away.

'Are you going to look at the rest of my work?' Baxter said, quite unmoved by his outburst.

'No.'

'Are you telling me that you can't sell it?'

Charlie shrugged.

'Are you the owner?' she grinned. She looked as if she suspected the whole operation might be a hoax, an elaborate practical joke.

'I'm the artist.'

'Jesus!' Baxter shouted. She seemed amazed by his confession. She spun on her heels and swept at the gallery walls with her arms. 'Why do you waste your time painting scenes from travel agents' windows?' she demanded. 'What's wrong with you? Why don't you paint from life?'

'I don't have a life,' Charlie retorted. 'I'm far too busy painting postcards.' It was meant to sound like a smart remark but as he said it he knew it was true.

'Don't you ever do figure work?' Baxter asked him.

'What sort of figure work?'

'Life studies. Nudes. How can you hope to understand form until you've mastered the nude?'

Charlie said nothing. He'd made several brave attempts to copy figures from the best of *Skirt Lifter* magazine. But the copies had not been a great success – it was difficult to consider a nude wearing a wig and a Playtex™ girdle.

Baxter retrieved the portfolio and rummaged through her drawings. She pulled out a pen and ink study of a naked woman with breasts as long as cucumbers. A page of clenched fists. A watercolour of several feet. A sheet of charcoal penises. She spread them over the gallery floor so that Charlie could admire them.

'Look at the figure in that picture!' she said, turning with contempt on Charlie's Dutch Windmill in Tulip Fields and prodding at the canvas with a slender finger crusted with rings. 'Is that a man or what?' She frowned and wrinkled her nose in disgust. 'It looks like a carrot in clogs.'

'I taught myself,' Charlie said, stung by her criticism. He'd been rather pleased with his simple Dutch peasants. 'I never went to life class.'

'So what did you do at art school?' Baxter said sarcastically. 'Cake making and carpet weaving?'

'I never went to art school,' he said at last. He lunged forward, making the chair legs clack on the floor, spreading his hands on the desk, defeated. She had made him feel like a fraud.

'So what?' she said brightly. 'I'll sit for you.'

'What?'

'You want to learn to draw from life? I'll sit for you. There's nothing to it. I do it all the time at college.'

'You pose in the life class?' Charlie marvelled. 'You pose in front of your friends?'

'Friend or foe. It's all the same to me. It doesn't hurt,' Baxter grinned, delighted by his expression of horror.

Charlie looked for her face through the tangle of thick black hair and tried to read her eyes. He thought she was only mocking him.

'Why should you want to help me?' he said suspiciously. 'You think my work is puerile.'

'It's not that bad,' Baxter laughed gently. 'You've got a wonderful sense of balance and colour. It's not how you paint – it's what you paint that's wrong.'

'I don't know,' Charlie said doubtfully. He swung in his chair and squinted at the carrot in clogs. He didn't want to appear too anxious for fear the girl would doubt his intentions.

'Suit yourself,' she said briskly and began to gather her drawings into their battered portfolio.

'Do you really think I could master it?' he said quickly, fearing now he had hurt her pride.

'You'll love it,' Baxter promised. She smiled and threw back her head, pulling off the straw hat and combing her fingers through her hair. 'It will really open your eyes. All that fat and gristle. It's disgusting. It's beautiful.' She looked so excited that, for a moment, Charlie thought she might peel off her cat skins and give him a demonstration.

'I'd have to pay you,' he said. 'It would have to be a proper arrangement.'

'I don't need the money,' Baxter said scornfully. 'I'd like to help you.' She paused and nibbled her lower lip with the cutting edge of her teeth. 'And if I help you,' she added cautiously, 'perhaps you can help me get my work into the gallery. What do you think?'

22.

A few days later Baxter Pangloss returned to the Church Street Gallery and Charlie was there to lock the street door and take her upstairs to the studio.

'Is this really where you live?' she asked, walking around the crooked rooms. She was wearing a dress she had cut from discarded bathroom curtains and a skullcap of red china beads.

'This is it,' Charlie said proudly. He'd spent the previous evening scrubbing floors and washing windows. He was pleased and surprised by the transformation.

'What's that!' Baxter screeched when they reached the kitchen. She stood and stared in horrified delight at a dirty glass tank that was balanced on the top of the fridge. A tiny child's face stared back at her through its murky world of embalming fluid. Its hands were pressed against the glass and its blue eyes bulged as if it were straining to smash the tank walls and escape.

'It's a mermaid,' Charlie said.

Fat Harry had insisted on bringing his freaks to live with them. The mermaid floated on top of the fridge. The cannibal lived in the bathroom. The cockatrice lurked beneath Harry's bed. Charlie hadn't dared to inquire about the fate of the two-headed sheep.

'Would you like a sandwich or something?' he said nervously. 'Would you like a drink?'

Baxter shook her head. 'It's time to work,' she said and grinned.

She found her way into the sitting room, sat down on the sofa that served as a bed and began to unbutton her dress.

Einstein

Charlie had set up his easel beside the chest of drawers. He stood behind the easel, tightened the clamps, adjusted the legs and stared at the blank sheet of paper already pinned to the board. His shirt pocket sagged with pencils, crayons, sticks of charcoal and a Swiss army knife.

He began to divide the paper into eight equal parts. At the top of the paper, in the first two sections, he drew a balloon to suggest a head. Beneath the balloon he drew something that looked like a wire coathanger from which were suspended a display of curious sausages. Shoulder sausage. Arm sausage. Leg sausage. The sausages dangled the length of the page. But when Charlie stepped back to review his work he could see that something was wrong. The first foot sausage wouldn't fit the paper. He tried again. This time he divided the paper into sixteen equal parts and reduced the size of the balloon.

'Charlie,' Baxter called softly. 'How is it coming along?' Ten minutes had passed in silence.

'Fine,' Charlie said, scribbling. 'You were right. Everything is so much easier when you draw directly from life.' He had abandoned his pencil in favour of a thick blunt charcoal stick. His fingers were black. There was charcoal dust in his eyes and nose. He scribbled furiously, snapping the charcoal into fragments, smudging the sausages with his thumb. Was it hot in the room or was it his imagination? His collar felt damp against his neck.

'Charlie?' Baxter said again.

'Yes?' Charlie said.

'Why haven't you looked at me?'

Charlie stopped scribbling. The charcoal fell to the floor. Slowly, very slowly, he tilted his head and peered around the easel.

Baxter was sprawled in the sofa, naked, grinning, supporting herself on one elbow and hiding her pubic bush with one hand in a rather good imitation, she felt, of a famous painting by Edouard Manet. She was still wearing her little skullcap and was turned, very slightly, at the shoulder so that Charlie might take full advantage of the tilt of her big white breasts. She was surreptitiously feeding herself liquorice allsorts from a bag she had hidden under a cushion and for the rest of his life Charlie would associate the sweet scent of liquorice with this moment and the pleasure Baxter took in teasing him and his own confusion and the way he had kept his eyes cast down, afraid that they might betray him and the shame of his desire.

'You can't learn anything unless you look at me,' she said impatiently.

Charlie blushed and looked at her feet, from the bulbs of her heels to the chipped opalescent lacquer on the nails of her slender toes.

'What have you been doing behind that easel?' she said, jumping up and walking on tiptoe towards Charlie's drawing. She peered at the string of sausages and wrinkled her nose in disgust.

'That's a mess,' she declared flatly.

'I was just getting the hang of it,' Charlie blustered. 'Trying to get the feel of it.'

She turned to him, lightly touched him on the arm and pulled a pencil from his pocket. 'There's no structure,' she complained.

'I was coming to that,' Charlie said.

'You start with the structure,' Baxter said. 'Watch.' And she quickly drew a skeleton in a corner of the page.

Charlie stood beside her and watched. He watched her frown in concentration. He watched the flick of her wrist and the swing of her arm as it pulled and joggled the heavy breast. Skull. Thorax. Arms and legs. A few quick strokes and it was finished. She made it look simple.

'There!' she grinned, returning the pencil. She walked back to the sofa and arranged herself in the cushions.

'Don't look at the paper,' she called to Charlie, who was already retreating behind the easel. 'Look at me.'

Charlie emerged from his hiding place, sat down on the carpet and balanced a sketching block on his knees.

'Just try to think of me as a bag of bones,' she said, tossing him a liquorice allsort.

'Bones,' Charlie said.

'Two hundred bones,' Baxter said. 'When you've found them you can start to dress them with fat and muscle.'

'Fat and muscle,' Charlie repeated.

'And don't exaggerate my titties,' she cautioned him. 'Men always make too much of my titties.'

By the end of the afternoon she had taught him how the shoulder girdle is connected to the spinal column and the spinal column is connected to the pelvic girdle and the pelvic girdle is connected to the thigh-bone and the thigh-bone is connected to the leg-bone and the leg-bone is connected to the ankle-bone until, when she had finished, he had worn his charcoal sticks into stubs and she was nothing but a wonderfully articulated skeleton laughing goodbye and pausing to kiss him as they walked downstairs.

'You learn quickly, ' she said, pulling away, leaving him breathless and too shocked to speak.

Here ended the first lesson.

23.

Why had Baxter fallen in love with him? How did she come to lose her heart to this quiet barber's boy when she could have possessed almost any man she desired? She was so striking, so handsome, that she needed only to snap her fingers to have men running in circles, fawning and throwing flowers. They wrote her atrocious poems and long, anguished declarations of love and begging letters and suicide notes. She tossed aside the poems and letters but kept the suicide notes taped to the glass of her bathroom mirror.

Baxter was bored with beauty. And Charlie, to her surprise, never once compared her mouth to a bruised rose or her eyes to dark and mysterious pools. He was frightened of her beauty, of course, like all the other men she had encountered in her short but brilliant career. But Charlie, unlike the others, never managed to turn his fear into verse and found, instead, the magic words that she wanted to hear more than anything else in the world.

He told her she was talented.

No one had ever told her she was talented because it wasn't true. She was beautiful, yes, and so confident in her manner that she might have been accused of conceit. Her talent, however, was small. But Charlie, who had taught himself to paint, was overwhelmed by her easy, professional manner and casual draughtsmanship. She was the most accomplished artist, in fact the only artist, he'd had the good fortune to meet.

When she returned the following afternoon she was wearing a black silk dress, salvaged from a charity shop, white ankle socks and bright green shoes. She had tied her hair into bunches.

97

Einstein

Charlie stood by the easel pretending to sharpen pencils already sliced down to hypodermics and peeping at her while she undressed and dropped her clothes on the floor. He tried to imagine her in a classroom, naked on a little stage, while students jostled to gawp at her beauty. He wondered if it was any easier for them, sitting handcuffed to drawingboards, while Baxter Pangloss challenged them to draw the maps of their desires. He supposed that true artists, real artists, with their fine and lofty views, must be immune to the fever that infected him. Did they walk their rooms at night, unable to sleep, pricked awake by wild dreams?

'Are you ready, Charlie?' Baxter said, waiting for him to look up and meet her gaze.

She was standing in a pair of black silk panties, tied at the waist with lengths of red ribbon. She had bought them that morning. The price tag still dangled from one of the legs.

'I'm ready,' Charlie said.

Baxter pulled the ribbons. The confection fell apart and drifted smoothly to her feet, springing a wonderful bramble patch of gleaming pubic hair.

'They're new!' she said, bending down to scoop the panties into her hand. She grinned and waved them at Charlie.

'They're pretty,' Charlie said carelessly, as if such trifles were hardly worth his attention.

'They cost a fortune!' Baxter said with immense satisfaction. She clambered aboard the sofa, wriggled coquettishly into the cushions, sighed once or twice and fell asleep.

Charlie set to work on his drawing and his concentration was so ferocious that soon he was settled into a trance. The world was the size of the room, the sunlight slanting over the sofa, the enchanted girl, the magic marks he scratched on the paper that grew like a kind of spell as if, by catching her likeness, he might possess her body and soul.

These were some of the happiest moments in Charlie's life. But he didn't know it at the time. It was a shame. If he'd known that the world was going to end and that he'd find himself pleading for mercy from an eight foot monster with a head like a pumpkin, he might have taken the trouble to snatch a few more of these brief days of pleasure.

Baxter stirred and opened her eyes. She stretched her spine and yawned like a cat.

'Charlie,' she called. 'Are you still there?'

'I'm here,' Charlie murmured softly.

'Take off your clothes.'

'Why?'

'I want to make some drawings of you.'

Charlie peered anxiously at his own drawing and chewed the end of his pencil.

'I'm still working... ' he said in alarm. Everything? Did she want him to take off everything?

'I'm bored,' Baxter complained, standing up and walking to the window.

She found her shoes and performed a little hopping dance as she struggled to spear them with her toes. She made no attempt to recover the rest of her clothes. The forgotten silk dress remained a shadow on the floor.

'I've nearly finished,' Charlie said.

'You can finish me another time,' Baxter said. 'I must have been sitting for hours. You sit down while I do some work.'

So, behind the shelter of his easel, Charlie reluctantly pulled off his clothes, gulped at the air and hoped to smother his excitement. He moved forward like a man creeping over wet shingle into a freezing sea. But somehow, between Charlie stepping towards the sofa and Baxter moving towards the easel, their hands touched, their arms entwined and they fell, hopelessly entangled, onto the carpet and she was shrieking obscenities and biting him and pushing his face between her legs.

Here ended the second lesson.

24.

Fat Harry knew that something was wrong as soon as he entered the gallery. He had come home with a bellyful of beer and a big commission from the Best of British Hotels™ Group who wanted forty oil paintings to decorate some of their restaurants. Romantic views of manicured English country gardens that would give Best of British™ customers an appetite for the roast pork dinners and frosted pineapple puddings. He'd also persuaded the men of the Universal Rubber Corporation™ that Charlie should paint twelve of their fifteen factories. Harry had brought home photographs of the rubber plants: identical concrete fortresses surrounded by razor wire and towers of tractor tyres.

It was long past midnight when he unlocked the door and crept into the gallery but even by the light of the street lamps he could see that something was wrong.

The French vineyard, the Spanish harbour and the Portuguese storm clouds were missing and in their place hung a set of mysterious pencil drawings. They were meticulous studies of bird and animal carcasses and some kind of queer fruit that looked, to Harry's bleary eye, like rows of old men's penises. What was happening here? This didn't look like Charlie's work.

He switched on the gallery lights. The pencil drawings ran the length of one wall. The other walls were covered in large, square canvases of brightly coloured nudes.

Fat Harry hauled himself upstairs to the attic, threw open the door and knocked Baxter Pangloss to the floor.

'Who are you?' he demanded, glaring down on the terrified girl he found sprawling at his feet.

Einstein

Baxter kicked out her legs and screamed. She had just emerged from the bathroom and had been attacked on her way back to Charlie's bed. She was wearing a lot of lipstick and a lick of novelty underwear.

'Charlie!' Baxter shouted.

'Harry!' Charlie shouted. He came running from the bedroom, looking startled and trying to keep his pyjamas closed.

'Calm down, it's all right!' he said, turning to Baxter. 'It's Harry. It's only Harry.' He managed a smile and bent down to help the fallen girl recover her modesty. But Baxter shrank away from his touch, sobbing and chewing her fist.

He reached out to embrace Harry but the big man snorted, pushed him aside and blundered into the sitting room.

'Oh, my Gawd!' Harry bellowed, when he'd snapped on the light. He tottered forward and peered at the picture on the easel. His face was purple with indignation. 'That's disgusting! What are you trying to do to me, Charlie? You want to break my heart?'

'What's wrong?' Charlie demanded.

'Nude women!' Fat Harry roared. 'You've been painting nude women behind my back!'

'He's drunk!' Baxter said from the safety of the door. She watched the intruder grasp the easel, clinging to it for support while his legs performed a rubbery dance.

'They won't buy paintings of nude women!' Fat Harry raged. 'You're wasting your time with this kind of rubbish. People don't want to stare at a lot of women's arses while they're trying to eat and drink in sophisticated surroundings. It's enough to turn their stomachs.'

'Get out!' Baxter shouted. 'Charlie, tell him to get out!' She stamped her bare feet like a sulky child.

'He lives here,' Charlie said.

'Who are you?' Harry wheezed, turning on Baxter as if he were looking at her for the first time.

'This is Baxter,' Charlie said. 'She's a painter. We've been working together – I thought you'd be away until the end of the week.' He hadn't expected this confrontation. He tried to wave Baxter into the sanctuary of the bedroom but Baxter refused to meet his eye.

'So that's it!' Harry said bitterly. He moved away from the easel and began to sail the room like a stricken galleon. 'I travel the length of the country trying to find you honest work, and when I come home you've forgotten me and taken up with a fancy woman!' He sounded like a wounded wife, betrayed by a lecherous husband.

'I finished a couple of Snow Drifts in the Apple Orchard. I didn't neglect the business.'

'It looks like it,' Harry said mournfully, shaking his arm at the evidence on the easel.

'I'm tired of painting pictures from postcards,' Charlie blurted, glancing at the half-finished canvas. A pale ghost of Baxter stared back at him, a nearly naked nympholept, flaunting her legs in a faintly sketched chair. 'It's not enough. I can't waste my life painting views of windmills and ruined castles. I'd rather be a barber.'

'You haven't got the talent to be a barber!' Harry roared. 'Your haircuts were horrible.' He chopped at his scalp with the flat of his hand and nearly knocked himself to the floor.

'My paintings are horrible!' Charlie shouted, moving between the easel and Harry, instinctively protecting his work.

'Your customers like them,' Harry said, nursing his head. 'They like a nice view. It's not my fault.'

'And if they wanted paintings of pampered pets, I suppose you'd make him paint portraits of poodles,' Baxter sneered.

Einstein

'That's a good idea!' Fat Harry said. 'That's a very good idea.' He turned and stared at the source of this unexpected inspiration. He frowned. 'Who are you?' he demanded.

'My name is Baxter!' Baxter shouted.

Fat Harry staggered forward and stretched out a tattooed hand as if trying to introduce himself, lost his balance and grabbed at the girl for support.

'Keep away from me!' Baxter shouted. She twisted and turned but felt him fumble, catching her by the little chemise.

'You're the one in the paintings with the stupid grin and your tits hanging out!' he gasped as her underwear came apart in his hands. He looked at the hand and scowled, stepped forward, wagging his wrist as if he had cobwebs stuck to his fingers.

'You bastard!' Baxter hissed, wrenching at the strands of lace. 'Touch me again and I'll kill you!'

But the sight of Baxter, sweetly naked, long limbs loose with fright and fury, failed to set Harry on fire. 'I'm feeling very peaky,' he belched. 'I think I'm going to puke.' His face softened to a sleepy smile and he started to walk in circles, vaguely searching for the bathroom.

Baxter shrieked and flung herself at him, collided with a table and knocked a pewter vase to the floor. The vase bounced, slopping flowers across the carpet. She caught hold of Harry's arm and sank sharp teeth into his wrist, the lipstick bleeding from her mouth.

'Charlie!' moaned Harry.

'Leave him alone!' Charlie shouted.

Fat Harry bellowed with pain, capsized and buried Baxter beneath him. He didn't know what was happening. He couldn't understand why he'd found himself laid out to rest, with a squirming woman under his shirt and his face in a pile of rotting flowers. He tried to regain his balance but the floor was lurching and he couldn't organise his hands and feet.

'Charlie!' Baxter moaned.

'Leave her alone!' Charlie shouted.

He tried to rescue Baxter by catching one of her legs and wrenching her to safety. But Baxter was thrashing and screaming so much that he lost his grip, received a nasty kick in the face, and had to content himself, instead, with pulling on Harry's ears.

It was some moments before Harry was aware of this fresh assault on his person; then he let out a terrible trumpet, gave his head a mighty shake and flung Charlie hard against the table.

Again Charlie tried to pull Baxter free and again she frantically kicked him away. But now she was making peculiar gurgling sounds in her throat and her fight was growing feeble. So Charlie picked up the empty vase and briskly smacked Harry's head.

Fat Harry shuddered, gave a long and sorrowful whistle, as if steam were escaping through ruptured seams, and rolled slowly against one wall. Charlie jumped up and threw down his weapon.

'You've killed him,' Baxter whispered, as they stood together staring down at the corpse. 'Oh, Charlie, you've killed him.' Her face shone with excitement and she cupped her breasts with her hands as if shielding them from the sight of death.

Charlie looked frightened. A moment ago he had been half-asleep, safe in the dark, waiting for Baxter to settle beside him and now, in a few swift movements, he'd become a monster, a murderer, standing in torn pyjamas, lonely, confused, staring down with wild eyes at the broken body of the man he had always called his friend. Everything seemed blurred and distant. He couldn't remember what had happened. He knelt down and rummaged in Harry's fat for the ticking of his heart.

The corpse snuffled and started to snore.

'He's breathing again,' Charlie whispered. 'I think he's fallen asleep.'

'Quick!' Baxter hissed, clapping her hands. 'Let's get out of here before he wakes up.' She turned and ran around the attic, searching for her clothes, exhilarated by the danger.

'Where?' Charlie said.

'You can stay with me,' Baxter said, wriggling into her skirt. Charlie didn't know it, but she had a mews cottage in Chelsea with a small yard and a smell of the river. 'I'll look after you. But quick, get dressed.'

'We can't just leave him here,' Charlie said. He looked sadly down on his battered companion. His face was grey and his ears were crimson. His fine silk suit was smeared with lipstick and rotting flowers. They should wrap him in a blanket and put a pillow under his head. Yes. Let him dream his drunken dreams. It would all seem different in the morning.

'I'm frightened, Charlie. He looked so crazy. I'm frightened he'll kill you,' Baxter said. And she pressed herself against him and kissed him, very hard, on the mouth and ran away to fetch his shoes.

25.

'You should be ashamed of yourself!' A small voice cried from a corner of the room.

They turned to find the ghost of Charlie's mother sitting in a little chair and scowling at her wayward son. She looked just as dusty and dishevelled as she had on her first appearance and she still hadn't found her missing shoe.

'How could you?' she said, shivering with rage and indignation. 'How could you?'

'What?' Charlie said, rubbing the sleep from his eyes.

'How could you let yourself be deceived by such a horrible little trollop?' she demanded bitterly. 'Where did we go wrong with you? Didn't we always do our best? Didn't we give your everything? Didn't I feed you myself, with real mother's milk, even though it made me feel sick, because the doctor said you'd grow up to be some sort of pervert if I denied you all that biting and slobbering and made you drink from a nice clean bottle like any sensible modern baby? And later, didn't I play with you and read you stories? You had all the Mr Wiggly books. Didn't I make all the sacrifices that a mother could make for her son? Did you ever hear me complain? Never. And didn't your father love you to distraction and give you everything that money could buy, even though we couldn't afford it and sometimes had to go without, including the Little Snippety Barber's Shop outfit for Christmas complete with badger hair brush and plastic razor blades? And he wasn't a young man, Charlie. He found it difficult being a father. God alone knows, he found it hard enough being a husband. But he was proud of you. He had plans. And

107

look what happened! As soon as we've gone you fall straight into the arms of the first little madam who flutters her eyes and lets you unbuckle her brassiere! It breaks my heart, Charlie. I'm glad I never lived to see you make such a fool of yourself... ' Her voice faded into a graveyard whisper. She looked very small and lost.

'I was young,' Charlie said unhappily. 'She was interested and I thought I was in love.'

'You should have stayed with that nice Mr Harry,' his mother muttered. 'He wanted to help you. If you'd listened to him you could have been very comfortable. Very comfortable. I liked him. And I liked your paintings. You had a real talent for windmills.'

Einstein stared at the ghost, grinned and cocked his ears. He squeezed from his hiding place under the table and trotted forward, his nostrils flared and quivering, amazed by her sweet, unearthly scent.

'Keep him away from me!' she warned Charlie as the mongrel approached her chair. 'You know I was always allergic to dogs. They bring me out in a rash.'

Einstein hesitated, crawled forward on his belly and began to lick at her naked foot. She tasted of ancient pavement, warm leather and blowsy summer roses. He was bewitched.

Geraldine laughed and curled her toes as she tried to push him away. But the draught that was stirred in her skirt made him growl with excitement and he pushed his wet nose between her legs. Geraldine shrieked and beat her skirt with her fists.

'Einstein!' Charlie shouted.

Einstein cringed and skulked away. 'I can't help it,' he grumbled to himself. 'I'm a dog.'

The Mariner suddenly jerked back his head and let out a shattering sneeze.

'Bless you,' the ghost said, smiling and smoothing her petticoat.

The Deep Time Mariner snuffled and pulled something that looked like a Buck Rogers Atomic Torch from the pocket of his flying suit. He directed a narrow beam of light in circles around the room.

Charlie ducked and buried his face in the crook of his arm. The light faltered and died. The torch emitted a piercing whistle.

'This air is poisonous!' the Mariner said in disgust as he returned the torch to his pocket.

'He doesn't keep the place clean,' Geraldine sniffed. 'Look at those curtains. They haven't been washed in a month of Sundays. This room is a disgrace.'

'How can you breathe this filth?' the Mariner demanded. He shook his head and lumbered to the door.

'What's wrong with it?' Charlie said. He tried to keep order. But it wasn't so easy when you lived with a dog who liked to take his meals from the carpet.

'Wrong with it?' the Mariner roared. 'It's full of sulphur dioxide, nitrogen oxide, carbon monoxide, dust, soot and heavy metals! It's absolutely filthy!' He snuffled and rubbed his leathery nose. 'I'm leaving before I do myself a mischief.'

'Wait!' Einstein barked.

'He hasn't finished telling his story,' Geraldine complained.

'Leave him alone,' Charlie said. 'I'm tired of this rigmarole. Clear out and leave me in peace.'

This sudden change of heart took everyone by surprise.

'Don't be a fool,' Einstein said. 'Tell him the rest of it.'

'There's nothing else to tell,' Charlie insisted.

'That's not true!' Einstein growled. 'Do you want to die from modesty? Tell him the rest of it. Your life was full of incident. All sorts of strange things happened to you. There was Baxter the bumptious boggart. Baxter the burbling basilisk. You married Baxter. And that was almost as weird as striking up a relationship with one of Harry's freaks. And then I came to live with you and tried to keep you out of mischief. And then the house was filled with hundreds of grizzling squabs.'

'I want to see my grandchildren,' Geraldine insisted. 'I always wanted lots of babies. But all your father could manage was you,' she added, looking sadly at Charlie.

'I wasn't the father,' Charlie protested.

'What do you mean?' his mother said sharply.

'They weren't my children,' Charlie said.

'You mean she took a string of fancy men?' Geraldine said in a shocked whisper. 'Is that what you're trying to tell me, Charlie? Oh, you poor lamb! Don't you want to tell your mother what happened? Don't you think she'll understand?'

'And don't forget the episode with the chicken factories!' Einstein chuckled. 'That was a real song and dance.'

'What's that?' the Deep Time Mariner said. He turned, cracking his head against the lampshade and glaring at Charlie through the grey cascading dust.

'You tell him,' Einstein said and scuttled for the safety of the table.

'Chicken factories?' the Deep Time Mariner growled, jabbing at Charlie with a slender finger.

'Ambrose Pangloss!' Charlie shouted. He was trembling with fright. 'He made me do it. He gave the orders. It wasn't my fault. I did it for Baxter...'

26.

They are staring down into a large and darkly furnished office. The carpet is the colour of raw liver and the walls are lined with green silk. Beneath the window, where the blinds are drawn against the sun, there is a desk the size of a grand piano cut from slabs of mahogany, inlaid with oak and walnut. There is nothing on this desk but a telephone and a small lamp. The lamp, cast from bronze, throws a pool of light on the telephone that never rings.

The phone never rings because this is the office of a man who is thought to be so important that no work can be found important enough for him. He does not place his own telephone calls, nor write his own letters, nor drive his own car, nor wash his own shirts, nor trim his own fingernails. This is the measure of the man's success, a mark of his importance. It is enough that he is here, at his desk, captain of a mighty industry.

The man who sits behind the desk is Ambrose Pangloss, tyrant tycoon and living inspiration behind the Pangloss Chicken Empire. He is fifty-four years old, fighting fit, with a perfect out-of-season tan and immaculate steel-grey hair. He wears hand-made Italian suits, white linen shirts and stands five feet eight in his spotless Elevator™ shoes.

He is the man behind the Pangloss Melting Moments™ Oven Ready Chicken, the original Fancy Chicken Tidbits™, Mexican Chicken Surprise™, Roast Chicken Fingers™, Spicy Chicken Drumsticks™ and Chopped Chicken Sausages™. Children love his teatime treats. Housewives adore his nourishing dinners. The supermarket freezers of Europe are stuffed with his fat and heavy-breasted birds.

111

Einstein

He has given his life to chickens and they have given their lives for him. He owns the companies that breed them, feed them, slaughter them and market them. He also owns a chicken fertiliser company, a paper packaging company and a chain of fast-fried chicken restaurants.

The office in which he sits is at the top of a monolith of glass and steel, stuck like a stake in the heart of London. Behind him, when he cares to raise the blind, he has a view of the Thames and the dome of St Paul's Cathedral. Beneath him he has a harem of beautiful and dedicated secretaries waiting patiently for him to press the button concealed in the carpet at his feet. Beneath the secretaries he has a squad of senior executives, many of whom he knows by name, and beneath them a swarm of junior executives, many of whom look familiar to him, and beneath them he has never needed to venture.

He had not been born a wealthy man. His father had been a small-time chicken farmer and Ambrose had never forgotten those early years of misery. As a child he'd been made to rise at dawn to clean out coops, scrub down dropping boards, mix the feed and remove the corpses. When his father had died, Ambrose was working in the chicken sheds from dawn until dusk, seven days a week, to support himself and his crippled mother. By the time the old lady died, Ambrose Pangloss was already making a success of his life and he could thank God that his mother had lived to see it. But the poverty of his childhood continued to haunt him.

Now he sits in a green silk office with the world at his feet. He has come to understand that everything serves a purpose. His own suffering has led him to strive for great riches. The darkest days in a man's life are merely the shadows cast by the brilliance of his opportunities. Everything follows a grand design and he is one of the architects.

It is ten-thirty in the morning. In a few minutes he will press the button in the carpet and one of his secretaries will open the door and introduce his daughter to him. His daughter, Baxter, will be wearing a gauche collection of rags, despite a generous dress allowance, and her attitude towards him will be deeply supercilious, which is no more than he has come to expect. This does not trouble him. She is playing the part of the tortured artist. Children must experiment.

But this morning will be different from other mornings because Baxter will be presenting her odious new beatnik boyfriend. Charlie Tilson or Neilson or Nelson. She has warned her father of this encounter and he is prepared for it. Baxter placed a message with one of his senior secretaries and made an appointment to visit the office. She often pays visits to ask for money or little favours but this is the first time she has asked him to approve one of her boyfriends and from this he concludes, as he stares at his reflection in the polished mahogany desk, that this young man may be the one she intends to marry.

He contemplates the marriage of his only daughter and the prospect pleases him. He regards such an arrangement as a cure for all her filthy habits and adolescent grievances. She needs the discipline. The young man will be some sort of artistic nincompoop, no doubt, but this does not dishearten Ambrose Pangloss. The man who invented the Melting Moments™ Oven Ready Chicken is not to be defeated by a little yobo in plimsolls who thinks it will start raining banknotes because his hand found its way up a Pangloss skirt. If there is to be a marriage, and he has decided that there will be a marriage, then this young loafer must be transformed into the perfect husband, devoted father and fanatical executive in the Pangloss Chicken Empire.

He smiles. He lives in the happiest of worlds where everything, with the application of his chequebook, can be arranged for the best. And his daughter, like her mother, deserves nothing but the best. When the interview is complete, and he estimates that it will take no more than fifteen minutes, he will leave the office and go home to tell his wife the good news.

His wife will not speak to him but he continues to tell her what's happening around them because it makes him feel closer to her and there is always the possibility that the doctors are wrong and she will recover her senses. She has not spoken to him since she was dragged unconscious from the wreckage of a Peruvian air liner that fell from the sky over Lima while she was attempting to travel alone on a grand tour of the world.

When Ambrose Pangloss had learned of his wife's misfortune he had not wasted a moment indulging in grief or self-pity. He had immediately made arrangements to have his wife flown home in a chartered hospital plane and engaged the finest Swiss engineers to install a life support machine in the comfort of her own bedroom.

She has been connected to this machine for seven years.

There were valuable lessons to be learned from the tragedy and Ambrose Pangloss counts his blessings:

1. His wife survived a disaster in which one hundred and seventy Peruvians perished.

2. The accident resulted in dramatic improvements in the design and function of life support machines.

3. Swiss engineers also build excellent slaughterhouses.

He has done everything to help his wife and now he will do everything to help his daughter. He presses the button with the heel of his shoe.

27.

The scene changes abruptly. The office folds and fades away and they find themselves looking down on an ugly concrete house. The house stood alone in a green field site surrounded on every side by the grey industrial suburbs that sprawl on the outskirts of London.

At a distance the house resembled the hulk of an ocean liner, dragged ashore and sunk to its gunnels in grass. A salt-bleached wreck of funnels and narrow sun decks. But on closer inspection the house embraced all the conceits of a Hollywood hacienda, decorated with Spanish tiles, etched glass and elaborate wrought iron shutters.

The house had been a wedding present, built on a priceless plot of land only thirty miles from the city. Ambrose Pangloss had chosen the architects and spared no expense in its grand design. He considered no detail too small. Nothing had been forgotten. He'd ordered triple-glazed windows, air-flow central heating, mirrored walls and polished cherry wood floors for the bedrooms; a kitchen with a range of full-sized restaurant equipment and handmade Italian bathrooms with climate control and clusters of halogen chandeliers. To protect his investment, he'd installed a security system involving a lot of laser beams and automatic steel shutters.

When Charlie and Baxter had arrived the builders were finished but the house needed carpets and furniture.

Confronted with such a challenge Baxter had felt obliged to quit art school, as her father had intended, and settle down to the urgent business of choosing curtains and kitchen cupboards. Her first purchase was a big brass bed.

Einstein

Charlie, dazed by the changes in his life, was content to sit in the bed, exchanging caresses and Ideal Homemaker magazines. They had stumbled into the twilight zone of genuine Shaker stencil kits, Elizabethan cushion covers, illustrated place mats, silent curtain rings and solid teak outdoor furniture shipped direct from the Indian Ocean. There were real Victorian tapestry hangings, handcrafted Black Forest barometers and special containers for pot-pourri. There were even storage jars engraved with the names of their future contents: Pasta Shells and Preserving Sugar. So many methods of filling a space. Homemakers abhor a vacuum.

The marriage ceremony had been a brisk exchange of contracts, followed by a champagne and smoked chicken supper and a honeymoon in Marrakech, where it rained for seven days and Baxter wouldn't leave the hotel.

It was Charlie's first venture into the world beyond the smothering streets of London and he was impatient for foreign shores. He'd taken a camera, notebooks, maps, phrase books, pocket guides and a brand new watercolour box. He was bright and excited and armed to the teeth. This was the start of the great adventure.

Baxter had been to France, Spain and Switzerland but never before travelled so far south and was quite convinced that civilisation stopped at Gibraltar. They spoke English in Gibraltar and you could eat the food and drink the water without an instant dose of the squitters and gaze out at the smoke of Africa from a safe and respectable distance.

Morocco gave her the spooks. She had travelled the length of Europe like a seasoned cosmopolitan but here she found herself lost, surrounded by mysteries she couldn't fathom, a prisoner in a tourist hotel. A cheap and nasty tourist hotel. There were cats roaming the restaurant and no proper night-club or shopping arcade. It was a loathsome place. She wanted nothing more than escape.

'It's horrible!' she shuddered, whenever he suggested they go out to visit the mosques or make a tour of the souks. 'The streets smell like shit, the food tastes like shit and everyone speaks in a foreign language. The whole damned country gives me the creeps. It's a pain!'

Charlie had discovered that Baxter measured her life in pain. Anything tiresome was a pain. Anything difficult was a pain. Challenges were a pain. Art school had been a pain. Her father continued to be a pain. Morocco was a startling world of totally unexpected pain.

'They speak French,' Charlie said.

'So what?'

'I thought you spoke French.'

'I don't speak that sort of French,' she retorted and rolled her eyes in that supercilious manner she had always reserved for her father.

'We'll soon get the feel of the place,' Charlie said hopefully. 'Don't you want to see the Sahara?' Tribesmen, camels and cargoes of spices. A desert so vast it could hide North America under its sand.

'No!'

'The mosques,' Charlie pleaded.

'No!'

'We can't miss the famous Koutoubia Mosque.' Take my hand and walk with me for behold we have entered the secret city of minarets, tombs and palaces.

'No!'

'We may never have the chance to come here again,' Charlie grieved, pressing his nose against the window of their hotel room and gazing down on the rain-sodden lawns.

Einstein

An old man wearing a polythene sack for a hat was raking leaves from the boiling surface of the swimming pool. A colony of wet cats was watching him work from their shelter in a stack of upturned chairs.

'Good!' Baxter said. 'I never want to go anywhere again!'

'You don't mean that.'

'Trust me! I wish that we'd never left home. It's a pain!'

She was slumped in a chair, arms hanging loose, legs askew, a studio portrait of boredom. She had thrown herself into lethargy with spirit and energy. She rolled her head and sighed. She yawned and picked at the ends of her hair. She raised herself up and threw herself down again. She was trapped and restless. The bedside radio played nothing but Perry Como tapes or tunes from the Arabic hit parade and the television, to her disgust, would broadcast nothing but African football. It was such a pain that she wanted to scream.

Charlie was disappointed. It had been his own idea to come to Marrakech. He'd imagined how they would spend their mornings exploring the souks to haggle for rugs and silver bracelets and how, in the afternoons, they would seek the shadows of pavement cafes to sip at glasses of sweet mint tea to emerge through the jasmine-scented twilight into the famous market square to gawp at the snake-charmers, fire-eaters, jugglers, dancers and desert traders.

It had been a bad idea. He felt angry with himself for suggesting it and mad with Baxter for hating it with such determination. But when she reached out for him, to turn him away from the window, and kissed his face and conducted his hands on a guided tour of her bathrobe, he knew he would forgive her anything. The desert and mountains could wait for them. There was time. This was the morning of their lives.

'It's raining,' she whispered as she moved him slowly towards the bed. 'It's stupid to walk in the rain.'

28.

He was happy to be married but he wanted to return to work. He'd had to stop painting until a room could be found that would make a suitable studio. Baxter would plan it for him.

'As soon as we've finished the decorating we'll put a studio in one of the north rooms,' she promised him. 'You can work there undisturbed and have a chance to really develop some of your own ideas. You're going to love it, Charlie. And I'll sit for you whenever you want and we'll play music and make love every afternoon and get drunk every night and dance naked in the garden whenever the moon is full. And you'll be doing real work – no more sugar-coated landscapes.'

'And what about your own work?' he asked anxiously. Her portfolio was gathering dust. She hadn't touched it since quitting art school. He was half-afraid she had lost her commitment.

'What about it? You think that getting married is going to stop me painting?' Baxter said indignantly. 'As soon as I'm ready I'll find a room of my own and you can sit for me.'

She sat beside him now in the new brass bed. She was wearing her Hot Bitch Rubber Harness purchased at great expense from a Chelsea fetish fashion store.

At a glance it looked like a skin-tight red rubber diving suit but the limbs were welded to a wasp-waisted corset that might have come straight from the pages of a specialist mail order catalogue. Her breasts protruded through a pair of black rubber rings that clasped them so tight they looked alarmingly hard and swollen. The back of the harness was cut away to leave her buttocks exposed. There was a mask with holes cut out for the eyes, mouth and nose and a sinister ventilation nozzle set at the back of the skull. There were straps and hoops at the ankles and wrists that seemed to have no regular purpose and even Baxter had dared not inquire about their true function, although she supposed they must be designed to secure her limbs to sweet contraptions of torture. She could be spread upside down from hooks in the ceiling or held like a slave from chains in the wall.

The costume had baffled Charlie when she'd brought it home. He didn't know what to make of it. Did she suppose that he harboured desires for women in bondage, or had she bought it for the hell of it, in the way that she chose the rest of her wardrobe? What did it mean when your wife walked around in a bright red rubber sausage skin? Was it fetish or mere charade, confession or passing fancy? He wasn't complaining. He didn't want to discourage these brief but passionate flights of fancy.

He'd loved the sight of her in the French maid's uniform. The glossy black stockings and puffed white knickers like a froth of stiffened egg whites. He'd been sorry when she'd torn the skirt during a bedside breakfast skirmish. He'd relished the spangled boots and the buckskin shirt of her cowgirl rodeo outfit, despite the bullwhip and cutting spurs. During a few brief weeks he'd ruined a smirking schoolgirl in pigtails, molested a starchy, pale-faced nurse after hanging her helpless in traction and fondled the strong yet yielding thighs of a mortified Mother Superior. He'd risen to every occasion with a lechery brinking on madness, but he wasn't certain how to respond to a hot bitch rubber wife.

Baxter for her part never considered for a moment that Charlie would be puzzled by her exotic wardrobe of disguises. There was no mystery. It had nothing to do with him. Nothing. She was mounting her own exhibition of erotic comic strip art for the sake of the adoration of shadows held spellbound in the bedroom mirrors. This was Baxter as Batman's Bride. Baxter the Battling Amazon. Baxter the Slippery Slut of Sleaze.

It had taken her twenty minutes and a tin of dusting powder to get dressed that morning and the effort had so exhausted her that she'd had to retire to bed. But Baxter loved it. Behind the mask she felt lewd and dangerous. The Hot Bitch Rubber Harness clasped her like a cannibal lover, licking the salt from her skin and sucking greedily at her bones. Its muscular embrace was hot, relentless and suffocating. The bold display of her buttocks and breasts only heightened her state of arousal.

'Don't you adore the smell of warm rubber?' she murmured, raising a brightly polished arm and offering her hand.

'You smell like a winter's dark afternoon of raincoats and wet umbrellas,' Charlie grinned, reaching out to catch the hand and kissing the pungent fingertips.

'Gas masks,' Baxter said. 'Waterproof sheets and lunatic's pillows.' She pulled her hand away and caught him securely by the throat, trapping his breath and making him choke.

'Party balloons,' Charlie croaked.

'Truncheons, mouth clamps and torture chambers,' Baxter said. She was suddenly astride him, pulling herself forward and squashing his face between her hot and heavy breasts.

'Rubber ducks,' Charlie mumbled and laughed, a deeply muffled rumble of pleasure.

'Dead men's gloves,' Baxter whispered and shivered. 'Dead men's gloves and strangler's shoes.'

Charlie spluttered something that she couldn't understand. But she felt him reach out with his hands, groping for her buttocks beyond the clinging ribs of rubber.

29.

The days slipped away and Charlie continued to play the buffoon in Baxter's bedroom pantomimes. But as the time passed he considered his new surroundings and began to feel uneasy in them. The Pangloss Chicken Empire had paid for the house and furniture, laid the garden to lawn and filled the freezer with Fancy Chicken Tidbits™. Now Charlie began to wonder how they could afford to live in such idle luxury. It seemed to him that the house was a monstrous machine that would soon demand money with menaces.

'This place is too big,' he complained one night when Baxter sent him downstairs to investigate some phantom in the woodwork and check the locks on the doors and windows.

They had switched off the laser security after triggering the alarms and finding themselves locked in the bathroom for hours until the rescue services had arrived to cut through the steel shutters.

'Was anybody down there?' she muttered, half-asleep, her face obscured in a cobweb of hair.

'No,' Charlie said.

'So what took you so long?' she murmured, reaching out for him with one of her evil-smelling arms.

She was still wearing her Hot Bitch Rubber Harness. The contraption had perished and welded itself to her skin. She was too embarrassed to tell Charlie. He would eventually have to cut her out with a pair of bacon scissors. She would emerge, slippery and stinking, as wrinkled as a newborn baby.

'I got lost. I took a wrong turn at the top of the stairs,' he said, miserably, pulling the blanket over his ears.

'Did you check all the windows?'

'Yes.'

'And you locked all the doors?'

'Yes,' he whispered, creeping forward stealthily to grope for her hot and rubbery comforts.

'You're cold!' she gasped as she shrank from his touch and slipped once more into sleep.

He lay awake in the dark and counted the cost of the good life. He had his money from the Church Street gallery – Harry had bought his share of the business – and that would keep them secure for a time, but then he would have to find some kind of work. He had a wife and a house to support.

Charlie liked to think of himself as a simple working man. His father had worked as a barber and his grandfather had worked in a pickle factory where he'd suffered a heart attack, drowning in a vat of malt vinegar – a few weeks short of his eighty-third birthday – so the factory had felt obliged to pay the funeral expenses and arrange a cold beef and pickle supper for the widow and mourners.

He had seen a snapshot of the old man – a small, dainty figure in shirtsleeves standing on a seaside promenade and scowling in the sun as he smoked a Woodbine. He held a small child by the hand. A scowling child in a black woollen swimsuit, leather sandals and a brutal, kitchen chair haircut. The reason, Charlie had always supposed, why his father had been destined to become a barber.

His great-grandfather had worked in the coalyards of the Great Northern Railway and shovelled coal for forty years, retiring with emphysema, a silver watch engraved with his name, a bottle of sherry and his own shovel. The stationmaster had made a speech, explaining how he could use the shovel to work in his cottage garden to grow prize-winning vegetables. Golden years of spinach and cabbage, potatoes, leeks and onions the size of human skulls. The old man didn't have the breath to stand and express his gratitude.

His great-great-grandfather had worked on the land and lived in a fine brick stable, sleeping on a mattress of straw with his wife and other beasts of burden. He had a slow and stubborn body. His face had been weathered like leather, whipped by the wind and burnt by the sun. He picked stones from the fields, scared crows from the crops, repaired buildings, laid hedges and built fences. He was thirty-seven years old when a carthorse threw a fit, startled from a troubled sleep, and trampled him to death.

They hadn't been important men engaged on affairs of state, but they had been honest and true to themselves. They'd all taken pride in their work and they'd worked hard and hadn't stopped working until they'd dropped down dead. Charlie was proud of them. He liked to imagine that he was part of some grand tradition. He wanted to be a painter and make his own way in the world. But if he couldn't support Baxter with his earnings as a painter, then he'd have to take some other kind of employment. He wasn't comfortable without labour. It didn't seem natural. It didn't feel healthy.

If Charlie could have traced his family back another twenty million years he'd have been surprised to find that he came from a large and happy tribe of dedicated idlers. For millions of years his ancestors had done nothing but loaf around in the trees, eating fruit and hoping that it wouldn't rain. They had eaten when they were hungry, slept when they were tired and copulated without restraint whenever the mood was upon them, which was often since the only work involved in earning the next meal was the effort of reaching out an arm to pick at the nearest branch. When the food ran out they stirred and stretched themselves, yawned and moved to another tree.

Charlie's own convoluted method of filling his stomach and hiding from storms, involving, as it did, a lifetime's drudgery of little lendings and borrowings, not to mention the part it played in the relentless destruction of wilderness, the poisoning of lakes and rivers, the draining of wetlands, the flooding of lowlands, the stripping of jungles into deserts, the slaughter of animals, birds and fishes, insects, plants and microbiota, would have seemed insane to them.

But Charlie was a long, long way from his family in the forest and the forest was burning and he was sitting in an ugly concrete fortress somewhere at the end of the world. He had to find some kind of work. They couldn't live on love and Fancy Chicken Tidbits™. But whenever he tried to express these concerns to Baxter she would only laugh and shake her head and stop his mouth with kisses.

30.

Ten days later Ambrose Pangloss called at the house. One of his senior secretaries made the appointment. He would arrive at nine-twenty and stay for thirty-five minutes.

It was a cold Monday morning with a frost gleaming on the great lawn. Beyond the distant garden walls rooks flapped like prayer flags in the skeletons of trees. Charlie and Baxter dressed themselves for the occasion and did their best to clean the kitchen and bedroom.

At nine-twenty precisely they watched the Pangloss Mercedes glide silently to the house and deliver its tiny tycoon to the freshly painted front door. He looked smaller away from his office.

They offered him coffee and biscuits and then, after a little polite conversation in which they inquired after the health of Mrs Pangloss to be told, cheerfully, that all her systems were working and her fuel pipes had lately been replaced which had brought the colour back to her cheeks, they set him loose to patter about the house.

He inspected the rooms, approved Baxter's choice of furniture and bestowed his blessings upon them. And then, since the visit seemed complete, they began to walk him back to the door.

His daughter leaned forward to peck the top of his head, because she knew it annoyed him, his son-in-law shook him by the hand, and Ambrose Pangloss turned to leave. But as he opened the door something made him hesitate and stare thoughtfully at Charlie.

'What do you know about chickens?' he said, as if suddenly struck by a great idea.

'Nothing,' Charlie said.

'What do you know about the wheels of industry, the engine of commerce, the triumph of trading nations?'

'Nothing,' Charlie said.

Ambrose Pangloss nodded and smiled. 'Good,' he murmured happily. 'That's good, Charlie. I think you're the man who can help me.'

'No!' Baxter snapped. She stepped quickly between the two men. 'He's not interested. I want him to be a painter. You can't have him. I won't allow it,' she said fiercely, glaring down at her father. A pair of dangerously high-heeled shoes had turned her into a giantess.

'I'm not going to steal him from you,' he said in surprise.

'You're not even going to borrow him,' Baxter warned him. 'He's mine and you're going to leave him alone.'

Ambrose Pangloss shrugged and smiled. 'I understand,' he said mildly and glanced at his watch.

Charlie was mortified. What was happening here? How could she be so angry at this natty little napoleon? Her father had given them everything for their comfort and security.

'What's wrong with you?' he hissed as they watched the chicken millionaire stroll back to his limousine. The chauffeur snapped to attention and offered a brisk salute.

'Don't be a pain,' Baxter said impatiently. 'Do you want him to think that he owns you?'

'We owe him something,' Charlie said. 'You don't even know what he wanted... '

'He wants to run our lives,' Baxter replied in disgust. 'He's turned himself into our landlord and now he's arrived to collect the rent.' She pulled off her shoes and threw them across the floor.

'But he's been so kind,' Charlie said.

'He can afford it,' Baxter said. 'Shut the door and forget it. Come on, Charlie, let's go back to bed.'

But Charlie ran out into the frost.

'No, wait!' he shouted. 'I'll be glad to help you.'

Ambrose Pangloss grinned like a cat and turned away from the limousine. 'It's a fine morning,' he said. 'Why don't we take a walk around the garden?' And he took Charlie by the arm and led him across the field.

'Do you like to eat chicken, Charlie?' he inquired confidentially when they were a little distance from the house.

'Yes, sir,' Charlie said. They'd been living on nothing but chicken for weeks.

'That's right,' Ambrose beamed. 'Everyone likes to eat chicken. It's good and wholesome.'

They walked for a time in silence, Ambrose secure in his cashmere overcoat, Charlie in shirtsleeves shivering.

'Do you know how many people there are in the world, Charlie?' Ambrose said suddenly. He turned and looked back at the trail of black footprints in the silver grass.

'No, sir,' Charlie said.

'Billions. Untold billions. And they all eat chicken. Some of them won't eat pork and some of them won't eat beef but they all say yes please to chicken,' Ambrose said. A frown flickered for a moment across his face. 'And do you know how many Melting Moments™ we sell in a week? Three point eight million, Charlie. Three point eight million.' He sighed. His breath turned to smoke in the brilliant air. 'Everybody likes to eat chicken. Why don't they eat more chicken? That's the question…'

They reached the far corner of the garden where the lawn ran into a ditch beneath the high wall. The ditch was filled by builders' rubble, smashed bricks and broken shovels.

'That's bad,' Ambrose said, staring into the ditch. 'That's very bad.' But he wasn't disheartened. Great cities had been raised from rubble. 'I'll send someone down to clear it out and build something cheerful in this corner. A summerhouse with a veranda. It will catch the eye from the bedroom windows.'

'Thanks,' Charlie said.

'Do you know how many people work for me, Charlie?' the chicken tycoon continued, as they turned and retraced their steps.

'No, sir,' Charlie said.

Ambrose closed one eye and squinted at the sky, as if making celestial calculations. 'Thousands,' he concluded vaguely. 'Thousands of honest, hard working men with families to support. Large families. Women and children, the old and infirm. They depend on me to give them a living. They trust me. That's a big responsibility, Charlie. It's a terrible weight to place on one man's shoulders.'

'Yes, sir,' Charlie said.

Ambrose Pangloss nodded, amazed by his own importance. 'Do you know what I ask God when I go to bed at night?' he said softly. 'I ask Him how I can help those poor devils who work for me. I ask Him how I can make their lives a little easier for them. And do you know the answer, Charlie? Chickens. A four portion meal on two legs. The working man's feathered friend. We've got to make people eat more chicken.'

'Yes, sir,' Charlie said.

'I don't want to take you away from your sketching, Charlie. I know how you love your crayons. And it's a wonderful gift,' he added, smiling at Charlie with the kind of admiration a man might reserve for a tap-dancing chimpanzee. 'You're artistic and it takes all sorts to make a world. In fact, it's because you're artistic that I'm asking you this little favour.'

'But I don't know anything about the business,' Charlie protested.

'Exactly,' Ambrose said. 'You're a pygmy in a land of giants. You're floundering in the darkness of a pitiful ignorance, oblivious to the majestic beauty of a great industrial empire. And that's why you're so valuable to me.'

'Why?'

'Because you'll be looking at everything for the first time. You'll take a fresh approach. You'll be able to tell me where we have strengths and weaknesses. And you might come up with some bright ideas. Deep-fried chicken feet. Chicken neck savoury spread. Who knows? I'll pay generously for your time, Charlie. You could buy Baxter some decent clothes and a pair of sensible shoes. I know you'd welcome the money.'

He smiled at Charlie and wondered again how his daughter could find him attractive. He was so innocent, so eager to please, standing there, chilled to the bone, with his frost-bitten ears and wet carpet slippers. Battle-hardened by the boardroom, Ambrose Pangloss enjoyed a fight and Charlie had offered no resistance. There was really scant satisfaction in accepting his surrender. But he wasn't discouraged. He had settled Baxter in a fine new house with a garden and summer pavilion. And now he was going to transform her husband from an imbecile into a smart, young Pangloss executive.

Yes, everything would be arranged for the best.

31.

Despite Baxter's protests, Charlie had felt obliged to visit the Pangloss Chicken Empire. He couldn't see the harm in it. He was a painter, not a farmer, but if Ambrose wanted him to look at chickens, Charlie could hardly refuse his request.

The Mercedes came to collect him the following morning. His guide for the tour of inspection was a young PR man named Sam Shingles. As they sat together in the leatherbound silence of the big limousine, Sam explained to Charlie that the Pangloss Empire owned four superior poultry farms within fifty miles of London. These were called Sweet Orchard, Old Meadow, Larks Rise and Honeysuckle. He said their names reminded him of a team of prize-winning drayhorses and he laughed, in a nervous, gurgling way and started to chew his fingernails.

Sam Shingles was Charlie's age but he looked older and was already starting to lose his hair. He combed it into elaborate circles and pasted the outer rings to his ears. He smelt of toothpaste, mouth rinse, scented soap, hair spray and aftershave. He wore a silver feather in his jacket lapel. This little mascot was his badge of office and marked him out as a junior toady. He'd been programmed to sell the Wonderful World of Pangloss Chickens with all the passion of a 19th century missionary. Nothing could stop him talking. Nothing could stop him feeling cheerful. He wanted to win a gold-plated feather.

While Sam was explaining the history and virtues of Instant Chicken Dinners, Charlie watched the world gliding past the window. It was a world of building sites, factory sheds, storage bins, oil tanks, railways and junkyards. A dead and dreary land-

131

scape. The land lay cold and the sky was heavy with rain. But then, ahead of them, beyond a bend in the narrow road, sunlight sprang from the earth and shone through a group of chestnut trees. It was a brilliant column of light that dazzled the eyes and seemed to be aimed directly at heaven.

'That's Lark Rise!' Sam Shingles said gleefully and stopped eating his fingers.

The limousine turned into a gate and stopped beside a security post. Above their heads a huge hoarding, curved like a rainbow, was caught in the beam of light. Along the top edge of the hoarding, cut from letters of green and gold, was the legend: Larks Rise Farm. Home of the Pangloss Chicken. And beneath it, large as life but twice as lovely, was a wonderful painted farmyard. Fat and friendly chickens scratched for grain in the garden of a small thatched cottage, brown cows grazed in a buttercup field and behind the cows, the swollen hills were arranged like a row of dairymaids' buttocks. Among these hills was a tiny orchard and beyond, standing against a smooth blue sky, was a village of gingerbread houses. There were hollyhocks in the cottage garden and rabbits in the meadow and far away above the line of the distant village, a church with a sugar spire.

The driver offered a few words to the security guard who nodded and smiled and gave Sam Shingles a smart salute; and then the Mercedes was whispering down a curving ornamental drive of holly and rhododendrons.

A few moments later the drive opened into a courtyard dominated by another giant poster hoard depicting a similar farmyard scene but this time, in letters of gold and green, was the legend: Larks Rise Visitors gate.

'We're here,' Sam grinned, as a small door opened in the painted screen and a figure walked towards them. 'Welcome to the wonderful world of the pedigree Pangloss Chicken. That's

Farkiss. He'll show you around. I'll be back to collect you in a couple of hours. I know you're going to enjoy yourself.'

Farkiss, a fat man in a green bowtie, pulled open the car door and helped Charlie to his feet. He directed the baffled visitor towards the hoarding and urged him to enter through the little door.

Charlie stepped through the screen and stood gawking at a monotony of whitewashed office buildings, long factory sheds and towers of empty, metal crates.

'Where are they?' Charlie said, staring around the deserted concrete perimeter.

'What?' Farkiss said, supposing that his guest must have dropped something from his pockets and turning to search the ground at their feet.

'The chickens,' Charlie said.

'There!' Farkiss said in surprise, nodding at the factory sheds. He frowned at Charlie. 'Did you never visit a chicken plant?'

'No.'

'This one is a marvel,' Farkiss beamed proudly. 'It's frontier technology. You pack the eggs in one end of the plant,' he explained, throwing out his left arm, 'and six weeks later instant frozen chicken dinners come flying from the other.' He threw out his right arm and stood for a moment, with both arms outstretched, as if he wanted to embrace the entire factory, engines, cladding, pegs and rivets.

'Don't you ever let them out?' Charlie said, very disappointed.

'Let 'em out?' Farkiss laughed. 'Why should we let the buggers out?'

'You let them out to run around and scratch in the grass.'

'We don't have any grass. Besides, they wouldn't come out of there. You'd have to use dynamite to get them birds out of there. They have climate control, automatic feed, everything. The shock of

133

this fresh air would kill 'em. These are pedigree Pangloss flocks. They don't have the legs for running around and scratching and getting into mischief. Their legs have been scientifically designed. They're made for eating, not walking. That's the way we breed 'em. Come over here and I'll show you through Number Five Battery.'

They entered the battery through a set of hissing security doors and inside a small steel cabin Charlie was urged to borrow a nylon coat and shown how to tie his shoes into a pair of polythene bags fitted with welded rubber soles.

'Regulations,' Farkiss said. 'We're entering tomorrow's world. Are you ready?'

Charlie nodded doubtfully.

Farkiss punched a number into an illuminated keyboard and the inner door swung open with a blast of hot and stinking air. Charlie found himself stepping down a narrow corridor in a vast catacomb of dimly lit cages. The cages were stuffed with chickens. Their eyes glittered like a million specks of blood. Every cage was connected to a system of air pipes, feed troughs, sprinklers and defecation trays so that the interior of the battery had the appearance of one monstrous machine into which the birds had somehow strayed and become fatally enmeshed. They could squeeze their necks through the narrow bars but they no longer had room to stretch their wings. They were mad-eyed cripples, slumped, one upon another, gasping for breath, their beaks cut to stumps and their feathers broken.

'What's wrong with them?' Charlie whispered as he shuffled down the aisle. He had expected sweet artificial sunlight and yodelling cockerels and deep mattresses of straw. He had expected clouds of excited, scampering birds, exploding pillows of feathers. Here, in this fantastic twilight, there was no straw, no movement and no sound from the vast assembled flocks. There was nothing but the soft thunder of well-oiled machines.

'There's nothing wrong with them,' Farkiss said with a note of irritation. 'You're looking at fully ripe birds in the very peak of their condition.'

The heat of the battery had soaked him in copious sweat. His bow tie had wilted. Pearls of moisture hung from his ears. Beneath his nylon coat he was gently cooking in his own juices.

'But they're so quiet,' Charlie whispered.

'That's right,' Farkiss said. 'That's chemistry. We've introduced sedatives into their drinking water. A docile bird is a happy bird and a happy bird will tolerate being packed into greater concentrations.'

'Doesn't it do them any harm?'

'No!' Farkiss scoffed. 'These buggers are born addicts. Antiseptics. Antibiotics. Skin conditioners. Blood inhibitors. They'll take all kinds of punishment. These flocks are beautiful. Quick growth. Heavy yield. Standard weight. Beautiful. If we could get them to eat their own shit we'd have the perfect factory bird.'

He paused, peered into a cage and banged the bars with the flat of his hand. 'We get them to eat each other, of course, so they bury their own dead in a manner of speaking,' he said, as he unclipped the front of the cage and pulled out one of the prisoners. The bird was an ugly dwarf with a body the size of a grapefruit carried on plump and succulent legs. One of its eyes was missing.

'We collect up the corpses and process them back into feed pellets,' he explained, slinging the body into a passing rubber bucket. 'It's an art spotting the dead 'uns. Sometimes they look dead when they're alive and sometimes they look more alive when they're dead. That's why we use the Dead & Alive Men to check the cages every six hours. It's skilled work. Chickens are crafty.'

Charlie watched the bucket glide away on its steel track and vanish into the gloom.

135

Einstein

'We spray the pellets with vitamins, minerals and the Pangloss Special Recipe Natural Spicy Flavour™,' Farkiss continued, snatching a handful of feed from a trough. He pushed the pellets under Charlie's nose. 'Smell it. That's garlic, palm oil, bones and feathers. Smells good enough to eat.'

Charlie staggered, dazed by the heat and the stench of chickens.

'But this can't be very interesting for you,' Farkiss said finally, wiping his sweating face. 'I expect you'll want to see how we transform these humble birds into the world's favourite big flavour dinner.'

'I think I can imagine the rest,' Charlie said.

'You'll be amazed,' Farkiss said, taking Charlie by the arm. 'You haven't seen anything until you've seen the slaughter houses.'

32.

The music was deafening. It roared through the extractor fans, rattled the chains in the ceiling and banged on the chilled water pipes. It slapped Charlie full in the face and made all his bones vibrate.

Farkiss was beside him and his jaws were working but all that came from his mouth was steam. The sweat that had gathered in his eyebrows sparkled now as it turned to ice.

Six men wearing mufflers and leather gauntlets were pulling chickens from iron crates and hanging them by their feet from an automated ceiling track. There were hundreds of birds in the crates and hundreds more in the air. Alarmed by their shackles the birds struggled weakly as they made the only flight of their lives. Their eyes glittered and their wings fell open as they felt themselves shuttled across the ceiling towards the electric hammer.

'They're dead before – hit – ground!' Farkiss bellowed.

The hammer sizzled as it stunned the birds, banging their necks against a blade that sliced their heads from their bodies. The heads tumbled to earth, collecting in great twitching heaps along a gutter in the floor.

'It wasn't – this – old days!' Farkiss shouted. 'You couldn't trust – machines – old days. We – find that -- -- of the buggers -- plucked alive. Nasty! Bad for the girls!'

The dead were carried along the track to the other end of the slaughterhouse where row after row of young women sat waiting for the sky to rain corpses. The women wore hairnets and bored expressions. Their aprons were red with blood. Their faces were blue with cold. They held filleting knives in their hands. Some of them were singing.

Within moments of its arrival at the slaughterhouse a chicken could be hung, drawn and stripped down to a skeleton. The legs, wings and breasts were tossed onto conveyor belts, sprayed with disinfectant, spiked with chilled water and flavour concentrates, rolled in coloured paste, wrapped in polythene, checked, weighed and sent half a mile to the freezers.

The feathers were sucked up through a series of silver extraction hoses, carried aloft and blown, in relentless snow-storms, towards some distant part of the plant. The heads and claws were shovelled into grinding drums, mixed with entrails and turned by some diabolical magic into pellets of chicken feed. And while all this happened, while the chickens were having their throats cut and the dead-eyed girl were stripping out hearts and livers and lungs, the music swirled and blared around them.

Farkiss shouted something that was lost on Charlie but it made the nearest girl shriek with laughter. She looked up and grinned at Charlie. She was a thin creature with a crooked nose. Her face had been carelessly painted, a smudge of lipstick, two dark circles of greasy eye shadow. She was speaking, asking him questions, but he couldn't make out the words.

'What a girl!' Farkiss bellowed.

'What did she say?' Charlie shouted.

'She wants – know – you'd – excited if you got your – up a chicken!' he bellowed happily, making a fist with his hand and pretending to saw the air into logs.

Charlie shivered in disgust and tried to retreat but Farkiss had hold of his arm.

The girl shouted another question but still Charlie could not hear a word above the ear-cracking music.

'She says – wants – know how you'd like – stomach pulled out – arse!' Farkiss bellowed. 'She says that – all – visitors. What a girl! What – sense – humour!' He roared with laughter. He considered the killing floor as his private harem. They belonged to him, these tough, scrawny girls with their raw hands and vacant expressions. He was proud of them. He lingered for a few moments more and then marched Charlie away into the shadows of the great machines.

He led him to machines that devoured the broken carcasses and scratched the shreds of flesh from the bones, and machines that seized these little scraps and knitted them together again into tasty, bite-sized chicken nuggets. He showed him machines that took the bloody bones and reduced them to glue, and machines that drank this glue and turned it into rich chicken gravy. And beyond these machines there were other machines with unspeakable appetites and purposes. And beyond these machines the darkness and the distant, terrible thunder of freezers. And all the time Farkiss was shouting and steaming and gazing, with affection, around his kingdom of blood and bones.

Charlie staggered forward in silence. He was struck dumb with shock and cold. He concentrated on walking, taking slow, deliberate strides, looking neither left nor right, grinding his teeth, trying to swallow his nausea until, finally, Farkiss was leading him into another steel cabin and helping to remove his protective clothes.

'I hope you had a good time,' he said cheerfully. He sounded slightly dazed, as if they'd just come down from some bone-shaking fairground ride. 'It certainly gives you an appetite.'

'Thank you,' Charlie whispered.

'A pleasure,' Farkiss said, beaming with pride as they returned to the daylight. He guided Charlie through the poster hoarding with its wonderful farmyard scene and into the waiting limousine.

'You'll have observed that all the birds are taken apart by hand,' he said. 'Some manufacturers just spike them on rows of gutting machines but that doesn't suit the Pangloss principal. We put 'em together by hand, so to speak, and we like to take 'em apart by hand. It's the personal touch. It takes more time and it costs more money. I can't deny it. You could call me old-fashioned. I won't argue with you. But I think that when you take that extra bit of trouble the customer will always notice the difference.'

As Charlie scrambled into the car, Farkiss thrust a waxed cardboard bucket into his hand. The bucket felt heavy and warm.

'What is it?' Charlie said, hoping that he wouldn't be obliged to peek beneath the lid.

'A few fresh livers,' Farkiss said confidentially.

'Compliments of the Pangloss chickens,' Sam Shingles said.

'We had 'em plucked while you were walking around the plant. They're fat and juicy, believe me! And they don't come fresher. They're still warm. Try 'em with a knob of butter. It's a tasty treat for the whole family.'

'Did you enjoy yourselves?' Sam Shingle inquired, as they drove away down the ornamental drive.

Charlie nodded and wagged his head.

'Farkiss is a good man. There isn't much that Farkiss doesn't know about chickens,' Sam said, glancing enviously at the bucket of softly steaming livers.

Charlie closed his eyes, dropped his head between his knees and threw up over his shoes.

33.

The liver is a large gland essential to the maintenance of blood glucose levels, protein metabolism, the absorption of damaged red cells and the filtration of drugs such as penicillin and steroid hormones including estrogens and aldosterone. Waste products from the liver are excreted into the bile and stored in the gallbladder for discharge into the small intestine.

A Recipe for Chicken Liver Pate to serve four persons.
175 gm soft butter
1 large onion
225gm Pangloss Chicken Livers
1 small clove crushed garlic
Dash of brandy
Salt and pepper.

Melt a little of the butter into a heavy frying pan, slice the onions and gently cook until soft and transparent. Discard the stringy membranes and discoloured portions of the livers, taking care to remove any fragments of gallbladder. Add the livers to the pan and fry on a high heat. Add the garlic and dash of brandy. Season with salt and pepper to taste. Mince or mash the mixture into a paste. Blend the paste with remaining butter and pour into ramekin dishes. Allow the pate to cool and set firm. Serve with hot toast.

34.

Ambrose nodded and smiled. He was sympathetic. 'There's a certain degree of suffering, Charlie. It can't be denied.' He pushed a fragment of biscuit into his mouth, leaned back in his chair and stared at the opposite wall. 'But people have to eat,' he said at last. 'We have to accept their suffering for the general good of mankind. I won't pretend that the factories are perfect, but they're certainly the best factories available, believe me. They're clean, hygienic, Swiss engineered.'

He sucked his teeth thoughtfully, remembering Mrs Pangloss and the cold polished beauty of her life support machine. He would take home fresh flowers and put them beside her bed. An arrangement with plenty of fern and roses for their perfume and one of those fancy silk bows. He'd ask a senior secretary to ask a junior secretary to do whatever you had to do to order one.

'I don't care,' Charlie said. 'There's nothing you can say that will make me go back there again. Nothing.'

Ambrose blinked and looked at Charlie in surprise as if, for a moment, he'd forgotten he was there. 'I'm glad to hear it,' he said suddenly and smiled very brightly, revealing his teeth. 'Do you know why I'm glad to hear it, Charlie?'

'I've no idea.'

'It tells me that you should be working somewhere else in the company. We should be attempting to place you much higher on the corporate ladder.'

'I don't belong on your corporate ladder!' Charlie said abruptly, losing his patience. 'I'm a painter. I might be a lousy painter but it makes no difference. My task is to paint and try to make some sense of the world! And that's hard enough at the best of times without having my face rubbed in chicken shit! I don't like how you make your money. I've no intention of taking your money. And I certainly don't want to work for you.' He'd made the trip to Larks Rise merely to humour his father-in-law. He hadn't volunteered to become a Pangloss toady.

There was a long silence in which Ambrose Pangloss, smiling softly, gave Charlie the opportunity to regret this outburst. And Charlie sat scowling, feeling foolish, waiting to be dismissed.

'Painting,' Pangloss said, at last, considering the word in his mouth as if it had a peculiar taste he couldn't quite identify. 'Painting. That's a very artistic past time. I've always encouraged my people to make more use of their leisure hours. We once had a member of the board who made working models from cocktail sticks.'

'It's not a game for some wet afternoon!' Charlie said indignantly. 'It's my life!'

Pangloss smiled. 'But does it butter bread, Charlie? Does it butter bread?'

'I did it once and I'll do it again.'

'It's a large house, Charlie. A very large house,' Ambrose said gently. 'It gets cold in the winter, I imagine. And I don't suppose that Baxter is earning a living.'

'I'll find some other kind of work,' Charlie said unhappily. It was a mess. He wished now that he hadn't become involved. He needed to extricate himself without offending his benefactor.

'You should have more faith in your own abilities,' Ambrose said, attacking the rest of his ginger nut biscuit. 'Did you ever think that you might belong in Advertising and Market Research? It's fascinating work, Charlie. Absolutely fascinating.'

Charlie shook his head.

'A lot of writers and artists have made good livings in advertising,' Ambrose continued. 'Katie Pphart used to work for me in the early days. Did you know that?'

'Katie Pphart?'

'The famous romantic novelist. She wrote the slogan – Listen to those hungry sighs, when you show them Pangloss thighs! That was Katie Pphart.'

'Did she ever see the factories?'

'I don't remember,' Ambrose said. 'She seemed to live in a little world of her own.'

Charlie didn't doubt it.

'But I'm not going to put you into Advertising and Market Research,' Ambrose said at last. 'And do you know why I've made that decision?'

Charlie shook his head again.

'Because I've decided I'm going to place you in Future Forecasts,' Ambrose said triumphantly. He stared expectantly at Charlie, as if he had offered him some priceless gift and expected a moment of disbelief before the rush of gratitude.

'Forecasts? I'm no good at forecasts,' Charlie said, after another uncomfortable silence. If he'd been able to forecast the future he would never have found himself trapped in this office mumbling his excuses.

'Have you never wondered what the world will be like in the future? Have you never daydreamed about the cities of tomorrow with their sunshine domes and their moving pavements and how we'll dress and what kind of chicken we'll be eating and what kind of shows we'll watch on TV? Of course you, have Charlie. Everybody dreams about the future. And do you know what I dream about, Charlie?'

'I've no idea,' Charlie said. Hens as big as haystacks. Fighting cocks with diamond spurs.

'I dream that a Pangloss Chicken Dinner will be the first chicken dinner to land on the moon. That's my favourite dream. And that's what I'm asking you to do for me in the Future Forecasts department, Charlie. I want to pay you to daydream for me. I want you to summon all your creative energy, all your artistic inspiration, and imagine how we can secure a proper place for the Melting Moments™ Oven Ready in the wonderful world of tomorrow.'

'I don't know,' Charlie squirmed.

'You don't have to give me your answer immediately, Charlie. Take a few days to think it over and talk to Baxter. It's a very big decision. It's a very great opportunity.'

Charlie stood up to leave but Ambrose Pangloss hadn't finished with him. 'Sit down, Charlie. There's something I want to show you.'

'I'm late,' Charlie said miserably, returning obediently to his chair. 'Baxter is waiting for me.'

'This will only take a moment,' Ambrose said.

He opened a drawer in his desk and removed a waxed cardboard container. He placed the box carefully on the centre of the desk and held it lightly between his fingertips.

'Do you know what I'm holding in my hands, Charlie?'

Charlie shrugged.

'I'm holding a dream,' Ambrose said softly. 'A miracle. When this little box is opened there will be a revolution. There will be an end to world hunger and suffering and poverty. This box contains the answers to all our prayers.' He paused and tapped the box with his fingernails. His eyes shone. 'It also contains the key to immense wealth and influence. Can you imagine what would happen if this box fell into the wrong hands, Charlie? Can you begin to understand the implications?'

Charlie confessed that he understood nothing.

145

Einstein

Ambrose Pangloss smiled. 'Millions have already been invested in this little box, Charlie. Millions of pounds and seven years research. There are only twelve men in the world who know what this box contains. Twelve men. And I happen to own every one of them and their wives and families. But I'm going to share this secret with you, Charlie, because I know I can trust you. Why should I trust you? Because you're family and because you're an artist. You have vision. And this is a vision of the future... '

He flicked open the box and turned the contents over the desk. Charlie felt his scalp prickle with horror as his brain refused to believe his eyes.

They were staring at a four-legged chicken. An incredibly wrinkled ball of skin, about the size of a man's fist, mounted on four long fat-thighed legs. It had no feathers on its body and its eyes were a curious shade of blue. Startled by the light, the creature tried to scuttle away but became entangled in its own claws and fell against the telephone.

Ambrose picked it up very carefully, as if it were some marvellous toy, a fabulous automaton, and positioned it once more in the centre of the great polished desk.

'Isn't Mother Nature wonderful?' he whispered. 'Learn her secrets and anything is possible. Now that we've cracked the DNA code we can turn the working of every living thing on Earth inside out. Did you ever hear of the DuPont OncoMouse™, Charlie? It's an entirely new mouse. It was actually invented. It was a patent. Every time it sneezes the OncoMouse™ breaks out in tumours. They sell OncoMice™ to oncologists. Do you begin to understand the possibilities, Charlie? Do you feel your nerve ends tingle? Sheep the size of buffalo. Cows that can eat human waste. Pigs that can salt themselves into bacon. Biotechnology is the start of the Second Creation. The first company to succeed with a new kind of factory chicken will have total world market domination. You'll notice, Charlie, that there are no unsightly feathers. And why are there no feathers? Because that eliminates drudgery when we come to process the bird. Oh, yes, Charlie, we're entering a golden age.'

The monstrosity sank in a trembling heap on the desk, its neck outstretched and its beak snapping at nothing. The legs looked like so many fallen skittles.

'It's not perfect,' he admitted, taking up his coffee spoon and giving the bird a gentle poke, trying to prod it back into life. 'You can see, for instance, that the legs won't function. But that's a mere technicality. We think we can solve the problem by building a new kind of harness-cage. I'm designing it myself. I've called it the Apple Picker. The birds will be hung from a harness so their legs can dangle and ripen like fruit. Isn't that beautiful? Isn't that inspired?'

'It's filthy! A monster! You're breeding monsters!' Charlie shouted in horror. 'Why in God's name have you done it?' He stared at the repulsive little creature with a mixture of dread and fascination. He wanted to raise his fist, smash out its brains and put an end to its misery.

The chicken tycoon looked at Charlie in surprise. Nobody raised their voice to him. It must be Charlie's artistic temperament. 'We can double our capacity, double our productivity and double our market share overnight,' he explained patiently. 'Feed the world, Charlie. Feed the world.'

As they watched, the bird seemed to recover its senses and, in a furious burst of energy, went spinning in circles over the desk, pushing its body forward on the tips of its stunted wings.

Ambrose reached out to recover his prize and return it to the safety of the box. But before he had time to catch it again, the pathetic creature had fallen from the edge of the desk and tumbled into Charlie's lap.

35.

Charlie came out of his trance shouting and kicking his legs. Einstein looked bilious, crept into a corner and considered rejecting his chicken breakfast. Geraldine, mercifully, had fallen asleep and seen nothing of the horror show.

The Deep Time Mariner stared at Charlie and a look of terrible disgust flickered across his face. He knew that everything he had heard about the monkey-men was true. They were the most dangerous species in all the charted galaxies. He had encountered many cantankerous beasts during his work on the ark. The tiger, the shark and the mountain bear. The scorpion, snake and venomous toad. But these large apes were crafty and cruel and deadlier than the rest of creation because they were, all of them, raving mad. Rattle-headed smatterers. Babbling jobernowls.

Their brains were too big for their bodies and at some time in their history these big soft brains had told them that they were gods and set apart from the rest of the living world. And because they were gods among animals they came to believe they could disregard the natural laws that govern life and invent their own laws and make the world spin forward or backward, as the madness took them. They had also given themselves the authority to kill, mutilate, imprison and persecute every other species on Earth, including themselves, especially themselves, in vast numbers and with the greatest enthusiasm. Hatching monsters from hens' eggs was only one more crime in a long list of crimes against the universe to be perpetuated by these master torturers.

'What was your part this crime?' he demanded, kicking at Charlie's chair with a heavy, armour-plated boot.

'None! I had nothing to do with it!' The chair capsized, spilling him to the floor where he crawled around on his hands and knees, searching for a place to hide.

'Don't lie to me, you miserable ape!'

'I did nothing!' Charlie yelled, trying unsuccessfully to shelter under a little table. 'You were there with me. You saw what happened.'

Geraldine woke up with a squawk and frowned at her scuttling son. She was stupid with sleep. She had been dreaming of new curtains. She yawned and combed her fingers through her dusty, wind-blown hair.

'I didn't know they were breeding monsters,' Charlie insisted, seeking the dubious sanctuary of his mother's phantasmagorical skirt. Geraldine, fearing another fall, tried to whisk him away with her hand.

'But you were involved,' the Mariner growled, pacing the room. 'You were told of these things by the dwarf ape Pangloss and yet you did nothing to hinder him.'

'What could I do against him? I was in no position to change anything. I wasn't to blame for it.'

A cactus exploded, firing its bristles at the window. Einstein barked and scratched at the door.

'You're all to blame!' the Deep Time Mariner thundered, snatching up Charlie's abandoned chair and punching it into splinters with a blow from his mighty fist. He still needed to take the dog to the ark and he knew that Einstein would go nowhere without his ape and this gangling ape was quite incapable of providing one scrap of evidence that he, alone of the species, might be worth the considerable risk of preserving.

'How many of these horrors were created in your laboratories?' he demanded.

'I don't know. I think there were two hundred.'

Einstein

The Mariner stroked his huge green head. Something else now troubled him. No reports had been received of these pitiful four-legged freaks. Since the creature was an aberration, a nightmare fermented from a swollen brain, there would be no place reserved for it on the voyage of the Deep Time Ark when she slipped anchor and set sail from Mars. Was there time to file a report and send down a snatch-squad to search for it? What would happen if they failed to retrieve it? Would he have to make a declaration? Would it spoil his prospects of promotion? And the paper-work. Imagine the paper-work!

'Where are they?' he asked Charlie impatiently. 'What happened to these wretched birds?'

36.

The development of the Pangloss four-legged chicken became the doubtful privilege of the Future Forecasts department. Charlie was asked to report for work on the first day of the month.

The Pangloss Building was an ugly office tower planted in a square of windswept concrete to set it apart from the narrow street. He approached the building across a walkway spanning a moat that was choked with rubbish. On that first morning he paused on the bridge to catch his breath after the walk from the station, and stared down through the steel railings at the mounds of polythene and paper, drifts of polystyrene beakers, beer cans, bottles and dirty hamburger trays. Torn newspaper floated, suspended, in the draught from the air-conditioning vents.

As he lingered at the railings he saw something moving far beneath him. It was an old man wearing a knitted balaclava and a greasy dressing gown. He was bent like a sickle and clutched a bottle against his chest as he talked to a man in a cardboard box. The moat contained its own shanty town. There were people living down there in the filth, sleeping in packing crates, scavenging for scraps in the rubbish. Charlie started to walk again. He knew if he wasn't careful that he might be forced to join them. His first morning at work and already he was learning to fear the threat of redundancy, the plunge into unemployment, the spiral of poverty.

At the far end of the bridge he was stopped by a young security guard wearing leather gloves and a Polaroid portrait of himself clipped to his uniform. The guard checked Charlie's identity, made him sign the visitors' book and escorted him through an entrance hall containing enough white marble to dress a Roman palace. Huge chandeliers of sparkling, cut-glass eggs hung from massive ceiling chains and a gold frieze of galloping chickens ran the length of the polished walls.

'Third floor,' he said, when Charlie asked him for directions. On his previous visits he'd been treated like a celebrity and taken straight to the penthouse in the presidential lift. From this day forward he'd be expected to work his way to the top.

Charlie found his way to the third floor but was soon lost in a maze of identical corridors that ran between Global Marketing and Regional Accounts.

Baxter, despite her misgivings, had wished him good luck and sent him out that morning equipped with a plastic attaché case with real leather trim and combination security locks. She admired his determination to prove himself as a husband. It wasn't so bad. They'd have weekends and evenings together. He'd still have plenty of time for painting. And she wouldn't waste her days alone in the house. She planned to find her portfolio in search of ideas to develop. She'd always been rather pleased with the haddock.

Charlie had bought himself a dark business suit and a pair of sturdy black brogues. He already regretted the choice of shoe. They pinched his feet and made him hobble. When he finally found Future Forecasts he was sweating and out of breath.

He squeezed himself into a small reception cubicle, dominated by a large glass desk. A blonde girl with green eyes and a crimson lacquered mouth sat at the desk reading *Chinwag Weekly*. Her name was Lorraine. There was a low leather sofa placed directly before her where visitors might sit to admire her legs.

Lorraine was proud of her legs. They'd been shaved and polished to perfection. She wanted to be a swimwear model and have famous fashion photographers fighting to take her to the

Caribbean. Charlie gave her the letter of introduction that she opened while he sat in the sofa, panting and staring at her knees.

The department, when he finally made his entrance, was a large room bleached by the glare of a ceiling made from spluttering fluorescent tubes and divided into a number of work stations by frosted glass screens. The receptionist walked him as far as the nearest empty work station and sat him down at the desk. He placed his briefcase on the desk, untied his shoe laces and waited for something to happen.

On the first day he was given a red ballpoint pen, a black ballpoint pen, a doodle pad, a box of paperclips, a copy of his contract of employment, a leaflet about the healthcare scheme and a blue plastic feather with instructions for new recruits on how to attach the quill to a shirt or jacket lapel. Congratulations – you've just been made a Pangloss Chicken Crusader!

On the second day he was given a telephone, another box of paperclips, a security password for his computer, a copy of the fire regulations and an application to join the Pangloss Pension Scheme.

On the third day he was given a dozen empty document folders, another doodle pad, a green ballpoint pen, a blue ballpoint pen and a box of staples.

On the fourth day he was given a roll of Scotch tape, a packet of envelopes, a staple remover and a laundry marker.

On the fifth day he was given a small wire tray, a pencil sharpener, a leaflet explaining the leaflet about the health care scheme, a calendar and a desk diary.

On the sixth and seventh days he rested.

'What do you do at work?' Baxter said.

'I don't know,' Charlie said.

The following week he was taught to use the coffee machine and introduced to the forecasting team. They were a queer and suspicious group of men who liked to keep to their cubicles. They had all been working in Future Forecasts for a long time and seemed to be riding a carousel of little grudges and grievances.

The first forecaster had not spoken to the third forecaster for more than two years after a nasty incident involving a handy desk organiser moulded from green and yellow plastic. The desk organiser had been the personal property of the first forecaster and he'd scratched his secret mark on the base to guard against theft. The gadget had disappeared from his desk to be found, a few days later, in the third forecaster's cubicle but when he went to retrieve it he was challenged by its new owner and discovered the secret identity mark had been scratched away by a pair of scissors. There were angry words and threats of violence. The first forecaster had taken revenge by staying late one evening and stealing a Scotch tape dispenser. That would teach the bastard a lesson!

The sixth forecaster would not talk to the second forecaster because of some bitter dispute involving the coffee machine and a number of poisonous messages found on the conference room drywipe board. The messages threw doubts on the forecaster's parentage, the sanity of his children and the personal hygiene of his wife.

The fourth forecaster would not speak to the fifth forecaster because of a drunken argument involving some rather blurred images that Lorraine the receptionist had produced by sitting aboard the photocopy machine at the end of a drunken office party. The results looked like startled sea urchins pressed under glass and were worth a small fortune to her admirers.

Lorraine had tried to recover the prints but the forecasters would not surrender them. The fourth and fifth forecasters fought for possession. The scuffle had turned to a brawl. There had never been such excitement. The terrors and triumphs of office life.

The fifth forecaster would not talk to the first forecaster because of his quarrel with the third forecaster, the second forecaster would not speak to the fourth forecaster because of his quarrel with the fifth forecaster and the third forecaster would not talk to the sixth forecaster because of his quarrel with the second forecaster. It was a very confusing situation.

At last the first forecaster asked the sixth forecaster to tell the fourth forecaster to ask Charlie to read a pile of reports on what the world would be like in the future.

Charlie sat in his cubicle and worked his way through a hundred fabulous descriptions of a master race who wore sparkling nylon leisure suits and lived in floating cities.

The authors were paid to believe that, despite the evidence all around them, they would live to witness the dawn of a golden age. In this world of the future there would be no famine, no plague and no war to disturb the fun and games. There would be no Nature. There would be no wilderness. It would be a world of monorails, heliports and transparent cities in the sea. There would be no pain. There would be no labour. The landscape would be designed by teams of prize-winning architects, creating tranquil outlooks to be viewed through rose-tinted glass.

Perfect, happy men and women would sit around all day, smiling like people smile in commercials and watching two hundred channels of wrap-around hologram TV quiz shows with chances to win unearthly prizes like luxury weekend trips to the Moon. They would sit around all day and be entertained. They would do nothing for themselves. They would live in blissful bubbles of artificial sunshine and have cute little robots to wash and feed them.

The department's task was to find a way to make these little robots serve nothing but Pangloss four-legged chicken dinners. They were asked to speculate on the strength of potential consumer resistance, cosmetic enhancement of the product, the lower nutritional expectations of second and third generation consumers and a lot of other things that made Charlie wake up at night with a shudder.

They had barely finished planning their document when all the novelty poultry died. The birds had been engineered to grow extra legs but with the new legs came new diseases, tumours, fevers and blood disorders. They yielded no meat. The carcasses were destroyed and the scheme abandoned. It was a shame but even freaks were required to exist within suitable profit margins.

The forecasters heard the rumours but they thought it a pity to waste their hard work. So they carried on with it. The document was going to take them years and when it was finally complete, Ambrose Pangloss would have it weighed and dumped in the company shredder.

37.

The failure of the chicken experiment did not mark the end of Charlie's career in the Pangloss Chicken Empire. He thought he might be allowed to go home but Ambrose called him upstairs, by way of the presidential lift and contrived to get him involved in another of his schemes. Each job of work was treated as a personal favour, a trivial chore but one, nonetheless, that required Charlie's very special talents. Ambrose Pangloss had a gift for flummery. Whenever Charlie looked doubtful, Ambrose would mention the beautiful Baxter, the dream home and the cost of living until Charlie felt he couldn't refuse the requests of this genial gnome. The salary was large – although Charlie never thought of it as more than monotony money – the standard company benefits were widely regarded as generous and there were a hundred ambitious young men who would gladly have sold their grandmothers' teeth for a chance to be in his position. He was a lucky man. Everyone agreed that he was a very lucky man. He would have been mad to have thrown it away.

'Do you know what they found when they dug the foundations for this building, Charlie?' Ambrose asked him, leaning forward in his chair, propping his elbows on the desk and making a spire from his fingertips.

Charlie considered for a moment. The biggest plague pit in London. The rope and bell from the gates of Hell. The lost city of Atlantis. He shook his head.

'The remains of a Roman temple,' Ambrose said.

'What happened to it?'

'Nothing,' Ambrose said, in surprise. 'It's still there.'

157

Einstein

'It should be safe under concrete,' Charlie said.

'Nothing lasts forever,' Ambrose said, looking around the room as if he expected cracks to appear in the plasterwork.

Charlie had his doubts but said nothing.

'Do you know what they're going to find when they excavate this site in another thousand years, Charlie?' He grinned like a schoolboy stuffed with secrets. He had plans to insert a time capsule into the building's foundations. The time capsule would have a locking device that could not be opened for a thousand years. He didn't know that the world wouldn't last that long. If he'd known that the world was about to end he would probably have arranged for the capsule to be fired into space to take his story to the stars. The time capsule was intended to carry his glory into the future and show the people of tomorrow what a genius they had lost.

Charlie was told to work on the scheme, designing some jolly cartoon roosters to decorate a polythene pouch containing a freeze dried chicken dinner.

3 8.

'You did nothing to stop this butcher?' the Mariner said. He sounded astonished, as if he'd expected Charlie to raise an army and bring down the walls of the Pangloss Empire.

'I needed the work,' Charlie said. 'And what could I do against the system? It's too late. Someone flushed the lavatory and we're swimming in the vortex. Whenever we try to break the surface we find ourselves covered in shit.'

'You did nothing.'

'I wasn't big enough to make a difference. We live in an age without heroes.'

'Look at him!' Einstein scoffed. 'He's not Jean-Claude Van Damme!'

'Who?'

'He was a film star,' Einstein said. 'Famous for his polished bodywork and failure to master the language. He spent his entire adult life pretending to fight mutant robots or save the people of Earth from plague-ridden meteor showers. But you won't have heard of him. He's what we have instead of heroes.'

The Mariner snorted and turned away.

'What happens now?' Charlie said. He had pleaded for his life and merely succeeded in proving, even to himself, that his life was not worth saving. How had it gone so wrong? Why hadn't he seen the mistakes? What had happened to all those early dreams and ambitions? How could he have wasted so many precious years?

He remembered himself as a child, sitting in that distant classroom, painting bananas and oranges, and his life had stretched endlessly before him, an empty road of perpetual summer. He'd thought he would travel this road, innocent, brown as a gypsy, with no more luggage to hinder him than a picnic basket and painting box. He'd thought it was simple. He'd thought he would always be glad to be living.

Where had he lost his way on this road? How had he found himself trapped in an office, slumped at a desk, sick with boredom, drawing jolly cartoon roosters or making future forecasts into the marketing opportunities of chicken neck savoury spread?

The years squandered, watching the clock eat away his life, counting the hours, the days, the weeks, in paperclips and plastic cups of instant coffee. Now the world was at an end and all the clocks were about to explode and the Mariner was talking urgently to Einstein, begging him to leave while there was still time for them to make their escape.

'It's a long journey and we're late.'

'Give me a few more minutes.'

'Forget your monkey! You have other responsibilities. You have to follow your destiny. You are the future of your kind.'

'But the monkey saved my life,' Einstein protested. 'I can't run out on him. I can't leave him here.'

'No more nonsense! I don't believe a word of it!' the Deep Time Mariner shouted.

'It's true,' Einstein insisted. 'If it hadn't been for Charlie I would have been dead in a ditch. I was lost and starving. He found me and nursed me back to health.'

'You saved the life of this dog?' the Deep Time Mariner asked, scowling at Charlie. He suspected another fantastic web of vanity and deceit but he had to check the facts.

'I found him in the garden,' Charlie said. He opened his mouth as if he wanted to say more, but nothing came into his head.

'And nursed me back to health,' Einstein prompted, as if Charlie were a half-wit who had lost his memory. What he lacked in intelligence, he certainly made up for in stupidity.

'It's true he was looking rather scraggy,' Charlie admitted.

'He should have left you for dead,' Geraldine said, turning on Einstein. 'You nasty, dirty brute.'

'Shut your mouth!' Einstein growled. 'Hold your tongue or I'll chew you to rags!' He sprang forward, hackles raised, and threatened the ghost with his foaming fangs.

Geraldine let out a shriek and vaulted from the chair. She threw out her arms, drifted across the ceiling and started to fade away.

'Let me tell you how it happened,' Einstein said, turning back to the Mariner.

'No time!' The Mariner roared. 'No time!'

'You're forgetting your own responsibilities,' Einstein bristled. 'You belong to the greatest civilisation the universe has known. There has never been such a race of poets and philosophers. Your wisdom lit the stars and set the planets in their orbits. And yet you're condemning this monkey to death without an excuse me or thank you.' He growled, very deep in his throat, and whipped the floor with his tail. 'And you might have considered my own tender feelings before you tried to steal me away.'

'And the children,' Geraldine sighed. 'I never caught sight of the little children… ' She was very faint, a luminous patch on the ceiling.

'Tell me the story,' the Mariner sighed.

'Mine is a tale of adventure!' Einstein said, pricking up his ears and sitting to attention. 'Mine was a life of hardships and dangers.'

39.

Einstein had been the runt of a large litter born to a bitch in the cellar of a London pet shop. His mother had been born a mongrel, the daughter of a mongrel, and in her veins ran the blood of the poodle and terrier, the cocker and springer, the greyhound and tumbler, the house cur and turnspit, the Assyrian hunting dog, the Roman dog of war, the temple dog of Egypt and beyond, yea, even unto the wolf of the forest and the nimble jackal of the desert.

Einstein's ancestors had been warrior hounds of Attila the Hun, silken spaniels of the Chinese emperors, muscle-bound mastiffs of King Mwanga of Buganda. They had been starving pariahs, cracking open the bones of corpses buried in the mud of ruined cities. They had been pot-bellied pets of kings, sleeping on jewelled cushions, licking honey from the fingers of perfumed concubines.

Einstein, for his part, had been a yelping scrap of life, scratching at the bottom of a cardboard box. His first memory was the smell of the cellar, ripe with rabbits, kittens, white mice and parrots, horse cakes, fish flakes, biscuits and bonemeal. His second memory was the smell of the straw in the warmth of the crowded pet shop window. His third memory was a wickerwork cage and the flushed face of Mrs Flodden as she set him gently down on her bedroom floor.

Mrs Flodden was a widow who had purchased him as comforter for her large and lonely bed. She kept him in the top of her night-gown and fed him biscuits while they watched TV. She kissed him and squeezed him and set him loose to roam at night beneath her lace-embroidered sheets.

During the day she liked to sit in bed and read aloud from a tottering tower of library books. She had an enormous appetite for Katie Pphart romances and pocket digest editions of ancient and modern classics. The Katie Ppharts made him fall asleep with their drivelling accounts of swooning, pale-skinned women and dangerous, dark-eyed men, hopelessly trapped in all the elaborate rituals of courtship. But he learned to love the classics. He rode out with Don Quixote, pursued Moby Dick and followed the doings of Dombey and Son. He met Hamlet, Moll Flanders and Robinson Crusoe. He was introduced to the Hindu warriors, Greek gods and Russian princes. It was Mrs Flodden who provided his early education and for a time they were happy together.

She seemed surprised when he started to grow.

In the beginning he was content to burrow between her breasts, searching for sugar crumbs with his tongue. But as the months passed he changed from a trembling velvet ball into a whiskery ruffian who tore her night-gown, scratched her arms and sank his teeth in her fat.

It was Mrs Flodden who had called him Einstein because, as she told the engraver who had punched the name on the plate of a beautiful leather collar, her puppy was turning into a monster. She gave one of her little laughs. A high-pitched yapping. So amusing. The engraver looked blank. Einstein, she felt obliged to explain to this idiot of a man, was the famous beast in the Mary Shelley book of that name. The engraver didn't argue. He asked her how to spell it. It made a change from Randy and Rambo.

She continued to adore the young Einstein with his bristling moustache and wet inquisitive nose, but he was tired of Mrs Flodden's pillow talk. He was tired of catching his claws in her night-gown and tired of the games of hide and seek she played with his favourite biscuits. He longed to be running loose in the streets, mauling cats and exploring drains, and at the first opportunity he slipped through the widow's legs and escaped.

He lived on the streets and learned to beg food from the doors of hotel kitchens. It was a hard life but full of adventure. He hunted for cats in the alleys and courtyards and chased pigeons in public gardens. He slept secure in the basements of derelict buildings or fashioned nests from the rubbish that rolled in the streets.

These were the days of a thousand conquests. He surprised the shambling, swag-bellied Labrador with her chocolate eyes and her soft, drooling mouth; startled the nervous Afghan with her narrow shoulders and diamond collar and dainty tiptoeing stride; stunned the swaggering pit bull terrier with her stump of a tail held high like a flag, flaunting her broad and twitching buttocks; he sprang traps for the Pekinese and the corgi, the dachshund and the whippet. Such variety in the world! So many curious shapes and sizes. So much heat from so many bitches. Einstein always took his pleasure.

It was during this time that he met Arnold Belcher. The old man had been working as a cook in the kitchen of the Hotel Glorious, a tourist trap in Paddington. They stumbled upon each other one morning behind the hotel dustbins. Einstein was trying to salvage some pork ribs from a tangle of polythene wrappers. Arnold had just finished frying fifty egg and bacon breakfasts and had crept outside to enjoy a cigar. He was a small man in a greasy apron. He had a long face, very white, as if it had been poached and drained of its colour, and a tremendous gherkin of a nose. His arms were freckled with frying pan burns.

'I wouldn't touch them bones if I was you,' Arnold warned him. 'The rations in this place ain't fit to eat.'

He winked at Einstein and snorted smoke through his mighty nose and then, because the mongrel looked so hungry, slipped back into the kitchen to fetch him a slice of liver. This act of generosity earned Arnold Belcher a devoted friend.

When he returned to the dustbins that evening to smoke his after dinner cigar he found Einstein waiting for him.

'How d'you fancy a cockroach supper?' he said, bending down to scratch Einstein's ears. 'And somewhere warm to sleep the night?'

Einstein grinned and followed Arnold into the kitchen.

The floor glittered with cockroaches. They swarmed from every chink and crevice, ran up the walls and hung in festoons from the ceiling. They filled the breadbins to overflowing and clung in quivering chains to the locks on the pantry doors.

Einstein was astonished. He whimpered. He barked. He lowered his head and ran across the floor with his jaws clacking like castanets. Within half an hour there was nothing left of the infestation but broken shells and a litter of legs.

Arnold was so impressed that he let Einstein remain in the kitchen. He grew uncommonly fond of him. They slept together beside the ovens and lived on sweet tea and table scraps.

At the end of the summer Arnold Belcher left the hotel and Einstein went with him. They travelled north, to the sea, where they spent a season in the galley of a deep sea trawler. They sailed crimson seas that were stained with blood from the giant Japanese factory fleets and soft black seas spread with oil so deep that they that burst into flames and lit the night. They sailed seas that had turned as thick as glue from a plague of poisonous jelly-fish and sinister empty stinking seas where even the wandering albatross refused to cast a shadow.

The man and the dog were constant companions for nearly five years. They shared all kinds of feast and famine during their travels together. They worked trawlers and tankers and short-sea traders and, whenever they had to come ashore, found shelter in the kitchens of cheap hotels.

Arnold loved the sea. 'When the time comes to say goodnight, they'll wrap me into a nice clean apron and drop me into the deep,' he told Einstein one evening as they gazed out across the oily water.

The little dog growled and pressed himself against the old man's legs.

'I want the mermaids to have me,' Arnold said wistfully. 'I want them to sing me mermaid songs and wrap me into their cold embrace. I want a shroud wove from mermaids' hair.'

But when the time came, Arnold Belcher said goodnight in the kitchen of the Trumpet Hotel. It was a two star hotel in the outskirts of London. It had badly infected drains, a Polynesian cocktail lounge and last year's Christmas decorations still pinned in the corners of the restaurant ceiling. The hotel offered fixed price lunches and tasty toasted sandwiches. Arnold had been hired to plan and prepare the lunches.

The old man had been hacking at a frozen leg of mutton when the axe bounced and butchered his wrist. He yelped in horror and his teeth fell out. The teeth skittered across the table. The hand slapped the floor like a wet glove. It took Einstein by surprise. He'd been sleeping under a sack of rice. He was so shocked that he sprang forward, snatched up his master's ruined hand and carried it into a corner.

When the headwaiter arrived, Arnold was already dead. His heart had stopped. He was slumped against one wall with his apron covered in blood. There was blood on the ceiling and blood on his shoes. The dog was sitting beside him with the severed hand in his mouth.

They took the old man away and Einstein never saw him again. He stayed near the Trumpet Hotel for a week but the waiters cursed and threw stones at him. They thought he was a trouble-maker. They were afraid of him. They thought he'd brought a jinx to the kitchen.

Eventually Einstein took to the road, hunting for food in junkyards and ditches. The episode at the Trumpet had left him feeling confused and lonely. He tried to pick up the threads of his old, independent life. He didn't need comforts of home and hearth. He was a gentleman of the road, a ruffian, a buccaneer.

At first he thought he could hunt for carrion like his brother the fox and dig shelters in the earth. He was finished with the company of men. But he had none of the quick wits and cunning that kept the wild dogs alive. Scratching for scraps he had soon become chilled and sick with hunger.

And then one morning he found himself limping along in the shadow of a tall brick wall. He followed the line of the wall to a pair of wrought iron gates. When he poked his head through the bars he saw an ugly concrete house set in a wasteland of uncut grass. Faint smells of food came drifting from the house. A man was standing on the lawn. The man was wearing striped pyjamas and wet carpet slippers.

It was Charlie.

40.

I was strong, Einstein told them proudly. I was a seadog and trained to eat anything. But how long could I have survived in the wild? My coat was tangled and caked in mud. My pads were scratched and bleeding. When I saw Charlie that morning and caught the smell of fried eggs and sausages, hot toast and coffee, I nearly dropped dead with desire. I was foaming at the mouth. I managed to drag myself forward and offered a pitiful, submissive moan. I slobbered and thrashed myself with my tail. I sank down on my belly and begged. And Charlie knelt down to pick me up in his arms and carry me back to the house.

Another man might have turned away in disgust, alarmed by my frightful appearance. Another might have thrown stones at me and chased me from the garden. I was too weak to do anything more than accept the fate that awaited me. But Charlie cradled my stinking body in his arms and carried me away to the blissful fragrance of that early morning kitchen.

A small television, perched on a shelf, was tuned to a breakfast news show. An ocean incineration ship with 2,000 tons of toxic waste on board was breaking up in a North Sea gale twenty miles from Scarborough. A woman in false eyelashes and a satin track-suit was talking about a crash diet programme guaranteed to shed ugly fat in thirty days or your money back. There were food riots in the Western Sahara and flood warnings in Bangladesh. A famous world leader had died in his sleep. Someone said Have a nice day.

There was a toaster burning bread and a kettle spurting steam and a woman standing at the stove with a pan full of smoking sausages. She was a small woman with big breasts and a mane of dark, untidy hair. Baxter.

Why did Charlie find her so attractive? Her face, unpainted, was pale and unremarkable. She had large, slightly squinting eyes and a matron's chin that trembled like a turkey wattle. Her belly bulged through a dirty woollen dressing gown and she shuffled her feet in cracked leather slippers.

It's true, they were not, as Katie Pphart might have said, flushed by the fire of love's first embrace; but there was no excuse for the jowls, the paunch and the poisonous demeanour. This woman, his wife, only beloved daughter of the infamous chicken slaughterer, was a witch, a tartar, an acrimonious brabbler, a flatulent virago.

I was drooling into Charlie's pyjamas and doing my best to look wistful and winsome, in the hope of a morsel of something wholesome, when she turned and scowled at me with a look that withered my scrotum.

'What have you found?' she shouted, without taking her eyes from me. 'Don't bring it into the house, Charlie!'

'It's a little dog,' Charlie said gently.

'Was it hit by a car or what?' she demanded. 'Is it dead?'

'No,' Charlie said, smiling and scratching my muddy chin. 'I think he must be lost.'

But Baxter the ice queen found her heart unmelted. 'For God's sake, take it out of here! It probably has worms. It might have lice. It might even have rabies. Look! Look! Its eyes are different colours.'

'What difference does that make?'

'Clear out!' she shouted impatiently, threatening us with her sausage fork. 'Put it back where you found it and then go upstairs and scrub your hands!'

'But he's lost,' Charlie insisted, holding me tighter against his chest as if shielding me from her evil eye. 'I think he's starving. He's nothing but skin and bone. Can't we find him something to eat?'

'I'm warning you,' Baxter said. 'There's something wrong with it. Look, for God's sake, it's practically foaming at the mouth. Filthy little beggar. You'll go crazy if it bites you and I absolutely refuse point blank to visit you in hospital.'

'He's not going to bite!' Charlie shouted back angrily. 'I can't leave him out there in the garden to starve. I can't ignore him. He only needs a good meal and a little care and attention.'

'It needs drowning.'

'What's wrong with you?' Charlie demanded. 'We can spare him something to eat.'

'I'm not your skivvy!' Baxter screamed. 'Christ, you're such a pain!' Her wattle quivered with indignation. She flung the frying pan at the wall and suddenly burst into tears.

Charlie didn't know what to do for the best, so he just stood there with a starving vagrant in his arms and a fat woman in a tantrum and the sausages rolling over the floor. It was terrible. And then, very gently, he set me down, picked up the sausages one by one and placed them back in the frying pan. When he'd retrieved the breakfast, without a word to his wife, without another glance at me, he walked out into the garden with the frying pan in his hands.

I dragged myself after him. Baxter was busy blowing her nose into a Mickey Mouse™ tea towel but I knew that once she'd wiped her face she'd want to attack me with the kettle. She certainly wouldn't put down a plate and fry me a thick slice of smoky bacon. So I followed Charlie into the garden.

He was walking towards the summerhouse. It was a wooden pavilion with creaking veranda and peeling bargeboards. I followed him up the steps and into another world.

Light poured through the windows into a simple whitewashed room. A beautiful easel stood in the centre of the room and against one wall a trestle table loaded with brushes and bottles, tubes of paint, palette knives, boxes of rainbow coloured pastels, bundles of charcoal and rolls of rag. Empty canvases had been stacked beside the table. Against the opposite wall a horsehair sofa draped with a blanket seemed to serve as a makeshift bed. In a corner of the summerhouse a table had been transformed into a kind of kitchen with a camping stove and a water bucket. A man could survive, shut away in this place, for quite a considerable length of time.

Charlie had taken the frying pan and carefully balanced it on the stove. While he finished frying breakfast, and the sweet smell of pork fat and pepper once more tormented my senses, I tried to entertain myself by prowling around the room.

There was something wrong.

The bed had been frequently occupied. The blanket and pillow smelt strongly of Charlie. The kitchen had been used to provide many meals, according to the crumbs, raisins and tiny slivers of cheese rind, some no bigger than toenail clippings, that were caught in the cracks in the floorboards. All these signs spoke of an artist who lived for weeks in his studio, painting with furious energy, obsessed by secret voices and visions.

And yet the easel was empty. The canvases were empty. The tubes of paint bore no thumbprints, no wrinkles disturbed their straining waistbands. The brushes were clean. The bundles of charcoal still wore their immaculate paper collars.

The studio, I discovered, served as a hide-out, a retreat from an angry world. Charlie came here, not to paint nor even to ponder the pleasures of painting, but to get away from the chicken slaughterer's daughter.

Sometimes he would come here merely to rest and relish the silence of the afternoons and sometimes he would be forced to seek its shelter in the middle of the night after a sudden, explosive fight when all the mirrors in the house were smashed and his clothes sent sailing from the bedroom windows.

Einstein

Why did Baxter treat him so badly?

As soon as I'd recovered my health I began to keep her under close observation. It wasn't easy because she forbade me to enter the house and I had to live in the summerhouse where Charlie would prepare my meals and sleep with me through those long bitter nights when she tossed him from the marriage bed. But a dog is not without cunning and I made myself a frequent yet invisible guest in that god-forsaken ideal home.

At first it seemed they wanted for nothing.

They had silver in the kitchen and marble in the bathroom. They had chickens in the freezer and a television in every room. They had all the trinkets and trash that are advertised as lending meaning to life. Baxter even had her own studio at the top of the house. It was larger and better equipped than Charlie's room. But, like Charlie, she did not paint. Something had gone wrong with their lives. The passion and dedication, the enthusiasm they'd shared for the casual life of the artist, had gradually withered and died. They had everything they wanted but along the way they had lost all hope.

The chicken slaughterer was not to blame. He had done everything for the best and spared no expense in providing for their comfort. They were suffocated in comfort. And in the midst of this plenty they discovered a terrible emptiness.

Baxter looked at herself in the mirror and saw that, despite her Hot Bitch Rubber Harness, she was after all a butcher's daughter and she would never be a high society prostitute nor a portrait painter to the rich and famous nor even a footnote in the modern art histories. And she began to resent Charlie for snatching her away from her art school dreams and locking her in this concrete castle.

Charlie, for his part, caught sight of his reflection and no longer recognised the man who stared back at him. He still thought of himself as an artist, believed that he had been born a painter, but he looked like a worn-out office clerk wearing a non-crease city suit and clutching his plastic attaché case with combination locks. He was getting a little heavier, his hair was turning grey and he had a silver feather pinned to his lapel. He looked at his reflection and wept.

They were lost. They were somnambulists, moving from room to room in a trance. They struggled sometimes to shake themselves awake, fought and squabbled and threatened to leave; but they no longer had the strength to resist and would sink silently back into the depths of their poisoned sleep.

The world could come to an end without shaking them from their slumber. Indeed, the world was coming to an end and they watched it every night on TV. They saw the blood of the last elephant leaking into the African dust. They saw fire erupt in the last forests being cleared to make highways to nowhere. They saw oceans blazing with oil and beaches littered with the rotting corpses of unknown creatures from the deep. They saw men reduced to skeletons, crawling through fields of razor wire, scratching in vain for a few grains of rice. They saw monstrous worms with human heads slither from lakes of nuclear mud. They saw the Jabberwock, with eyes of flame, howl in the straw of lambing sheds. And when they caught sight of these things they yawned, flicked channels and turned to the game shows.

41.

Baxter was the first to break the spell.

I'd been living in the pavilion for a month or more and had already mastered the art of breaking into the house. As soon as Charlie had gone to work I'd worm a path through the over-grown lawn, prise myself through an open window and spend the time watching Baxter from a dozen cracks and crevices.

She slept late and once she'd dragged herself from her bed, wandered the house in her dressing gown. She divided the lonely days between eating, sleeping and watching TV. Sometimes she ventured as far as the studio in the attic but these were rare visits and, once there, she did nothing more than stand at the window to stare at the lawn.

And then, one morning, there was a ring at the front door. When Baxter went to answer it she found herself confronted by a huge grinning woman in a pair of canvas dungarees. This woman was built like a champion Turkish wrestler. She had a large loose mouth and dark protruding eyes, Her hair had been cropped to the scalp and her feet prised into a pair of shimmering snakeskin boots decorated with small brass bells.

'What is it?' Baxter snarled, scowling in angry disbelief at this pair of ridiculous ogre's slippers. 'If you're selling God you're wasting your time – we're Orthodox Satanists.'

The woman gave a trumpet of laughter, threw her arms around Baxter and lifted her clean from the ground.

Baxter started to scream and must have felt her ribcage bend for she promptly wilted, hanging loose in the woman's arms.

'It's Patch!' roared the assailant, dropping Baxter to earth again. 'Patch Armstrong. Don't you remember? We were at art school together. I was the one who made all those terrible beer can sculptures. They threw me out when I tried to exhibit a giant painting I made from some really weird photographs we found in Posing Pouch Magazine!'

'They threatened to call the vice squad,' Baxter said, the memories swarming in her head.

'And told me to see a doctor.'

'Those photographs were very weird.'

'My paintings were no bowls of roses.'

'You were the skinny one called Spider!'

'That's me.'

Baxter stared at the swag-bellied stranger and the shock must have frozen her face because Patch felt obliged to offer some explanation as she squeezed her immensity through the door and went jangling in search of the kitchen.

There were many sound reasons for Patch Armstrong's inflation. She argued that:

1) A woman's body was a cinema screen upon which men were encouraged to project their sinister power fantasies and to sabotage this cinema screen was an act of political sabotage.

2) Men wanted women starved to skeletons because the fashion industry was a sado-masochistic conspiracy between (A) powerful but emotionally-retarded industrialists with the imaginations of child pornographers and (B) weak-minded women prepared to be reduced to prepubescent waifs in return for the favours of these snivelling jackals of capitalism.

3) A woman's body, inflated to gigantic proportions, presented a challenge to all the traditional Judeo-Christian courtship rituals to which women had historically been expected to surrender and exposed men, for the first time, to the dangers imagined or otherwise, of physical and sexual abuse.

There were other reasons but Patch Armstrong was content to leave these verses unsung because she had found the fridge and was breaking into the salad box. She might look like a sixpenny side-show but she was, she claimed, a ruthless freedom fighter, a dedicated killing machine.

She told Baxter about the fat women tribes of West Africa and the Earth Mother cults of the Caribbean and a lot of other stuff that Baxter didn't really understand but it felt dangerous and exciting to have this woman in the house and she tried to encourage her to talk by sitting her down at the kitchen table and feeding her coffee and cake.

'No coffee,' Patch said, crunching on a celery stick. 'I used to have a serious caffeine problem. Remember the coffee I drank at college? I must have been on a gallon a day. But I broke the habit. Who wants to be an addict? Do you have any natural orange juice?'

'I've got some grapefruit juice,' Baxter said, turning to search in the fridge and check the damage to her salad box.

'Is it fresh-squeezed?'

'Fresh-squeezed from sun-kissed whole fruit. Keep chilled. Consume within six weeks of purchase,' Baxter said, frowning as she read the carton. She must have bought it months ago. She pinched open the wings and waved the carton under her nose.

'Fine,' Patch Armstrong said, stretching an arm. 'Don't bother finding a glass.'

'Do you want some cake?' Baxter asked, returning to the table and staring pessimistically at the glistening fruit cake she'd already unwrapped and arranged on a plate.

'Ugh! I don't know how you can eat that junk! It's nothing but white flour, sugar syrups and twelve kinds of animal fat. Disgusting.'

'I suppose it is rather rich,' Baxter said, looking disappointed. She picked at the cake as she took it away and slipped a sultana into her mouth.

'Rich? There's enough cholesterol in a slice of that stuff to turn your blood into toffee.' She threw back her head and took a long swig of grapefruit juice, squeezing the carton in her dimpled fist.

'Do you want something else?' Baxter said, sensing she should apologise for trying to poison her guest.

'I'll have another stick of celery, if you can spare it,' Patch gasped, wiping the sides of her mouth with her thumb. 'And maybe some toast and peanut butter? Do you have any wholegrain bread? You have to watch what you eat. Most of the food you buy these days is pure unadulterated toxic crap. It's nothing but rat bait. I haven't touched processed food in years.'

'What do you eat?' Baxter asked, staring in admiration at her visitor's prize-winning paunch. Wet concrete and steel rivets. Broken lightbulbs and razor blades.

'I'm on the Miracle Nature Diet™,' Patch said, slapping her gut. 'Lentils and grains, leaf and root crops, yoghurt and honey, no meat, white fish, no eggs, herb tea, fruit juice, garlic oil capsules, royal jelly, morning primrose, mineral salts, ginseng root and pots of blackstrap molasses.'

'You look good on it,' Baxter said, as she set about making toast. It certainly didn't allow her to starve. She could put a death lock on a mountain gorilla.

'You should try it for a few weeks,' Patch said. 'Clean out your system. Save your life.'

While the big woman prattled and fondled her fat, I managed to work my way under the table and settled silently under her chair. Her snakeskin boots leaked the sour odours of closed rooms, laundry baskets, incontinent cats and all the other miserable stinks of her own crapaudiere.

Einstein

Patch had called at the house to invite Baxter to submit a painting to the annual Women Against exhibition. These exhibitions were organised by a feminist group known as the Militant Mothers and Patch Armstrong was the leading light. The previous year they had mounted Women Against the Exploitation of Immigrant Mexican Textile Workers, which had not been a great success, and this year they hoped to broaden the appeal with Women Against the Horrors of War. Sixty women artists had been invited to contribute their work.

Patch Armstrong didn't bother to ask Baxter if she had continued to paint after leaving art school. Such doubts hadn't entered her head. Baxter Pangloss had been the star of the show. Patch took it for granted that the school's most beautiful student would now be enjoying a dazzling international success. And Baxter felt so flattered to be asked to contribute to the Women Against exhibition that without a moment's hesitation she boldly accepted the challenge.

'Where are you holding the show?'

'At the TWAT,' Patch said. 'The Women's Art Theatre. It's an old cinema we found near Russell Square.'

'When?'

'You've only got seven weeks,' Patch said, brushing down her dungarees and flicking toast crumbs into my ears.

Baxter looked doubtful. She didn't know if she still had the knack and Patch expected a masterpiece delivered in less than two months.

'I'm sorry,' Patch said. 'I know it doesn't give you much time. I had trouble finding your address. But it's going to be a tremendous show. We've got a women's mime group who are going to perform a piece they've written about Japanese prisoner of war camps and I'm hanging a series of abstracts based on some aerial photographs taken after the bombing of Dresden and there'll be a make-up artist who paints children to look like victims of chemical weapons and a woman who shaves her head and hobbles about naked, wearing nothing but a pair of melted plastic sandals pretending to be the survivor of the nuclear holocaust. She screams like a bitch and squirts blood from a rubber bottle. Tremendous. Will you do something?'

'I don't know. There's so little time.'

'It really would make such a difference.'

'I'll try,' Baxter said.

Patch looked pleased. 'Make it something really big,' she said and snapped at another slice of toast with her horrible, bone-smashing teeth. 'Don't spare their feelings. We want to give them nightmares for weeks.'

So Baxter set to work planning her war memorial to honour the women and children who had fallen in the world's great wars. It was hard for her to imagine the horror. She made countless sketches and studies but everything seemed to lack conviction. Her bombed landscapes looked like fruit puddings. Her dead looked like sunbathers basking in mud. Finally she abandoned her easel and settled on building a totem pole, strung with the broken bodies of babies. She was never a subtle woman.

She didn't tell Charlie about Patch Armstrong. She didn't tell him about the Women Against the Horrors of War exhibition. She was involved in her first important arts festival and she didn't want to share the glory. It was none of his business. She'd squandered enough of her energy trying to encourage Charlie to paint and now it was time to rescue her own wasted talents.

He came home one evening to find her sitting at the kitchen table surrounded by dozens of Burpie™ dolls. These dolls were fat rubber babies that belched when you gave them a squeeze. They were sold with a range of cute Burpie™ wardrobes. Burpie goes to the Beach™. Burpies Birthday Barbecue™. Baxter was stripping her Burpie™ dolls and inserting meat skewers into their chests.

Charlie walked into the room, stared at the carnage all around him and dropped his attaché case to the floor. He was appalled. He must have thought that the queen of sleaze had finally lost her marbles. I pushed my head around the door and offered him some encouragement with a series of blood-freezing howls.

'What are you doing?' he shouted. 'Jesus Christ, Baxter, what are you doing?'

Baxter looked startled, as if she'd been found in the arms of some muscle-bound lover. 'I'm working,' she said as she skewered another of her doomed rubber babies.

'But what is it?'

'Skewered babies.'

'Why?'

'They represent slaughtered innocence,' Baxter said, as if this were a perfectly sound explanation. 'I should have thought it was obvious.'

Charlie had no time to pursue his interrogation because, at that moment, Baxter caught sight of me trying to hide between his legs.

'Keep that animal away from the table, Charlie!' she shouted in alarm. 'I'm warning you – if it upsets my work I'll wring its neck!'

'He's only a little dog,' Charlie said, as if he were talking to a frightened child. 'He won't hurt you. He wants to be friends. He won't do any harm in the house – his manners are perfect.'

'Get out!' she screamed.

It's dangerous to argue with a woman brandishing a bundle of meat skewers. So Charlie found something to cook for supper and hurried down to the summerhouse with his faithful companion at his heels. When we ventured back to the house the mutilated Burpies were gone and Baxter was locked in the attic.

42.

'Oh, that's typical!' Geraldine said, rudely interrupting Einstein's trance. 'She sends Charlie out to work for her father and then settles down to a life of leisure. Why didn't you complain? You were the man of the house. Why didn't you stay home and paint? She was nothing special, despite all her airs and graces. Some of those drawings she made were disgusting!'

'It was just a dream,' Charlie said sadly. 'I knew, by that time, I was never going to be an artist. The world is made of men learning to live apart from their dreams.'

'Art is the desire to be different. The desire to be elsewhere,' Einstein murmured and farted.

'What?'

'Nietzsche,' Einstein said, looking surprised.

'You really are a very peculiar dog,' Charlie said.

'You should have talked to that nice Mr Harry,' the ghost sighed. 'I liked him. He wanted to help you.'

There was nothing much left of her now but a shadow floating against the ceiling. She drifted as far as the window and turned, kicking out her feet and swimming towards the opposite wall.

'I missed Harry,' Charlie said. 'I can't deny it. And he tried hard enough to make contact. He didn't hold any grudges. But I stayed away from him because I knew that he'd upset Baxter. Whenever he phoned she would always complain and want to pick a fight.'

'Jealous!' Geraldine said.

'He wanted to make her acquaintance,' Charlie said. 'And a few weeks after we were married he came down to visit the house.

It wasn't easy for him. But he came bearing gifts – flowers, champagne and a bottle of perfume.'

'A bottle of perfume!' Geraldine said. 'He knew his manners. Lovely. A proper gentleman.'

'No,' Charlie said. 'He bought the perfume in the market. The trader was an old friend who mixed all sorts of fake French perfumes in the back of an East End warehouse and sold them in fancy bottles with badly printed labels. He'd been doing it for years.'

'Did Harry know the perfume was fake?'

'Yes,' Charlie said. 'But it didn't make any difference to him. He loved fakes. His freaks were fakes. He was proud of them. He couldn't see anything wrong with it.'

'It's the thought that counts,' Geraldine said.

'Yes,' Charlie said. 'It's the thought that counts and the trader thought that Harry was setting out on some romantic episode and he liked Fat Harry and wanted to help him so he slipped him his largest bottle of Domination – a full pint measure – with a free gift hidden inside the box.'

'What happened?' Einstein asked.

'Baxter was impressed. She loved the flowers and adored the champagne and then she opened the perfume and found her mystery gift.'

'What was it?'

'A pair of lacy black rayon panties embroidered with scarlet valentine hearts'

'Good grief!' Einstein whistled.

'Baxter was furious. She thought that Harry wanted her to wear them. She thought that I had told him about the Hot Bitch Rubber Harness. She thought we had planned it together.'

'Conceited trollop!' Geraldine said. 'That's typical of the woman. She thought she was so attractive that every man she came across wanted to fondle her apricot!'

182

Charlie blinked and stared at the ceiling. Where had his mother learned such expressions?

'So she threw him out?' Einstein said.

'Yes,' Charlie said. 'And then time passed and I wasn't painting any more and I was working for the Pangloss Chicken Empire and I felt too ashamed to approach him.'

'You wanted to be an artist,' the Mariner said. 'But you worked for a chicken butcher.'

'Yes,' Charlie said.

'Why?' the Deep Time Mariner said.

'I don't know!'

The Deep Time Mariner shook his huge head and sighed. The lives of these queer little monkey-men were so short and they seemed to squander their time in finding ways to deny themselves the pleasure of the days.

'He had responsibilities,' the ghost of Geraldine shrilled. 'He had a wife and a big house and he wanted to start a family. That's why he worked for the chicken butcher. Nobody forced him. It was his choice. And he should have been counting his blessings instead of carping all the time and sleeping with that horrid dog. He was never satisfied. He should have listened to his father. He could have been a barber and had his own business and everything. He could have been somebody.'

'I wanted to be a painter!'

'You worked for a chicken butcher!' the ghost of his mother screamed, shaking dust from the curtains.

'Can't you keep her under control?' Charlie pleaded, turning to the Deep Time Mariner.

'She came from your head,' the Mariner said, sweeping at the air with his long thin hands.

Geraldine shrieked and darted away, knocking a picture from the wall. It was a small nude study of Baxter sitting in an armchair, an early watercolour from their liquorice allsorts period. Charlie rushed forward to save it but failed and trod on the glass.

'Did you see Harry again?' Einstein said, trying to maintain some sense of order.

'Yes,' Charlie said, carefully picking Baxter from the fragments of glass and helping restore her modesty by pushing her under a cushion. 'One afternoon I slipped out of the office and went down to the Church Street Gallery.'

'And he was still there?'

'Oh, yes,' Charlie said. 'He was still there but he'd returned to his old trade. The place was full of freaks.'

'He was clever. He didn't need you to support him,' Geraldine said from the ceiling.

'He had never needed me,' Charlie said. 'His freaks had been discovered by the London art critics. Some of them praised him and others attacked him and that created enough excitement to guarantee his success. He was the eye of his own thunderstorm. The critics called his work New-Structuralism and Nuclear-Dada and all sorts of similar nonsense. The art schools were now full of kids stuffing cats into cod fish and building giants from cow bones.'

'Horrible!' Geraldine said.

'It was crazy,' Charlie agreed. 'It felt as if the whole world was suddenly anxious to admire the ugly and the deformed.'

'But Fat Harry was famous,' Einstein prompted. 'He'd become something of a celebrity.'

'Yes,' Charlie said. 'After I walked out on him he had to do some fast thinking. He didn't want to go back to a life on the road. But he knew that if he mounted his side-show in the gallery and sold tickets at the door that the police would raid him, charge him with obscenity and probably destroy his work. So he called the cannibal The Unknown Political Prisoner and he called the mermaid Memories of the Madonna and he wasn't asking the hoi polloi to come to gawp at them. He was sending out invitations for people to buy them. And buy them for fancy prices. It wasn't a freak show. It was a sculpture gallery. It was so simple it was really an act of genius.'

'Did you approach him?' the Deep Time Mariner asked.

'Did you talk to him?' Einstein said.

'We went out to have a few drinks and talk over old times,' Charlie said. 'But everything had changed.'

43.

They are peering down into the cocktail lounge of the latest
London night-club and restaurant. The cocktail lounge is called
the Greenhouse Effect. It's the big sensation. The newest and
smartest watering hole. The floors have been laid with a bright
green artificial turf with clusters of polypropylene palms standing
in corners. Beneath the palms are polythene penguins. The lights
are low and the music is loud. Parakeets swing in wickerwork
cages suspended from the bamboo ceiling. A polar bear holding a
surfboard is striking a pose behind the bar. The owners are trying
to sell the idea that global warming will create a new kind of
paradise. A tropical Garden of Eden. There will be no winter.
Everyone will bask in the warmth of perpetual summer and
wallow in coral seas.

Fat chance.

Charlie is sitting at the bar with his Senior Statesman™ plastic
attaché case balanced on his knees. He is drinking a Radioactive
Waist – a sweet rum punch served in a goblet frosted with sugar.
He looks hot and uncomfortable. It is three o'clock in the afternoon. He is watching a waitress in a sequin-encrusted swimsuit
serving drinks and a little bowls of salted nuts, potato chips and
dishes of skinny green olives.

The waitress is a young woman with a large red mouth and a
head of perfect strawberry-blonde curls. She looks a little like
Marilyn Monroe. There are five waitresses in the club and when
he looks at them in turn, he discovers that they all look just a little
like dead actresses from Hollywood's Golden Age. There's
Marlene Dietrich busy mixing Martini Melt Downs and Bette

Davis selling cigarettes. Mae West is standing at the club door, sharing a private joke with Jean Harlow.

The owners had advertised for six identical Dorothy Lamours wearing sarongs and hibiscus flowers to serve the tables in paradise. But that had proved impossible and they'd eventually had to settle for these assorted legends in the standard Hollywood colour: blonde. There was no room for brunettes in this corner of paradise.

Charlie is sitting with Harry "Enrico" Prampolini, the famous sculptor and man about town. It was his idea to visit the Greenhouse Effect. Harry has brought Charlie here because he wants him to know that he can afford the good life. Harry still believes in the good life. He is wearing a fine silk suit and a Rolex the size of a golfball. The pockets of his jacket are crammed with Cuban cigars. His wallet expands in a hundred pleats – an accordion of gold charge cards.

'Remember the old days?' Harry says, full of good humour as he sloshes back his second or third Catatonic Converter.

'I'll never forget them,' Charlie says.

'You painted them and I went out there and sold them. It was a clever racket, Charlie. A very clever racket. I found I could sell 'em so fast that you couldn't meet the demand. You threatened to stamp out your landscapes with stencils. Remember?'

'It wasn't such a bad idea,' Charlie says, smiling as he remembers the little attic and Harry's approach as a salesman.

'You've got to laugh,' Harry grins.

'There were good days,' Charlie says.

Harry looks at Charlie and feels proud to be his friend. Charlie is now a big success in the chicken industry and he's heard that it's a cut-throat business. He tries to make him talk about his work but Charlie seems reluctant to give anything away.

'Do you make those Texan Chicken Burgers with the authentic Cowboy Sauce?' Harry asks him. 'I've always had a weakness for Texan Chicken Burgers.' Harry enjoys his food, he can talk about it for hours, and the food he enjoys the most – like everything else in his life – is heavily processed and counterfeit.

'No,' Charlie says. 'They're made for Mr Rooster™ by Animal Meat Machine Retrievals. They're not part of the company.'

'That's a pity,' Harry grins. 'I thought I might have a fighting chance of winning a lifetime's supply. You can't lick that Cowboy Sauce!' he adds, remembering the advertising. 'Are you the people who make those new chicken cocktail weenies?'

Charlie shakes his head. ' That's Mr Rooster™ again,' he says.

'They're good!' Harry tells him, smacking his lips at the memory. 'And they come in three party flavours. Smoky bacon, beef and tandoori. You've got to laugh. Chicken that tastes like bacon. Don't ask me how they do it!'

Charlie doesn't ask and Harry is sensitive to silence. 'So tell me, how do you spend your time?'

'I just shuffle paper for a living,' Charlie mumbles unhappily. 'It's nothing very interesting.' He picks at a pretzel, snapping the brittle stick with his fingers, coating his tongue with dust.

'I suppose you have to travel,' Harry says, concluding that Charlie must be a top-flight executive, since most senior company men in Harry's long experience, didn't know or even much care if they were manufacturing marmalade or machine guns. They did nothing but write mission statements and read stock market reports. 'A lot of travel in your line of work. Paris. New York. Tokyo. Do they eat Texas Chicken in Tokyo? I don't envy you the travel. It's a terrible kick to the nervous system. Airport to airport. Boardroom to boardroom. It snaps the springs in your body clock.'

'I'd never volunteer for it,' Charlie mutters. How can he admit that he works in a cubicle with nothing more exotic in view than a set of Korean ballpoint pens?

'But it takes you away from home,' Harry says, trying to

smother a crafty grin by plugging his mouth with a Cuban cigar. Boardroom to boardroom. Brothel to brothel. Bombay to Bangkok. He hopes the poor devil is having some fun while he's away from home.

The waitress who is not quite Bette Davis bumps and grinds her way to the bar and strikes a match for Harry's cigar. Harry sucks and winks at the girl who twinkles back at him through the smoke, hoping she might have been discovered.

'You wouldn't have a lot of time left for Baxter,' he continues, dunking his paper parasol into the dregs in his cocktail glass. 'That sort of life is hard on a marriage.'

'It's not easy,' Charlie says.

Harry looks at Charlie and blows smoke rings at the ceiling. He doesn't doubt that Charlie's work must be important and confidential. Harry the mammonite understands the pressure that comes with success. He imagines Charlie as a young tycoon in a mighty business empire. He can tell that he's an important man by the size of his plastic attaché case.

Charlie looks at Harry and feels ashamed. He doesn't know what to say to him. He doesn't know how to explain. Perhaps it's the booze or the stifling heat or the ear-bursting noise that makes him feel like he's drowning. He wants to throw his arms around the fat man's shoulders and talk about art and God and dreams. He wants to go back to their life in the attic and be given a second chance to play the game in a different way. He needs salvation. He needs a friend. He wants Harry Prampolini to take his hand and drag him ashore. And all they talk about is chicken.

He sucks up his Radioactive Waist and hurries back to the office.

44.

'You should have gone back to him,' Einstein said. 'You could have worked together again.'

'He wanted to take me to Frankfurt to help him with his new exhibition,' Charlie said, 'although we both knew it was impossible and, anyway, by that time Baxter was already…'

But Einstein had stopped listening. He swivelled towards the window, cocked his ears and flared his nostrils. His whiskers quivered like telegraph wires. His face puckered into a grimace and he threw back his head and howled.

'What is it?' the Deep Time Mariner asked, bending over the little dog. 'What's wrong?'

'I don't know,' Einstein said, smacking his nose with his tongue. He gulped nervously and turned back to the window.

A storm was approaching from the south, a rolling fortress of cloud that cast a shadow over the city and sent bolts of lightning bursting like mortar shells into the streets. Violent squalls raced ahead of the battery, banging on doors and cracking windows, squeezing chimneys until they sneezed soot.

As the storm rolled over the rooftops the city was suddenly plunged into darkness.

Charlie felt the carpet move under his feet. The room seemed to swell and shrink again, as if the building were gasping for breath.

'What's happening?' he shouted through the uproar.

But Einstein and the Mariner had no answer. They were staring, dumbfounded, at the window.

It was raining fish.

They were tiny, rainbow-coloured fish falling through a crackling, luminous rain. And with the fish there were small spider crabs and somersaulting squids squirting necklaces of ink and plummeting jellyfish trailing ribbons and nameless horrors of the deep with human heads and stinging tails. As they watched, the street was filled with flapping bodies, the walls of the buildings were gilded with fish scales, the gutters were running with blood.

'Quickly!' the Mariner snapped, turning from the window. 'Who will finish this story?'

45.

The totem pole of skewered Burpie™ dolls was the centrepiece at the Women Against the Horrors of War exhibition and Baxter was soon surrounded by adoring Militant Mothers. Few of the Mothers were artists. There were one or two who called themselves potters, an occupation that Baxter despised as a morbid desire to shape turds from mud, but the rest of them were strictly employed with the maintenance of their own reproduction. They were making their own world of children. They were raising an army of toddlers. Their wombs were constantly blazing kilns from which they shaped life in their own image.

Baxter was shocked to discover that Patch Armstrong was the mother of four fat bawling infants, each child claiming a different father. There were many reasons for this rampant fertility.

Motherhood was the natural fulfilment of women, whose bodies were miraculous machines built to reproduce themselves, quickly and efficiently, filling the world with future Mothers.

Motherhood was not the duty of wives dependent on jealous husbands but the joy of independent women who could use strategic multiplication to influence the affairs of men.

Motherhood was a form of magic greatly feared by the tribe of men who perpetually tried to frustrate fertile women with pornography, contraception and abortion.

There were other reasons but Patch was content to leave these verses unsung because Baxter would find them in the Militant Mothers publications, *A Window on your Ovaries* and *A Voyage down your Fallopian Tube*.

It wasn't easy being a Mother without a husband's sponsorship or a sympathetic employer prepared to establish a working crèche. The Mothers struggled in poverty, many trapped in single rooms and living on modest state stipends.

'The state owes every Mother a living,' Patch said. 'Children are the future of the world. What would happen if we stopped having children? Can you imagine the consequences?'

'I guess I've never really thought about it,' Baxter said.

'Everything would fall apart. Industry would collapse. The economy would stagnate. We'd be in big trouble. Why can't they understand that? When the state interferes with the future by persecuting Mothers and children it casts the seeds of its own destruction. We should all be paid decent wages and given contracts of employment. There should be incentive schemes and paid holidays and all the rest of it. We're the most important industry on the planet!'

She was wearing a cotton sling, attached by a system of straps to the front of her dungarees and in this sling sat a silent, staring baby. Baxter, made uncomfortable by the monotonous scrutiny of this unblinking infant, tried smiling at it. The child looked astonished, as if Baxter had breached all established laws of etiquette, and gave her a disapproving scowl.

This child was the result of a chance encounter with one of the following:

1) Harry "Enrico" Prampolini, the famous Nuclear Dadaist, who had refused to make a donation to one of the Mother's fund raising campaigns and then, in an act of swift revenge, had been coaxed to donate his sperm instead through a brisk but effective knee-trembler. Harry had no trouble in rising to the occasion since he'd always been attracted to fat/ bearded/ tattooed women.

2) George Carver whom Patch had found working in a deep pan pizza restaurant and who had managed, briefly, to tickle her

fancy with anchovies and garlic bread. For Patch there was something deeply erotic about a man forced to work in a kitchen.

3) Douglas MacArthur Figgens, a brooding young man who had spent many years nursing a crippled, insane father and who had insisted that she flog him with a wet towel before mounting her invasion of his person. She'd been more than happy to oblige.

No-one knew who had fathered the child and Patch didn't give a damn. She'd already forgotten their names. It was her child and she would fashion its life. Patch Armstrong agreed with Oscar Wilde that fathers should neither be seen nor heard, although she would have hated to have found herself in agreement with a man of any description.

'Do you have a smidgen more of this cheese? It really is delicious,' Patch said. 'And maybe some olives?' She had abandoned her Miracle Nature Diet™ in favour of the Paradise Protein System™. She had found it in a magazine. She was eating cheese, bananas, peanuts and milk.

Baxter took the empty plate and cut another slice from the Stilton. She felt dwarfed by the bulk of Patch Armstrong, a stoker at work on a giant boiler.

'We really need a nursery where the Mothers can meet once or twice a week and learn to relate to each other as women. Do you understand? We want to work through our fundamental problems until we're a self-sufficient group with a coherent strategy for the future. We want to raise our personal worth assessment levels. Don't you think that's important? And we want to encourage our children to expand their social awareness in a non-hostile, non-sexist, non-political environment. We want them to be liberated from all the debilitating prejudices and neurotic nihilism of the state educational system. And we also need a place where we can have herbal massage and primal scream classes.'

'What happens in a primal scream class?' Baxter ventured.

'You sit on the floor and scream,' Patch said, stuffing her mouth with olives and cheese.

'There's plenty of room here,' Baxter said. 'You could have one of the big rooms at the back of the house.'

'It's a great offer and I appreciate it,' Patch grinned, brushing aside the suggestion with a little wave of her hand.

'I mean it,' Baxter said.

'But we'd stop you working,' Patch said. 'We like to make a lot of noise when we get together. We have to vocalise our feelings.'

'It won't make any difference to me,' Baxter shrugged. 'I keep my studio in the attic.'

'It would be the perfect arrangement,' Patch agreed, cracking an olive stone with her teeth. 'But shouldn't you ask what's-his-name?'

'Charlie?'

'Yeah.'

'Why? It's my house. Anyway, what does he care what happens here? He spends most of his time in the garden.'

'What's he doing out there?'

'God knows!' Baxter said. 'Honestly, he's such a pain!'

'Men are strange,' Patch agreed. 'That's why the Mothers like to keep the children away from them.'

As she spoke she unbuttoned a pocket in her dungarees and one of her breasts fell out. It was a painfully swollen gourd, as richly marbled as the Stilton that its owner had just devoured. The nipple was a crumpled leather thumb. She pulled at the nipple and used it to stab at the baby's face. The infant struggled, opened its mouth to complain, caught the nipple and clung to it.

'What about the fathers?' Baxter said, trying to pull her eyes away from the sight of the bulging pap.

195

'What about them?'

'Well, don't they care what happens to their children?' Baxter said. 'Don't they want to interfere?'

'Are you kidding?' Patch said scornfully. 'Most of them don't even know they are fathers. They're from the wham, bang, thank you ma'am school of screwing. And if you told them they were fathers they'd probably want to forget it. But a few of them – the really jealous bastards – create hell and make life hard for everyone.'

'But I thought there were laws,' Baxter protested.

'Oh, yeah, there are laws,' Patch said carelessly. 'But we're working on it.' And then she told Baxter about the Militant Mothers' demands for a universal sperm bank where a woman could be impregnated, under proper medical supervision, without obligation to the donor or having to endure the wrangles of all those men who thought they owned the fruits of your labour just because they delivered the seed.

Baxter listened with a mixture of delight and incredulity. She imagined a universal sperm bank as a kind of Pangloss Chicken Battery where impatient Militant Mothers clambered into empty cages, hoicked up their skirts and spread their buttocks over nests of glistening caviar. The eggs were warm, golden, the size of pearls. The nests were deep and secure, like upturned feather hats. The Mothers poked their heads through the bars and clucked defiantly at the world.

'It's beautiful!' Patch boomed when Baxter finally led her to the empty back room.

It was a dismal corner of the house. A long, unlovely room with a brick fireplace, a pine plank floor and windows overlooked by a dense thorn hedge. Charlie had wanted to build a library here. The room contained a solitary bookcase, its shelves thickly lined with dust. It was a waste. Neither of them came to this room. Now it could be transformed into a real nursery filled with cushions and boxes of toys and a finger painting table and perhaps a beautiful rocking horse and the sounds of laughing Mothers and children.

'It looks so bare,' Baxter said sadly, as she looked around the empty walls.

'We'll bring some campaign posters and decorate,' Patch said, walking to one of the windows and using a finger to wipe a spyhole in the dirty glass. 'It will be perfect if we keep it warm and cover the floor. Do you have any carpet? And a few armchairs? And some bean bags? Do you think we could hang a swing from the ceiling?'

'I could paint the walls!' Baxter said, suddenly full of inspiration.

'There's nothing wrong with them,' Patch said, peering at the pattern in the wallpaper. 'I've always liked tulips.'

'No,' Baxter said. 'I mean I could paint a mural for you. Children love pictures, don't they? I could paint something big and colourful.'

'You've already done enough,' Patch said. 'We couldn't ask for more. What about your own work?'

'Painting is my work,' Baxter said. 'I want to do it. Besides, I've never attempted a mural. It would be a challenge for me.'

She could already see a Noah's ark stranded somewhere beneath the ceiling and a prancing carnival of animals ascending in spirals from the skirting boards. Elephants, giraffes and kangaroos. Lions and leopards and polar bears. And, at that moment, with a painful jolt of loneliness, looking at this Mother with the child buried warmly between her breasts, Baxter was suddenly aware that she wanted to be part of their nursery world.

46.

I was there! Einstein said indignantly. I was there and saw everything. They came from every direction and filled the house with their screaming snot-smeared spawn. Twenty full-grown monkey-women with seventy-six grunting carpet-crawlers. Can you imagine the noise of it? Can you imagine the smell? Charlie was spared the full horrors of this invasion since, by the time he'd dragged himself home from the office, there was little left on the battleground but a few broken toys and a sour miasma of soft dung and puke. It meant nothing to him. But his faithful four-legged friend was in the very thick of it.

Why did they do it?

Why were they so determined to breed and having taken delivery why did they treat their whelps with such concentrated adulation? It didn't make sense to me.

Infancy serves no purpose. It's an apprenticeship to be endured before animals are qualified to take their place in society. It's a state of affairs to be tolerated but not encouraged by parents. And yet it was obvious that these Mothers were not urging their children towards independence. On the contrary, these Mothers crawled around on their hands and knees, laughing and talking to themselves in a queer and primitive patois. They were teaching their infants to behave like infants. They had no intention of teaching their brats the secrets of self-sufficiency. They didn't want to be rid of them – they wanted them to remain as helpless, boggle-eyed dug-hangers. The Mothers described the ignorant and sorry condition of their whelps as the blessed state of innocence and were quite prepared to murder in order to preserve it. They seemed to believe that drooling, gum-smacking babbledom was the path that led to paradise, a divine blessing, a gift from Almighty God.

It came as no surprise to find that the Mothers themselves looked very much like overgrown whelps. They were flushed and petulant creatures with a taste for whimsical nursery clothes and pastel-coloured shoes. They wore smug smiles and button badges with stupid slogans. Baby on Board. The Incredible Bulk. Motherhood for these women was the true purpose and function of life. And who dared contradict them?

By devoting their days to the arithmetic of tomorrow the Mothers hoped to determine the future. But the Mothers weren't going into the future. They were sending their offspring into the future, like generals sending troops out to fight a war that couldn't be won. Their children were supposed to be the new hope for a hopeless world. They were the future concert pianists, Hollywood heroes, cosmetic surgeons and liver sausage millionaires. They would succeed where their parents had failed. They would be remarkable. They would be remembered. They would all be beautiful and brave and have brains the size of melons. The Mothers had made them from their own flesh and blood. They had invented them to conquer the world. They didn't know the world was coming to an end.

They knew, of course, that the world was full of sick and starving babies. But they were Chinese and African and Indian babies. That was different. You couldn't include the unlucky ones born in the slums of San Paolo, Mexico City, Calcutta, Bombay, Addis Ababa, Brazzaville, Bogota, Bangui or Cairo. Some of these people were so poor they didn't have washing machines or freezers. It was so primitive – how could they hope to raise children in such unhygienic conditions? Small wonder they caught such disgusting diseases. As far as the Mothers were concerned they might have been a different species forced to survive on another planet where they had no Heinz™ or Johnson & Johnson™ or any kind of welfare programme. It was terrible but the Mothers couldn't help everyone. They had enough trouble making their fat, best Western babies. You didn't see fat, best Western babies sick and starving, paraded on poster hoardings with bulging bellies and eye sockets swarming with flies. Thank God, it was still a safe and happy world for them. And the Mothers knew that as long as Ronald McDonald™ appeared on TV nothing was wrong.

A million years ago Nature had programmed their on-board computers to urge them to breed at any cost, and no one knew how to cancel the programme. The Mothers believed in eternal life, in God's great game of Pass the Parcel. Their children granted them life after death. Fuck today and live tomorrow. And even if they had sensed that something was wrong, it would merely have served to make them breed with greater vigour and concentration, hoping to outflank catastrophe by sheer force of numbers. Such was their dedication.

Motherhood was everything. It lent them the power and the glory. It gave them command over life and death. And it also provided a safe retreat from the terrors of the adult world. Surrounded by children they became like children, fortified in a nursery world of sweet milk puddings and Lego bricks.

A few of the Mothers had axes to grind, there's no doubt about it. One of the Mothers, a small woman with tight ginger hair and a history of unhappy love affairs, wanted to organise a study group for the Mothers who needed trauma therapy for the damage she felt had been inflicted upon their original state of grace during the brief but unpleasant moments of physical penetration by the men who had fathered their children. These moments might have been brief but they certainly must have done some mischief. The therapy lasted six weeks and included confidential counselling, colonic irrigation and pillow-punching sessions. Her little class of bowel-wrenchers could really make the feathers fly.

Another Mother was planning to raid a number of private abortion clinics to liberate unborn babies. She'd had a leaflet printed starring an unusually featous foetus with a face like a Burpie™ doll. Beneath this half-baked bundle of joy were instructions for making Molotov cocktails. A recipe she had found on the Internet. Her idea was simple and savage. The clinic consulting rooms would be bombed and during the confusion the reluctant mothers would be snatched from the beds, driven to a secret location and held until they delivered their babies.

A third Mother was trying to outlaw the sale and distribution of contraceptives because they encouraged men to think of women as sexual playthings and cheated them of their birth rights. Since contraception was the only protection the women had against several murderous male diseases, it was argued that men be required by law to carry medical cards. She already demanded that her own suitors take fitness and endurance tests. She'd weighed their balls before she'd agreed to play with them. You needed to be a determined man to rummage in her dungarees. She wanted to breed from champions.

But, for the most part, the Mothers were content to shut the door on the outside world and play with their rag dolls and plastic rattles. They crawled about on the floor in delirious games of peek-a-boo while Baxter moved among them with her brushes and paints, splashing at her Noah's ark mural.

47.

'What's that?' the Mariner said sharply.

'Where?' Charlie said, peering into the room where the Mothers were leading their toddlers in a game of primal screams.

'The window!' the Mariner said.

Charlie looked up at the nursery window and saw nothing but the thorn hedge he had planted and a narrow glimpse of the garden beyond.

'I can't see anything.'

But the Mariner grew very agitated, trying to squint around the corners of Einstein's dream. They were watching the world through the eyes of a dog and it was a keyhole view of giant babies, women's ankles and flat rubber shoes. The window was beyond Einstein's reach.

'Concentrate!' the Mariner roared impatiently, nudging the dog with the tip of an armour plated boot.

Einstein whimpered and started to shake. He was so frightened he shook himself out of the trance.

The Mariner cursed and lunged at Charlie, clasped him roughly by the shoulders and sent him crashing to his knees.

'Concentrate!' he roared.

Charlie felt as if he'd been thrown against a powerful electric fence. His limbs thrashed wildly out of control and sparks popped from his crackling hair. He hit the ground with such a force that he bounced and cracked his head. He lay where he had fallen, eyes closed, fists clenched, with the world still spinning around him.

When he finally opened his eyes he was staring at a brilliant summer sky. He could smell the sweet, sharp scent of grass and the heavy perfume of old-fashioned roses and heliotrope. For a time he didn't move but remained where he had landed, staring up at the clean and empty sky. When he turned his head he wanted to find himself stretched out on a grassy bank in a secret corner of his own garden. He wanted to find he had woken from a long and angry nightmare. He thought, in a moment, Einstein will come snuffling to find me, rasping my hand with his wet tongue; Baxter will appear from the house with a frosty jug of lemonade and she'll sit beside me with her skirts softly fanned on the grass and we'll be in love again because we'll be at the moment before the moment when it all went wrong and, this time, it will be different and we won't make the same mistakes.

He sat up slowly and looked around. He was sitting in his own garden. It was a warm summer's morning. To his left he saw Einstein jumping and plunging through a bed of flowers, his jaws snapping at flies. When he turned to his right he saw Einstein, again, peering at his other self from the safety of a holly bush!

He wiped his hands across his face, frightened by the sheer intensity of this new and startling illusion. The glare of the sunlight was burning his eyes. A grasshopper crawled on his naked foot.

'What happened?' he groaned, as the Deep Time Mariner came trampling from the undergrowth.

'I brought you back to the garden,' the Mariner said cheerfully. 'I thought you might care to show me around.'

'Are we really in the past?' Charlie whispered, pointing at the two dogs who were now sitting side by side and striking identical attitudes.

'Yes,' the Mariner said.

'I don't like it!' Charlie muttered. You didn't have to be a genius to know that if you trespassed in the past you were likely to encounter yourself approaching from the shadows. And, caught by your living reflection, the shock always killed you. Doppelgangered! It didn't seem to bother Einstein, but he was a dog. It was always different for dogs.

'Did you create this garden?' the Mariner asked him.

Charlie nodded and clambered to his feet. They were standing among the terraces he'd made when he'd cut the ornamental ponds. Beyond them a glade of flowering trees framed a view of the summer pavilion. Behind them the house was securely hidden by banks of exotic shrubbery.

The Mariner beamed with pleasure. His green leather face seemed to darken and glow. 'It's a fine day,' he said gently, sniffing the air. 'Let's take a walk.'

So Charlie followed the Mariner through a maze of overblown rhododendrons with the Einsteins trotting behind them.

48.

Charlie had transformed the rough acres of pasture that surrounded the house into a fabulous garden. Beneath them, through a clattering curtain of tall bamboo, lay a pool of dark water where fish the colour of apricots splashed among roots of fragrant lilies. Beyond the pool an ancient Chinese funeral urn, overflowing with ivy, stood in a brilliant silver sea of rosemary, lavender, sage and thyme.

This was not a manicured garden of shaved lawns, clipped hedges and neat herbaceous borders. Here was a wild and over-grown place. There were thistles wreathed in honeysuckle and deep, dusty nettle beds and creaking cabbages that stank and jostled the roots of the roses. And everywhere there were narrow paths cut through thickets of firethorn and bramble that led down to little pagan shrines, half-buried statues and curious grottoes.

The Deep Time Mariner stalked through the garden, inspecting all its secret corners and nodding his approval at every new discovery until finally he came upon a sun-drenched clearing set in a circle of scented shrubs and sat down to rest with the Einsteins beside him.

'Monkey-men were born to be gardeners,' he said peacefully, stroking one of the little dogs, and he asked Charlie all manner of things about the garden's design and the many plants that surrounded them.

Charlie did his best to answer these questions although the proper names of the plants escaped him and fleabane, loosestrife and lambs' tongue meant nothing to the Mariner. But he was thankful for this interlude in his trial, which he sensed was drawing to the wrong conclusions, and he wanted to keep the Mariner's interest. So he tried to remember how the garden had first taken shape and what had inspired him to build it.

It was difficult to explain. He supposed there had come a time in his life when he'd wanted to nurse the earth in his hands. It was almost as if some deep and primitive instinct had been stirred in him, some faint tribal memory that had whispered to him to stop running in circles and sit down in a quiet place to feel the planet moving beneath him.

But what had triggered this desire? Had it been his time in Future Forecasts, designing a chicken for tomorrow where everyone would find themselves trapped in a lonely, virtual world of TV sex and shopping, that had made him relish the bone-cracking frosts and the squalls of soft, summer rain? Or had Baxter and the noise of the Mother's menagerie driven him to seek the solitude of the orchard and the potting shed? He didn't know. It wasn't important. The days belonged to the Pangloss Chicken Empire, the house belonged to Baxter, but the garden belonged to him. It was a living work of art. An original creation. And he had created it.

Einstein had shown him the way to the garden. Forbidden to enter the house and bored in the pavilion, he had spent the greater part of his time running through the long grass, barking and jumping at Charlie or scratching for beetles and spiders. It was Einstein who had led him to the pond. At the time it had been no more than a shallow ditch filled with leaves and a vinegar of winter rain. But it held the promise of a clean pool that might flash with fish and dragonflies. A marvellous and secret place. So Charlie bought himself a spade and went out one weekend to cut the ditch into shape.

It felt good to be working in the open air with the cold wind stinging his face and the wet soil under his fingernails and soon he found he'd dug a series of ponds, and the earth from these excavations would become the banks and terraces that he'd fill with fruit and flowers.

When he'd first lifted the turf with his spade and peeled it back to reveal the bare soil he had felt a vague unease, as if he'd exposed the floor beneath a vast green carpet and could expect to confront, beneath the bare floor, all the heavy machinery that made the planet spin in space.

As the section of lawn was lifted Baxter had screamed and scolded him from the safety of the ranch style dream home, but he knew she never left the house and would have to be content to shout at him from the windows.

'Why are you digging up the grass, you crazy bastard?' she had shouted from her throne beneath the rafters. She'd been washing her hair and her head was still wrapped in a turban of towels. She looked like a dyspeptic sultan.

'I want to plant it,' Charlie had shouted back at her.

'It's already planted!

'I want to plant a proper garden.' He paused, squinting up at the house, shielding his eyes with his hand. He thought she'd get the idea. He naturally thought she would share his vision.

But Baxter didn't understand him. 'We already have a proper garden - it's called a lawn!' she screamed, pulling at her turban in rage.

'It's not a lawn. It's just the remains of the field,' Charlie had shouted back at the window and he bent once more to his spade. It was going to take a lot of hard work to bring this soil back into condition.

'That's a fully-landscaped lawn you're destroying! There's nothing underneath but dirt. Do you know how much they cost to put down? Do you realise the damage you're doing?'

'Cow pasture. It's just cow pasture,' Charlie had argued, slashing at the grass with his spade. 'I'm going to turn it into a garden.'

'Don't be such a pain! You're wearing your best office shoes and you've managed to cover yourself in mud! Do you think I'm going to clean that jacket? Are you drunk or what? Have you gone mad?'

'I'm planning to grow fresh vegetables. Good wholesome food whenever we need it. And a goat for the milk and perhaps a few chickens for their eggs.'

There was stunned silence for a moment while the full meaning of his words were absorbed by his unhappy audience.

'Why are you trying to frighten me? Is it because of my friends? Is that it? Are you jealous of my friends? If you don't stop this nonsense at once, I'm warning you, I shall go and phone daddy!' Baxter had screamed and then, because she was shouted hoarse, she had slammed down the window and sulked.

Everything Charlie planted had flourished. Rare tropical fruits and vines miraculously thrived among the potatoes and turnips. There were orchids in the spinach beds and jasmine trailing through the onion patch. Charlie didn't know the rules of gardening so he planted everything he could find, buying countless packets of seed, sprinkling the wizened specks of life into the dark and clinging soil, watching the seedlings unfurl themselves, sprouting towards the sunlight. Nothing disappointed him.

He loved this quiet garden as he'd loved nothing else in his life. He loved the creeping thistle and ragwort as much as the precious buds of the first magnolia flowers. He loved the blackbirds in the apple trees and the mice in the strawberries and the deep-throated frogs in the gloom of the grottoes. It was his work. It was his small patch of paradise.

'It's good to be back,' Einstein sighed, bracing himself against his front legs and stretching his spine so taut that the knot in his tail uncoiled like a spring.

'Yes,' Charlie whispered. 'It's good to see it again.'

'You'd better make the most of it,' the future Einstein said, turning to his earlier self who had fallen asleep in a clump of marigolds.

'Why?' Einstein said, cocking an ear and tilting it in Einstein's direction. 'What's going to happen?'

'You'll soon be driven out,' Einstein said.

Einstein sat up and sneezed. He was covered in grass seeds and prickly burrs. His whiskers were dusted with pollen.

'We're turned out of the garden?' he said. He shook his head and his jaws fell open. He couldn't believe it.

'Yes.'

'But where do we go from here?' Einstein said. He was shocked to his marrow. He thought he was in the garden forever. He'd had enough of high adventure. He was nothing but an old seadog who had come ashore to rest his bones.

'You wait,' Einstein said, in a very superior tone of voice. 'I can't tell you. But you'll find out when the time comes and, believe me, you're going to hate it.'

'Is he a Deep Time Mariner?' Einstein asked suspiciously, as he slobbered at the feet of the Jolly Green Giant.

'That's right,' Einstein said.

'Good grief!'

49.

As he sat there in the long summer grass, mollified by the drone of bees and the monotonous rattle of insects, the Deep Time Mariner grew sentimental and was moved to tell Charlie something of his own people and their history beyond the stars.

'Long, long ago,' he began, 'before this little solar system had been discovered, there was a time called the Time of the Ancient Gardeners. The Ancient Gardeners lived on a planet in the Cyclops Cluster where they mastered the mysteries of the universe. They made the first maps of the stars and unscrambled the chemistry of their sun. They taught the birds of the air to sing and the fishes to swim in the sea. They knew many secrets and exercised many wonderful skills that have long since been forgotten, even by the Deep Time Mariners. And while their nearest neighbours in space were still killing and eating each other in the mucilaginous swamp, the Ancient Gardeners used their gifts to create a paradise for themselves in a garden that covered six planets. They pacified the volcanoes and cured the boiling, sulphurous lakes. They filled the valleys with forests and covered the mountains with painted flowers. They were accomplished draughtsmen and architects. They built elaborate crystal fountains, mirrored halls and intricate puzzles and mazes. And, wherever there was shelter, they raised immense crops of fruits and vegetables. They were especially proud of their cabbages.'

'Cabbages?' Charlie said.

'Cabbages,' the Mariner growled. 'They might mean nothing to you, monkey-man, but they're as rare as hens' teeth in the gardens of the Cyclops Cluster.'

'What happened to these Gardeners?' one of the Einsteins asked.

'They had already returned to the dust of the stars before the time of the Mariners. But the Mariners knew of the Gardeners and kept their laws and their gardens. It was the dream of the Mariners to continue the work by planting other planets in the great eternity of space. And so they embarked upon an epic voyage of discovery to the far corners of the universe, collecting all kinds of rare plants and animals to create their gardens of paradise.'

'And the Earth?' Charlie said, gazing around him at an extravagance of leopard mint and cow parsley. A butterfly, bright as a flake of rust, hung trembling from the lace of a flower.

'The Earth was one of the first and most beautiful gardens to be established in this galaxy,' the Deep Time Mariner said. 'And will be the first to perish, if you don't count the Great Moon of Mali.'

'What happened to the Great Moon of Mali?'

'It was destroyed,' the Deep Time Mariner said, 'by a certain kind of voracious weevil. The weevils ate the roots of the plants that sheltered the fruits that fed the birds that nourished the soil that supported the trees that caught the rain that filled the lakes that supported all the life on the moon.'

'Shocking!' the Einsteins muttered, shaking their heads. Tweedledum and Tweedledee. The terrible twins of Eden.

'We were disappointed,' the Mariner confessed. 'But that was nothing compared to the shock of learning what had happened on Earth. Here we found that monkey-men had dropped from the trees and were everywhere trying to murder each other and shoot, net, harpoon, drown, gas and starve every other creature they found on the planet.'

'Crazy!' the Einsteins barked together.

'Their brains were addled,' the Mariner confirmed, fixing Charlie with a crimson eye. 'And from the slobgollion sloshing around in their skulls they had created all sorts of fantastic lies to support their cruelty and conceits. They invented gods in their own image and asked them to bless the destruction. They shut themselves away in the vaults of vast cities and when they sensed the planet was dying they built crude and dangerous machines in a vain attempt to conquer the stars.'

'Remember Laika,' one of the Einsteins said. 'The first dog to be shot into space.'

'They strapped her into a Sputnik,' the other Einstein said, 'with wires sticking into her brain. Sailing in circles above the Earth while her masters watched her starving to death.'

'Charlie built this garden,' the first Einstein said, sensing now that it might be time to draw the Mariner back from the brink of a dangerous melancholy.

'Indeed,' the Mariner murmured. 'Monkey-men were born to be gardeners.' He took a huge breath and seemed to relax again. He tilted his head and blinked at the sky.

'He laid all the paths and planted the orchard. He never stopped working,' Einstein continued. 'It was his dream. When it was finished he wanted to be buried here among the rhododendrons.'

'Where is Charlie?' the other Einstein said suddenly, sitting up and trawling the air with his snout.

'He can't be far away,' Einstein said. 'He always spends weekends in the garden.'

'Oh, no!' Charlie said. 'Leave me alone.' He jumped up and plunged into the shrubbery like a man throwing himself into the sea. 'We've seen enough. We don't belong here. What will happen when I meet myself? I want to leave this nightmare.'

'Wait and you might learn something,' the Mariner told him.

'No! I'll go crazy,' Charlie said. 'The shock will probably kill me.'

'Which one of you?' grinned Einstein, turning to wink at himself.

'What difference does it make?' Charlie shouted, with his head spinning from the thought of it.

'Pull yourself together,' the Deep Time Mariner hissed. 'You're far too primitive to see the ghost of your future.'

'I can see the two of them,' Charlie insisted, pointing at the two dogs who were grinning at him with a most exasperating expression on their hairy faces.

'It's different for me,' they said together. 'I'm a dog.'

'Concentrate,' the Mariner said. 'It's really very simple. If he saw you it would mean that he had acquired the gift of looking into the future.'

'Is that right?' Charlie said.

'Yes.'

Charlie nodded and considered the implications of these words for a few moments. 'So what?' he said at last.

'Do you remember meeting yourself while you lived here in the garden? Can you recall a warm summer's morning, long ago, when you stumbled upon yourself sitting in the shrubbery talking to a Deep Time Mariner?'

'No,' Charlie admitted.

'Exactly. And do you know what will happen in the next few minutes?' the Mariner asked.

Charlie shook his head.

'You can't look into the future,' the Mariner concluded. 'You have never, in the past, had the gift of looking into the future. It follows that your past self will not be aware of your present self but your present self will be fully aware of your past self since the experience of the past is already familiar to you.

And that should be easy enough to grasp, even for you monkey-man.'

'We'll soon know if it works,' one of the Einsteins said, yawning and stretching himself. 'If he's not in the pumpkin patch he'll be sleeping in the summerhouse. Let's go to look for him.'

50.

But the summerhouse was empty.

They climbed the steps and tiptoed into the sunwashed studio. Charlie gazed around at the familiar, shabby furniture. The dusty easel. The makeshift kitchen. The horsehair sofa that had served as a bed. A pile of freshly cut flowers lay spread on the kitchen table. A cheap glass vase waited patiently beside them. Charlie stepped forward and placed the flowers in the vase. Sweet peas and small wild roses. Their fragrance filled him with a brief, delirious nostalgia.

'You're not here,' the Mariner said. He sounded disappointed.

'He must be in the house,' one of the Einsteins said brightly, leaping onto the bed.

'Let's leave it,' Charlie said, haunted by the sight of his old gardening shoes standing sentry beneath a chair. 'It doesn't feel right.' If he was somewhere in the house then he would probably be with Baxter. He was nervous about meeting the ghost of himself and he was absolutely positive that he didn't want to see Baxter again. His moment of sentimental regret dissolved into panic.

But the Einsteins were already down the veranda steps with the Deep Time Mariner in pursuit.

'Move, monkey-man!' the Mariner shouted, when he sensed Charlie hesitate. 'You can't afford to be left behind. You've got enough problems.'

Charlie sprang into life and chased them through the garden towards the back of the house.

'There's nobody home,' he whispered with relief, as they peered through the kitchen windows.

'It's the perfect opportunity to look around the place,' the Mariner said. He was impossible. You couldn't argue with the creature.

'It's not very interesting,' Charlie insisted, as he tried the lock on the door. To his dismay the door swung open and the little party entered the house.

The kitchen was quiet. The remains of a meal were on the table. There was a stick of French bread, broken apart with its soft white interior pulled away; a block of butter, studded with crumbs, melting into a cracked saucer; a half-eaten tuna salad, smeared with congealing mayonnaise, composting in a china bowl. There were fragments of eggshell on the floor and the scorched smell of boiled black coffee lingered in the air. But Charlie and Baxter were missing.

'I can hear them!' one of the Einsteins whispered, suddenly freezing and cocking his ears.

'Where?' the second Einstein demanded scornfully. He had heard nothing. He was padding around the deserted room, lapping at crumbs, snuffling into the skirting boards.

'They're upstairs in one of the bedrooms,' the first dog said in great excitement and, before Charlie could stop him, he'd shot through the kitchen, his claws clacking on the treacherous stretch of Spanish tiles, and was running towards the main staircase.

There was a commotion in the master bedroom. Charlie and the Deep Time Mariner crept forward and peeked through a crack in the half-open door. The curtains had been drawn against the sun and the room was drenched in a warm twilight.

A naked man, a pale and scrawny Romeo, a knobbly leprechaun, was sprawled on the bed with Baxter sitting astride him. There were clothes and pillows thrown on the floor and a tangle of clothes on a little chair.

216

Baxter Pangloss, plump as a porpoise and wearing only a cotton vest, was squirming on her spindle-shanked lover and punching the mattress with her knees.

It was a moment or more before Charlie, peeping at the door, recognised the man as himself. How skinny and foolish he looked! How different he was to the man he imagined. He wanted to rush forward and cover the sight with a sheet.

'What the hell is wrong with you?' Baxter wheezed as she pummelled him hard amidships.

'I can't help it… ' Charlie grumbled as he caught his breath. 'I guess I need some encouragement.' She was giving him such a pounding that his teeth had begun to chatter.

'Help yourself!' Baxter snarled and without moving from the saddle she wrenched the vest from her shoulders.

Her big breasts swung loose as pastry and dangled over Charlie's face. He reached out gingerly and rolled them around with his hands.

'I can remember when you couldn't wait to get me into bed,' she continued, slapping her thighs against him.

'That was different,' Charlie gasped, busily tweaking her nipples as if he were tuning a radio.

'You're such a selfish bastard,' she muttered.

'I'm trying to co-operate,' he said gloomily. He couldn't concentrate. There was work to be done in the garden. He was worried about an attack of neck rot in the onion beds and a creeping leaf infection that had started to threaten the roses.

'But she's not wearing her oxygen suit,' the Mariner whispered in some surprise.

'What are you talking about?' an Einstein whispered. 'She doesn't have an oxygen suit.'

'I saw her wearing it,' the Deep Time Mariner insisted. 'It was red rubber with some sort of ventilation system around the vital organs.'

'She threw it away.'

'Why?' the Mariner demanded. 'I don't understand'.

'I'm not surprised,' the Einstein grinned.

'You've fallen out!' Baxter screeched. She stopped pounding on Charlie and searched between her legs. She looked outraged. She scrambled from the bed and threw herself down on the floor.

'I'm not a machine!' Charlie complained, instinctively hiding his shame in his hands. 'I'm just not in the mood.'

'I can't wait for you to get yourself into the mood!' Baxter raged, scooping her breasts back into her vest. 'Why do you have to be such a pain? I suppose you'd like me to dress up in stockings and suspenders and have my titties dipped in chocolate! Is that how you'd like it, you pathetic little pervert? Would you like to see me helpless and hog-tied in some tacky peek-a-boo thingamee? Would that do it for you? Are you some creepy little schoolboy or what?'

'No!' Charlie said indignantly. It sounded good to him but he wasn't going to make the confession to someone who had him by the short and curlies.

'I'm not your plaything you can pick up or throw down whenever you feel like it, you preening panty-sniffer!' she shouted back at him. 'I'm not here for your pleasure!'

'No,' Charlie said. No argument.

'I'm a woman. I have to follow my natural cycles'

She stood up, her buttocks dimpled with rage, and walked to an empty crib in one corner of the room. It was an elaborate cage of ornately carved wood, smothered in lace and pink and blue ribbons.

Above the cage, a large hand-written chart had been pinned to the wall. This chart, carefully complied by Baxter with the help of the Militant Mothers, represented a mysterious tide table of her own vital fluids. Each day she would study these peaks and troughs like an astrologer reading the stars. She was determined that Charlie should stand and deliver at the most auspicious moments. His reluctance to perform this simple basic duty seemed, to her, a deliberate attempt to prevent her fulfilling her destiny.

'I can't wait for you!' she shouted, turning towards the bed. 'Don't you understand? Everything is critical. I've taken my temperature. I've checked my ovulation pattern. I've had a warm relaxing bath. I've done half an hour's transcendental meditation. Everything is ready but you!' She gathered her breasts through her vest, as if checking their weight and tension, before setting them loose again.

'I can't help it,' he insisted miserably, drawing his legs against his chest like a skeleton worked by strings. He was sulking now. What had happened to Baxter the Battling Amazon? Baxter the Slippery Slut of Sleaze? It was a long time since she'd shown any interest in him and, after such an abstinence, this clinical approach came as a rude awakening. She was cold and mechanical in his embrace. It made him feel that the operation was being performed under medical supervision. He wouldn't have been surprised to have discovered Patch Armstrong, smelling of hospital disinfectant, waiting for him with a towel and a set of clean pyjamas.

Desperate now to service his wife and prepared to seek any help he could find in rising to the occasion, he tried briefly to speculate on the erotic possibilities of Patch Armstrong dressed in some early *Skirt Lifter* fashion – a classic Ruby Keeler wig, the enormous undercarriage buckled into a Playtex™ girdle. Think of those heavy, heaving buttocks, warm as an oven, broad as the rump of a Suffolk punch. Concentrate! It won't kill you. Patch Armstrong is dressed to thrill. But it was the last flutter of fancy from a desperate man and failed to have the desired effect.

'There's something wrong,' he concluded and reached out to pull the blanket from the floor. 'It doesn't feel natural.'

Einstein

'What's more natural than making babies!' Baxter screamed. She snatched up a pillow, flew at her husband in a fury and began to beat him about the head with the whirling bag of feathers.

The Mariner was intrigued. His eyes glowed and his mouth snapped open in amazement, exposing the tip of his long black tongue. But poor Charlie, standing beside him, turned away and went to sit on the stairs. His face burned with embarrassment and his hands were shaking. The Einsteins followed him, gently arranging themselves at his feet.

A ridiculous performance.

51.

'It never stops!' the Mariner roared, sweeping Charlie and Einstein through the house and launching them into the sky. They flew up over the orchard, the garden shrinking away beneath them.

Six billion mouths to feed and still they breed while the planet shrivels around them. Worms in a rotting apple. The world eaten up by a struggling, squirming ball of worms. At the end of time will they turn on themselves and devour each other? Was there no war, no famine, no pestilence to stop these creatures spreading their curse? Was there nothing to be done against them?

The air was suddenly filled by phantoms. Charlie saw them bucking, heaving, clinging, scratching; bollock-naked wrestlers in a spiralling pillar of sexual frenzy. He saw them young, old, ugly, handsome, mad, sad and grotesquely deformed; he saw them rolling their eyes and grinding their teeth; he saw them clambering one upon another, clawing at penises, buttocks and breasts. He saw them flogging each other with canes, he saw them tormenting themselves with dildoes, he saw them shackled with ropes and chains, he saw them feasting like cannibals. He saw the sky turn black with them. He saw mothers with sons, fathers with daughters, the wretched with beasts that brayed and bellowed. He saw the voluptuous and the lascivious, the stupid and the cunning; he saw the lonely and the frightened, the violent and insane. He heard them snorting, he heard them squelching, he heard them gasping, he heard them screaming, a terrible storm of tumultuous shagging.

'Enough!' he cried. 'Dear God, enough!' And all at once he found himself back in his room with the dog and the giant beside him.

'And was an infant born?' the Mariner asked, glaring down at his bruised and frightened prisoner.

Charlie nodded.

'You continue to breed in the shadow of famine, while your fishing industries collapse, your grain stores dwindle to nothing, the forests are squandered for firewood and the living soil turns to dust? Your factories belch smoke. Your cities sweat fog. The water is full of poisons. The very air is venomous. What's wrong with you, monkey-man? Are you a total goober-brain? There are millions of you living in squalor, sleeping in pipes and cardboard boxes, denied so much as a cup of clean water, scratching for crumbs in mountains of cinders. There are millions more of you gathered together, starving to death on land already stripped to sand. And still you continue! Are you beyond the laws of nature?'

Charlie said nothing.

He remembered Baxter, grown from a dolphin into an angry, trumpeting walrus, sitting in a hospital bed surrounded by bundles of wilting flowers. Baxter with her books of names and paperback guides to the best in child psychology.

At first Patch Armstrong had tried to persuade her to give delivery in the kitchen, squatting in a birthing pool of herbal infusions while the Mothers sang songs of encouragement and shot the event on video.

'The most important, beautiful, primal, sacred moment in your entire womanhood shot in living colour with stereo sound and presented in a special souvenir box!' Patch the Mother Superior bragged, when she'd tried to sell the idea to a more than reluctant Baxter.

The new Mother shuddered. It was going to be hard enough without inviting a camera crew to crowd between her legs. 'I don't know,' she said. 'It doesn't sound very hygienic.'

Patch ignored her reservations. 'It's absolutely awesome!' she crowed. 'It's like having eyes in your arse.'

'Don't you think we should have somebody here with some sort of medical qualification?' Baxter said. 'I might need some help.'

'Why?' Patch said. 'It's so simple – just follow the laws of gravity.'

'But it's my first time,' Baxter said. 'I'm afraid there'll be complications.' Breach birth! Caesarean section! Blood on the walls! Bowels on the carpet!

'We'll help you,' Patch said. 'We're Mothers. We'll make it something you won't forget and when we've taken delivery we'll cook and eat the placenta.'

Baxter wasn't convinced that she wanted to be a part of this jungle jamboree but she didn't know how to tell the group. She knew she would die if she had to give birth in their stupid, inflatable rubber bath, but she didn't want to disappoint them. They'd already bought the scented candles.

She needn't have worried. When Ambrose heard of the pregnancy he'd lost no time in making reservations at the most expensive maternity hospital he could find in London. A private suite with closed circuit TV. Carpets on the walls and whirlpool bath. French and Chinese meals on a tray. Make-up and beauty consultants. The works. Baxter, for once in her life, didn't bother to argue with him.

Ambrose loved children. They were an investment for the future. Every child born in this wonderful world was an extra mouth to feed and a chance to enhance the profit margins. He was already hatching a scheme to send every new mother in the country a personal greetings card containing a wishbone from a Pangloss chicken.

The child had been born at two o'clock in the morning. Baxter had screamed and struggled and bitten the nurses. She abandoned her breathing exercises and her seven rules of relaxation. She cursed Charlie and God and the Militant Mothers. It was horrible. She hated it. She felt she was passing a pineapple gift-wrapped in razor wire.

Charlie had not been invited to watch the delivery.

'You've had your moment of glory, sailor,' Baxter had told him in the cab on the way to the hospital. 'I'm not having you stand and gloat while they turn me inside out.'

When he was finally summoned to her bed she had already given birth. He found her in a drugged sleep and the infant connected to a life support machine in the Peter Pan & Wendy Intensive Care Ward™

A nurse with thick ankles and soft canvas shoes had helped him into a cotton gown and taken him into the ward. She looked too young to be in charge of anything more challenging than a Burpie™ doll. She looked like she should have been at school. There were angry love bites on her neck and braces on her teeth. A gold bead gleamed on the side of her nose, her own reward for a recently pierced nostril. The bead shone like a small, ripe cyst. She had nothing to say to him. She led him through a maze of machines, her shoes making little sucking sounds against the floor.

Charlie stared around at the hundreds of incubators, the oxygen lines and monitors. It was like a Pangloss battery house. They were factory farming babies. In the Peter Pan & Wendy Fattening Unit the tiny inmates had climate control, soft lights, automatic feed, everything they needed to cling to life and grow to the perfect size and weight.

'Congratulations,' the nurse said, stopping beside an incubator and gesturing at the contents. They stared down at a roll of bandages, plugged into the parent machine by a clutch of brightly coloured tubes. Beneath a transparent oxygen mask glowered a face like a poisonous walnut.

'What is it?' Charlie whispered.

'It's a baby,' the nurse said, although she seemed to have her doubts. She half-closed her eyes and peered at the bandages again.

'What sort?'

'It's a girl,' the nurse said, checking a plastic clipboard that hung beside the machine.

'Is it normal?' he asked nervously. The child looked so frail that he almost expected to see the Dead & Alive Man come creeping along the rows of machines, swinging his heavy rubber bucket.

'What's wrong?' the young nurse said, glancing quickly at the monitors. She frowned. She checked heartbeat, ventilation and heat; colour, movement and weight; fluids, gases and solids. Everything seemed to be under control.

'It was early,' Charlie explained.

'That's why we keep them in these cookers,' the nurse said, smiling and showing her dentalwork.

'Why?'

'Don't ask me,' the nurse said with a happy shrug. 'I think it's all part of the Golden Delivery Service™. You paid for it. Why don't you check in the brochure? I don't usually work this ward.' Her face grew vacant. She had exhausted her knowledge of the subject. She walked away on her softly sucking shoes.

Charlie sat by the incubator, smiled down at the child and waited for the surge of fatherly love that he knew should overwhelm him. He knew that he should love the child, that it was natural and right to love children. The house was already filled by letters of congratulations from baby food and toddlers' fashionwear manufacturers, illustrated catalogues of educational toys and nursery furniture, free samples of powdered milk, rusks, stewed fruit, rubber teats, soap, shampoo and dusting powder. Babies were shown on TV shows as adorable household pets. They featured in advertising for detergents and disinfectants and malted chocolate sandwich spreads. Their wit and wisdom was a regular feature of women's magazines. Out of the mouths of babes and sucklings. Aren't they cute – the things they say! Children were born to inherit the Earth. They would be the guardians of its smogs and its oil slicks and nuclear dumps. Especially its nuclear dumps. They would have dominion over the barren sea, and over the foul air, and over the skeleton forests and over all the Earth, and over every creeping things that creepeth upon the earth. Yea, even unto the plastic airline tray and the wire coat hanger and the indestructible sock and all the other treasures of Man. One day, my child, all this will be yours.

He should have felt proud, he should have felt small in the sight of God, he should have hoped that this half-cooked meat pudding would bring salvation to a desperate world. He should have felt sentimental, foolish, astonished, immortal. He should have gone out to make himself drunk, wandered the streets, harpooned the mouths of gawking strangers with giant Havana cigars.

After a few minutes the nurse returned, hurried towards him and hooked his hand to the crook of her arm. 'Wrong baby,' she said impatiently as she moved him to another incubator. 'Why didn't you tell me?'

'I didn't know.'

'Congratulations,' she muttered, checking the new clipboard. 'This time it's a boy.'

He was staring down at an identical infant in an identical machine. He couldn't tell the difference. These new visitors to the planet all looked the same to him. Beneath the gauze and bandages, beneath the clusters of pipes and tubing, they reminded Charlie of processed chickens.

It was five o'clock in the morning. He felt tired and confused and lonely. He stood up to stretch himself and wandered aimlessly through the long rows of incubators. The monitors chirruped softly as he passed, blinking their green and orange eyes. He turned right and then left and quickly managed to get himself lost. He tried to retrace his steps but it was hopeless. His child was hidden in the maze.

He reached the main doors and went in search of the nurse but beyond the Peter Pan & Wendy Intensive Care Ward™ the corridors were empty. He found a flight of stairs and followed them down, through the deserted kitchens and past the locked dispensary, until he found himself out on the street.

It was raining. He pulled off the cotton gown, cast it aside and stole away, into the cold embrace of dawn.

52.

Later that day Charlie took himself to the office and was immediately summoned into the presence of the mighty Ambrose Pangloss. He found the tycoon, positively pink with pleasure, behind the mahogany slabs of his desk.

'Congratulations, Charlie!' Ambrose beamed, waving him into a chair. 'I phoned the hospital before breakfast. It's wonderful news. You must be pleased. No complications. Mother and baby doing well. If there's anything you need I hope you won't be afraid to ask me. This will mean some big changes in your life.'

'I think Baxter has everything under control,' Charlie said. He sat down and placed his Senior Statesman™ plastic attaché case on his knees. He smiled. His eyes glowed unusually bright. His damp suit was giving out a sinister smell. He needed a shave and a fresh shirt.

'That's my girl,' Ambrose smiled. 'Women instinctively understand babies. It's their natural condition. And do you know how many babies are born every day, Charlie?'

'No,' Charlie said.

'250,000,' Ambrose said. 'Imagine! That's a hundred and seventy something a minute. Every minute of every day. That's more than two a second. Why, that's faster than you can count 'em. Yes! It's all here in these population reports,' he said, tapping his fingernails against a bulging yellow folder on the desk. 'Millions of babies every week. A couple of dozen since we've been talking!

Charlie said nothing.

'And they all need to eat,' Ambrose said gleefully. 'I've been told that in the next ten years there'll be sixty-four countries around the world with populations too large to feed. But I want you to keep that to yourself, Charlie. We need to keep the competitive edge. This is the biggest marketing opportunity in the history of mankind!'

'No doubt about it,' Charlie said, without listening. He stifled a yawn by scratching the stubble on his chin. He was so tired that his smallest movements felt exaggerated, as if he were no longer secured by the laws of gravity and might float away, if pushed from his chair, with his feet never touching the ground.

'But what are we going to do about it?' Ambrose inquired, leaning forward confidentially and beaming at Charlie.

'We're going into baby foods?' Charlie suggested. You didn't need to be a genius to know what Ambrose Pangloss was thinking. He was always thinking of chicken.

'Baby foods!' Ambrose said triumphantly. 'It's the future, believe me. People make people. It's a growth industry.' He paused. A growth industry. That was a good one. He liked that. He must remember to write it down. He could use it in one of his speeches. 'The more babies there are in the world the better for everyone. We need expanding markets. But we've got to catch them young. Always remember, Charlie, that people no longer have lives – they only have life styles and life styles are dependent on a vigorous branding approach. Think about it. Drop everything else. Think about bottled baby foods. Chicken soup. Chicken broth. Chicken paste. Chicken spread. Cradle to grave, Charlie. Cradle to grave.'

Charlie left the green silk office and made his way down to the Future Forecasts department. It was ten thirty. Lorraine the receptionist glanced up at him from the pages of *Chit-Chat Monthly*, crossed her legs, frowned and consulted her watch.

Everyone else ignored him. The second forecaster was kneeling before the coffee machine with his hand up the sugar dispenser. The rest of them skulked in their cubicles.

Charlie walked into his own cubicle and sat down. Then he placed his attaché case on the desk, snapped open the locks and removed a hammer. It was a big claw hammer, with a red handle and a polished steel head. He held the weapon in his fist and smiled. It had taken him a long time to reach this exquisite moment of madness, but we boil at different degrees and Charlie had reached his boiling point.

His heart fluttered. The fatigue he had felt pressing down on him seemed to lift away to reveal a curious sense of elation. There was no rage. He felt happy and excited. The hammer would speak for him.

The telephone rang. The noise took him by surprise. He raised the hammer and hacked at the phone, spilling the handpiece from the cradle. He chopped at the flex and splintered the brittle plastic shell, sweeping the debris to the floor. That was a new way to answer the phone. And then nothing could stop him. He slashed at the wire trays, the appointments diary, the coffee mug filled with ballpoint pens and the multi-functional calculator.

He stood up to confront the glaring computer screen. It was running the new Pangloss screensaver: a line of pecking chookies that jerked across the screen like ducks in a shooting gallery. He turned sideways and swung the hammer like a pendulum, using the force of its own weight to take down the line of chickens. The monitor shattered in a fury of smoke and sparks. He twisted around and hammered at the frosted glass walls of his cell. The walls exploded, showering him in brilliant hailstones. He swung the hammer in circles over his head, bringing down the rest of the glass and chopping at the wooden frame.

When Charlie opened his eyes, the cubicle had disappeared.

He had cut himself loose. He stepped from the wreckage and looked around the empty department. There was silence. The other forecasters crouched, without breathing, beneath the shelter of their desks.

Charlie returned the hammer to his Senior Statesman™ and strolled from the building. He went home to work in his garden.

53.

The child was called Victor. As soon as he'd grown fat enough he was disconnected from his incubator and Baxter was permitted to take him home. The Militant Mothers were waiting in the nursery, which they'd hung with coloured ribbons and bunting, to hold a peanut butter party in celebration of the great event.

Charlie had been asked to attend the party – for half an hour's ritual humiliation or perhaps to witness some small point of law that confirmed or confounded his rights as a father – he couldn't guess why they'd called him. He arrived with a bunch of freshly cut flowers but it hadn't been such a good idea. When he'd entered the nursery one of the Mothers started sneezing and another had an asthma attack.

'Oh, look!' Patch Armstrong said archly. 'How sad. He's cut some flowers. I suppose he wants us to put them in water and watch while the poor things die. I think it's a crime to cut them down before they've had a chance to seed.'

Charlie stood with the bundle of flowers swinging loose in his fist and made several rapid calculations involving the target of Patch Armstrong's mouth, distance of strike and velocity. She sensed the threat and knocked him dead with a look she reserved for children who wilfully wet themselves.

'I can't breathe!' one of the Mothers gasped. 'Don't let him bring them in here!' She clutched at her throat and collapsed in a twitching heap of cotton. Her face turned a nasty shade of blue. She was squeezing out little strangled groans. Several of the Mothers ran forward and tried to calm her down by clucking and fanning her with their hands.

'Do something quickly!' someone shouted. 'This sort of thing is bad for the children.'

'Charlie!' Baxter shouted, from the other side of the room. 'Why do you have to be such a pain? Take all that rubbish away.'

'I cut them for you.'

'I saw enough flowers in hospital,' Baxter said. 'This isn't a blasted funeral parlour. What's wrong with you, Charlie? Why do you always have to be the centre of attention?'

So Charlie retired in disgrace and returned, without bearing gifts, to sit on a painted wooden stool while twenty curious infants came and smeared him with peanut butter. They sat on his shoes and dragged at his sleeves and tried to pull out his jacket pockets. One of their number, a little girl with a snot-plugged nose, managed to clamber aboard his knees and gave his ear a poke with a pencil.

Charlie clenched his teeth against the sudden jolt of pain and grinned at the child. He pulled the pencil from her grasp and snapped it into fragments, silently stuffing the splinters down the front of her Donald Duck™ vest. The child was horrified. She had been leading a charmed life. She had never encountered opposition. She couldn't believe it. She was outraged. She burst into tears and scampered back to her mother.

It was the first time that Charlie had been allowed into the nursery. He felt like a man who had blundered by chance into a women's changing room. Everywhere he turned he saw heavy, half-dressed women crawling around on their hands and knees. One of the Mothers was sorting through a box of plastic bricks, sitting cross-legged on the floor with her skirt bunched high around her thighs. She paused to stroke her knee, feeling the warmth of the sun through the window. Another Mother, with a short ponytail and wire-rimmed spectacles, was playing a game of peek-a-boo in white cotton underwear. She had perky breasts and a slight paunch, a stubborn cushion of fat pushed from the waist-band of her pants.

Charlie cast furtive glances in every direction. His own computer software had been designed to make him focus on every sound and shape that might approximate a woman. He'd been programmed to twitch at every signal. Whenever he came within range of the target, the light in his brain would flash, the button was pressed and he blinked, firing the voyeur's unloaded camera. He resented this automatic reflex, the relentless search for titilla-tion, almost as much as the objects of his attention, these plump erotophobic creatures, despised him for it. He knew it was madness. But the programme was running. He didn't know how to cancel it. And Charlie had been taken by surprise, he hadn't been prepared for this lazy exhibition of unbuckled women. He felt hot and wretched as the blood was stirred in him. He was in enough trouble without looking for it.

One of the Mothers caught his eye and he quickly checked himself, concentrating his mind by counting the bars on the climbing frames. An animal mural filled the walls with elephants in striped pyjamas and pigs wearing pork pie hats. The floor was covered in chewed cushions, towels and rubber sheets.

Finally Baxter came forward with a blanket bundle in her arms. She was dressed to look young and radiant. Baxter the Suffering Madonna. Baxter the Innocent. She was wearing a long white night-gown – in contrast to the other women who seemed happy to play in their underwear – with full sleeves and a high buttoned neck. Her hair had been gathered into a pigtail draped neatly between her shoulderblades. She unwrapped the blanket and introduced Victor to his father.

The child gurgled and tried to put its foot in its mouth. It didn't look too bad now that the wrinkles had disappeared and its head had a halo of fine white hair.

'Say something,' Baxter prompted. 'This is your son. Isn't there something you want to say?'

'Hello,' Charlie said, leaning forward and peering into Baxter's perfumed arms. He was sharply aware that he'd just been replaced in the grand scheme of things. Here was the child who had come to bury him. This was the fruit of his own brief season. Here was winter's messenger to wither the hope and promise of a summer he had neglected to taste. They were closing the turnpikes. They were locking the windows and doors. His dreams of adventure were finished. He had lost his moment. He felt the nausea rise in his throat. What had gone wrong? He had everything he could desire. He was, as everyone liked to tell him, a very lucky man.

'Haven't you forgotten something?' Patch Armstrong said. The rest of the Mothers fell silent. The children stopped crawling and bawling. Everyone looked expectantly at Charlie as if he were about to shout Surprise and shower them all with gifts.

'No,' Charlie said.

'Isn't there something you want to say to Baxter?' Patch said, folding her arms against her chest and tapping her foot in a pantomime of impatience.

'What?' Charlie said, hauling himself from the painted stool and spilling crumbs from his clothes.

'Thank you!' a chorus of Mothers shouted.

54.

There's no doubt that, given time, Charlie would have learned to love this child. And he might have settled down with Baxter who, given time, would fall in love with him again, in a more mature and gentle fashion, having finally convinced herself that all his personal agony stemmed from the day when he saw his mother flying through an open bedroom window. And they would become a happier and wiser couple, given time, content to devote their lives to Victor the surgeon and concert pianist and gracefully growing old together beneath the hollyhocks. And Ambrose Pangloss would find God, given time, and use all his money and influence to establish homes for waifs and strays and persuade Patch Armstrong (who would find and marry Harry Prampolini) to run the homes with the Militant Mothers, and everybody would walk, hand in hand, happy and exhausted, smelling of attar of violets, into the final pages of one of those Katy Pphart novels that Mrs Flodden used to read to young Einstein. Anything could happen, given time.

But this is a story about the end of time.

55.

Charlie went back to the summerhouse. He didn't want to stay in the house – the Mothers complained that the sight of him curdled their milk.

At nine-twenty the following morning the Pangloss Mercedes broke a path through the undergrowth and delivered the chicken slaughterer to the house. Ambrose inspected the grandchild, approved Baxter's choice of women friends and bestowed his blessings upon them.

He didn't enquire after Charlie since he thought his son-in-law was at large in the farthest outposts of empire, working on bottled baby foods. Baxter, if she gave it a thought, knew that Charlie's golden feather allowed him the freedom to work as he pleased. They both believed that Charlie was a long way from the house. And Charlie, watching the limousine from the safety of the wooden pavilion, wasn't going to argue with them.

Ambrose hadn't heard the rumours from Regional Accounts that Charlie had taken an axe into Future Forecasts and threatened to butcher his colleagues. There were whispers, in Global Marketing, that Charlie had murdered someone and drowned himself in the river; but the police were not informed because the company feared a scandal. The stories spread from floor to floor but Ambrose Pangloss heard nothing. He was too important to be troubled with gossip.

That same night a maintenance crew had been called to rebuild the cubicle and fit a new desk and telephone. The next day a wire tray and a red ballpoint pen appeared on the desk and by the end of the week it looked as if nothing had changed.

237

'You should clear this jungle,' Ambrose complained, nodding towards the orchard and the rhododendron grove. 'You've let it grow wild. I don't know what's happened to the place. It's a shame. There's nowhere to park the car anymore.'

'It's Charlie,' Baxter said. 'It's just another of his crazy schemes. One moment he thinks he's Gauguin and the next he's pretending to be Kate Ability Brown.'

'It's a mess,' Ambrose said. 'Why don't you let me send someone down to clear it out.'

Baxter smiled sweetly and squeezed his arm. 'You're such a big sweetheart,' she crooned. 'We really want a proper playground for the sake of the children.'

'It's natural,' Ambrose said. He liked the idea of Baxter as mother. She looked so serene in her pretty smock and neat little plastic sandals. A complete woman. 'They need fresh air and sunshine at that age,' he said cheerfully. 'When you were small you played in the garden for hours. Do you remember?'

'But we can't let the poor liddle things out there... ' Baxter prompted, pouting and looking forlorn.

'It's dangerous,' Ambrose agreed. 'They could eat something and poison themselves. They could fall in the water and drown. I'm surprised that Charlie allowed this to happen. It's very careless of him. You need a big lawn and a sandpit – children always love sandpits – and a few swings and a climbing frame.'

'I don't know,' Baxter said doubtfully. 'You find doggie-doodles in the grass and horrid nasty spiders and worms and all sorts of horrible creepy-crawlies that iddy-biddy babies might put in their liddle mouths.'

'Well, what do you suggest?'

Baxter hesitated. She chewed her lower lip and gazed thoughtfully out towards the firethorn thicket. 'We could pave it,' she said at last.

'That's drastic,' Ambrose said. He'd been thinking of elegant English lawn, croquet hoops and a barbecue corner.

'If we paved it we could hose it down every day with lots of nice hot soapy water and then we'd always know that it was clean enough for the eeny-weenies,' Baxter said. 'And you'd always have somewhere to park the car,' she added, pinching his arm.

'It makes sense,' Ambrose nodded. You had to make sacrifices for children and it wouldn't do any harm to have somewhere to park the Mercedes.

'But I can't wait for Charlie to do it,' Baxter said flatly.

'Leave it to me,' Ambrose said. 'I'll organise something for you as soon as I get back to the office.'

Baxter smiled and pecked his ear.

Charlie, of course, could hear nothing of this conversation. When the limousine had driven away he crept from the summer-house, collected Einstein and went back to work in the cabbage patch.

56.

The demolition began while Charlie was out near the south grotto, clearing ground for his poultry house. He'd settled on a favourite variety of cross-bred pullet and was planning to let the birds run loose in the orchard, so he'd need nothing more elaborate than a night roosting ark with nest-boxes, feeders and drinkers. When the birds were settled they'd soon be earning their keep in eggs. He could use their old bedding for compost. If the poultry proved a success he might consider making a beehive. Raw honey and wax for candles. Anything seemed possible.

It was a bright, crisp morning. There were cowslips showing in the long grass. The apple trees were shedding their blossom like canopies of melting snow.

When he heard the sound of the engine he stopped work, turned and looked at Einstein. The dog was standing on a grass bank, his ears cocked and his muzzle trawling the air.

'What is it?' Charlie said.

The little dog growled and stamped his feet. He looked anxious. He could smell diesel fumes. He could sense trouble. The ground beneath him seemed to vibrate.

Before Charlie could speak again there was a terrible crashing of undergrowth, a jangle of chains and a plume of oily black smoke drifted across the tops of the trees.

He picked up his spade and ran through the garden with Einstein hard on his heels. They slithered down ditches and scrambled up rockeries, chasing the line of the wall towards the wrought iron gates. They came charging through the shrubbery and then stopped to stare in horror.

A dirty yellow bulldozer, slashing a hole through a holly hedge, was uprooting a small magnolia tree, smashing the earth around it like pie crust.

'Get away!' Charlie shouted, stumbling forward into the path of the great machine. 'Get out of here, you crazy bastard!' He waved his arms, swinging the spade above his head, like a frenzied samurai swordsman.

'What a fugging mess!' the driver shouted back at him from the window of his cab. He was a little stump of a man with a square head and a mouthful of broken teeth. He switched off the engine and scowled down at Charlie.

'What the hell are you doing here?' Charlie shouted. He fell to his knees and nursed the tree in his hands. The trunk had been twisted, the few flowers shattered like luminous fragments of porcelain, the roots exposed among the great sods of upturned soil.

'Are you the fugging gardener in this fugging place? It's fugging diabolical. It's going to take me fugging hours to root out this fugging mess. This machine is too fugging small for the fugging job, that's the fugging problem. You need fugging dynamite for this fugging job. No fugger bothers to tell me nothing.'

The noise of the bulldozer brought Baxter and some of the Mothers marching from the house. They gathered, a little distance away, and shouted encouragements to the driver.

'Morning, ladies!' he beamed. He couldn't believe his luck. A house full of fugging women. He looked them over, stripped them down, and made little clicking sounds with his tongue. He liked the one with the big gut and the mane of curly hair.

'What's the matter?' Baxter shouted. 'Why have you stopped the engine?'

'Are you the governor?' he called down to Baxter. He wasn't going to make a move without a nod from the governor. The turnip-head with the spade looked like a fugging lunatic.

241

'Yes,' Baxter told him.

The driver winked and grinned at her breasts.

'What's happening here?' Charlie demanded, trying to choke back his anger. He stood up and turned to his wife. He was covered in mud and leaves. 'Is this your idea?'

'Daddy wants the place cleaned out,' Baxter said, moving slowly back through a strawberry bed.

'But this is my garden! It's mine!' Charlie shouted. 'It's beautiful. You can't touch it.'

'Leave her alone!' the driver shouted. He didn't want a fugging lunatic spoiling everything. They ought to keep him chained to his bed. A house full of fugging women. This was his lucky fugging day.

'Shut up, Charlie!' Baxter snapped. 'It's not a garden. It's a filthy overgrown wasteland. Look at it! God knows what's lurking out there in the weeds. And it's not healthy for Victor and the rest of the children to have all these pools of stagnant water around the house.'

'They're dangerous and they're full of horrid, slimy things,' one of the Mothers added, a moonfaced creature with her hair in braids. She was wearing a Hans Christian Anderson smock embroidered with a cartoon crocodile. She pouted at Charlie and stuck out her chest. The crocodile flexed its rubbery jaws.

'They're my ponds!' Charlie shouted. 'I've planted them and stocked them with fish.'

'I don't care if you've stocked them full of flaming flamingos, you stupid selfish bastard! I want them filled!' Baxter screamed. 'They're death traps. I'm going to have this wilderness paved – I will not have my children crawling about in the dirt! If you thought more of your career and less about your stupid hobbies you could have been a junior board director. Daddy had plans for you. He was going to make you something important.'

'I quit!' Charlie shouted.

'What?'

'He said he quit,' a tall, cadaverous girl in a mottled rabbit skin coat shrilled at Baxter.

'I'm no longer working for Pangloss!' Charlie shouted. 'I've quit. I've finished. I've walked out.'

'I don't believe you,' Baxter said nervously. 'He never mentioned anything to me... '

'It's true.'

'But what about your wife and child?' another of the Mothers demanded. 'You can't leave them to starve. Get a grip on yourself, man. Have you no common decency?'

'They won't starve!' Charlie said. 'I've planted my early potatoes. We can cut the winter spinach and kale. I've already lifted the leeks and potatoes.' If the year went as planned they'd be harvesting beans and carrots, cardoons and onions, melons and quinces, bunches of chervil, chives and lovage. They'd be making sweet cordials, fruit wines and vinegars, sauces, chutneys and relishes.

'I'm not eating that filth!' Baxter shouted. It was preposterous. He was joking. 'Are you joking?' He must be joking.

'We can be self-sufficient!' Charlie shouted back at them. 'We can feed ourselves.'

'He's trying to grow his own food!' the cadaver shrilled and was suddenly convulsed by a high-pitched twittering laugh.

Charlie lost his patience and shook his spade at the Mothers. He was trembling. The fury swelled in him, stretching his spine, and gave him a sinister strutting gait as if he were walking on tiptoe.

'Look out!' the cadaver cried. 'He's found a shovel. Quickly, someone, phone the police!'

'He's gone crazy! He's gone crazy!' the moonfaced Mother shrieked, clutching at her braids.

Her companions grew alarmed. They conducted a ragged retreat through the middle of the bramble patch, snagging their skirts and scratching their arms and legs.

'Now look what you've done!' the moonfaced Mother wailed triumphantly. 'Are you satisfied? I'm bleeding!' She held up her arm and punched at the sky with her fist. Wounded. A savage attack on an innocent woman. She could probably have him arrested and forced to pay damages.

'I'm going to call daddy!' Baxter shouted and the Mothers started running for the safety of the house.

'You want me to sit here all day sugging my fugging thumb?' the bulldozer driver called after them.

'No!' Baxter shouted. 'Start working!'

'If you start that machine again – I'm warning you – I'll take your head from your shoulders!' Charlie roared, raising the spade to his chest and advancing on the machine.

'Do me a fugging favour,' the driver grinned.

He switched on the engine, jolted the bulldozer forward and knocked Charlie to the ground. The spade went spinning into the brambles.

When Charlie tried to stand up again he found the driver looming over him, snorting and swearing, his fists raised against his face. They circled each other for a few moments, heads thrown back, chests puffed out, feet stamping the soft soil, like a pair of clumsy storks engaged in a courtship dance. Then the driver took a swing at Charlie and caught him a glancing blow on the chin that rattled his teeth and made him bite his tongue.

'You fugging fugger!' the driver leered, encouraged by the sight of Charlie bent forward clutching his face. 'I'll fugging kill you.'

'Get out of my garden!' Charlie hissed, wiping his mouth. The back of his hand was smeared with blood. He lunged at the driver, slamming both fists against his chest and knocking him to the ground.

The driver struggled into a sitting position, shook his head as if he were checking that none of its contents had shaken loose, looked up at Charlie and laughed. He was a man who enjoyed a fight.

He was destined to have the fight of his life when the time came and a firestorm swept through his lodging house. Stupid with sleep, he'd wrap himself in a wet sheet and blunder onto the smoke-filled staircase, find himself trapped by flames and fall to his death through a broken window. If he'd known what waited for him in the future, he might not have wasted his strength fighting Charlie.

'You caught me by fugging surprise!' he whistled, clambering to his feet. He was full of admiration. He limped forward and stretched out his hand to congratulate his opponent.

Charlie accepted the hand, the driver jerked him off balance and smacked him smartly on the nose.

Charlie sneezed blood and sank to his knees. The driver grabbed him by a hank of hair and pushed his face in the mud. Charlie started to suffocate. He thrashed out blindly, clutched at the driver's legs and managed to pull him down. They rolled together through the holly hedge, kicking and punching, scratching and biting, until they fell into a pond.

The shock of the freezing water seemed to finish the battle. They broke the surface and floated together like drowned lovers, tangled in each other's arms.

'Get out of my garden or I'll set the dogs on you... ' Charlie croaked at last, slapping the water with his fist. His knuckles were raw and swollen. His face was covered in blood.

'What fugging dogs?' the driver panted. 'I don't see no fugging dogs!' He struggled painfully to his feet, dragged Charlie ashore and kicked his head.

57.

Where was Einstein when Charlie needed him? Where was the whiskery warrior while his master was tilting at windmills? He had stolen into the house and was scampering lickety-splick up the softly carpeted stairs. He knew what was wrong. He understood the cause of the uproar and the reason for the destruction. It was wrapped in a cotton vest and a bonnet of antique lace. It was sleeping safe behind the prison bars of its fancy cherry wood crib, dreaming its mammaphile's dream.

He tiptoed into the bedroom, leapt at the crib and dragged the blankets to the floor. The baby blinked at the dog and blew a string of milky bubbles. Einstein seized him by the leg and tried to haul him overboard. But the baby was heavy and his limbs seemed to stretch like elastic. The dog pushed him into a corner and tried to nudge him through the bars. He balanced himself on the top of the crib and attempted to pull him to his feet. Nothing seemed to work. The baby gurgled and bared his gums. He enjoyed this tug o' war. Finally Einstein braced himself, clasped the baby's head in his mouth and flipped him into the air like a rabbit. The infant somersaulted from the crib and tumbled into the waiting blanket.

Einstein jumped down, seized a corner of the blanket and hauled the baby across the floor. To the dog's sensitive nose, the child stank like a Camembert. But he could be thankful, at least, that Victor didn't put up a fight. He planned to take the repulsive gnome and throw it into the nearest pond. He saw nothing wrong in this murderous kidnap attempt. He was a dog. He knew the fate of unwanted litters.

246

He had dragged the baby from the bedroom and was trying to work out a method of rolling the burden downstairs when Baxter and the Mothers came running into the house. They glanced up at the dog and the burbling baby and all together they started to scream. Einstein crouched at the top of the stairs and snarled down at them.

He watched Baxter move, very slowly, to the staircase and clutch at the banister for support. She seemed to glide forward, floating on air, and a strange light came into her eye. He recognised that light. It had shone in the eyes of the waiters in the kitchen of the Trumpet Hotel when they'd found him curled in a corner with Arnold's hand in his mouth. It was cold, malicious and full of murder.

He stopped snarling and folded his ears. He shifted his position slightly and pretended to study the opposite wall, as if he hadn't noticed the baby caught in his paws.

Baxter was barely an arm's length away and he was about to launch himself over her head and into the arms of the waiting Mothers, when she stopped her advance and squatted down on the stairs.

'Good doggie,' she whispered. Her voice sounded cracked and dry. 'Good doggie.' She held out her hand. Her fingers were shaking. 'No one is going to hurt you.'

He gulped and slapped his nose with his tongue.

'Don't move,' she whispered as her fingers grazed his whiskers. 'Stay there.' And she bared her teeth in a ghoulish grin.

Her fingers snapped at his throat and he vaulted over the banister. He yelped as he hit the floor, sprang to his feet and scuttled towards the front door.

'I'll kill it!' Baxter screeched. 'I'll kill it!'

One of the Mothers kicked out at the dog and very nearly cracked his skull. He whistled with pain and fell in a heap. He lay there, dazed and trembling, while the others ran forward to trample him.

'Don't let it get away!' Baxter shouted as she came running down the stairs with the baby in her arms.

'Someone fetch some rope!' one of the Mothers cried, snorting like a buffalo.

'Hit it with something!'

'Get the animal into a sack!'

Trapped in a circle of kicking legs, Einstein surrendered, quivered, whimpered and died. He closed his eyes and his jaw fell slack. He tongue unrolled on the floor.

'I think it's dead,' the Mother in the Hans Christian Anderson smock said with satisfaction. She poked him cautiously with her shoe. 'It must have thrown a fit or something.'

The Mothers looked rather disappointed and turned their attentions to the infant who, exhausted by so much excitement, had puked down his vest and fallen asleep. While they simpered at the sodden blanket, Einstein seized the advantage, sprang back to life and shot through the open door.

The garden was ruined. The bulldozer was cutting a trench around the house, churning the turf into thick coils of mud, smashing down shrubs and hedges. The driver, stripped to the waist, his body streaked darkly with mud, saw the mongrel dart through the garden, threw back his head and laughed. He'd expected a rampaging Rottweiler or a team of bone-brained Dobermans.

Einstein scrambled across the battlefield, through a tangle of roots and the choking haze of diesel fumes, towards the summerhouse. Behind him he could hear Baxter running in pursuit and the Mothers shouting for revenge.

58.

Charlie, retreated into the summerhouse, was crawling under the makeshift bed. He wasn't seeking a hiding place among the scraps of food and the cobwebs. He was searching for his old metal cash-box.

The battered black box had lain undisturbed for many years at the back of a bedroom wardrobe. Baxter, if she had noticed its existence, had never expressed curiosity about its history or contents. When Charlie had taken up residence in the garden, the box had followed him.

He prised open the lid to reveal a few yellow newspaper clippings announcing the opening of the Church Street Gallery; thirty small nude studies of Baxter, completed during the days of their courtship, watercolour, charcoal and pencil; the only letter she had ever written to him, green ink on perfumed paper, declaring everlasting love; an unframed photograph of his mother as a young woman standing in her father's grocery shop, a bundle of *Skirt Lifter* magazines, a woman's shoe and a .380 Beretta automatic.

The weapon felt clumsy and cold in his hands. His father had kept the gun, hidden away in the barber's shop, as a defence against intruders. It was heavier than he expected and he wasn't sure how to use it.

There were voices shouting from the house and Baxter stood panting at the summerhouse door. She glared around the room. During the chase across the garden she seemed to have grown taller and more terrible, like an uncorked genie, her body inflated with rage. Her hair had been blown into wild tufts that stood from her scalp like a head-dress of feathers and her mud-stained dress was splitting its seams.

The sight made the fugitive Einstein whimper and cringe beneath an armchair.

'Get up and get out!' she shouted at Charlie and her wattle shivered with indignation.

Charlie looked at his wife and said nothing. His eyes were empty. His face was a scratched and bloody mask.

'Are you listening?' Baxter shouted. 'We're finished! I've had enough of you!' She waved her arms and clenched her fists. Her breasts heaved like barrels on a tossing sea.

Einstein squeezed out a bloodchilling howl, poked his head from beneath the chair and snapped at Baxter's ankles. Baxter yelped and kicked back at him.

'Leave him alone,' Charlie said softly. He lurched forward with the gun in his hand. His feet felt heavy, dragging against him.

'What the hell is that?' Baxter demanded. She was looking at the Beretta but she didn't believe her eyes. 'What is it?'

Charlie wasn't listening. He had more urgent business. She tried to hold him back but he somehow pushed past her and staggered onto the wooden veranda.

The bulldozer was turning in clanking circles, its rusty tracks throwing out sprays of wet gravel, its shining blade cutting a trench through the garden. The driver glanced at Charlie from the safety of his cab, shook his head and bellowed with laughter. What a fugging performer. He didn't know when he was beaten.

'Switch off the engine!' Charlie shouted at him.

The driver took time to peer down at Charlie, caught sight of the weapon and scowled. 'Drop that gun, you fugging lunatic!' What a fugging lunatic. He'd found himself a fugging shooter.

'Switch off the engine! I'll shoot. I swear I'm going to shoot!'

'Fug you!' the driver yelled. He swung the bulldozer around in a cloud of diesel smoke and rumbled towards the summerhouse.

Charlie watched the heavy machine accelerate towards the veranda. A group of Mothers were running forward, spilling from the safety of the house, shouting and screaming for Baxter. The air was filled with smoke. The ground vibrated beneath him.

Charlie raised the Beretta, took careful aim at the face behind the mud-splattered windshield, braced himself and squeezed the trigger.

59.

'Is that it?' the Deep Time Mariner asked him.

'That's it,' Charlie whispered.

'What happened?'

'Nothing,' Charlie said. 'The gun wouldn't fire. I don't suppose it was even loaded. I stood there pulling on the trigger as the bulldozer hit the veranda and made the summerhouse capsize. The whole damned building blew apart, the walls burst and the roof came down.'

After that terrible morning he had taken Einstein and fled the ruined garden, driven away by Baxter and the Militant Mothers. He'd been too proud to ask Fat Harry for help, so he'd picked these gloomy rented rooms and settled down to salvage what remained of his life. He knew he'd been wasting his time. He knew that he'd made some big mistakes. His life, to that moment, had been a rapid downhill struggle. But everything was going to change. He'd found himself work cleaning tables at a Haughty Hamburger Restaurant™ and as soon as he'd saved a little money he was going to travel, he was going out to explore the world. He didn't know that the world wouldn't wait for him.

'This little life!' the Mariner hissed in disgust. 'The planet trembles on the edge of disaster and this is all you have to show me?'

'What did you expect?' Einstein growled fiercely. 'Did you hope to lay all the sins of the world at his feet? The world is made of men like him, scratching a living, marking time, regretting the past, dreading the future, all of them clinging to little lives of quiet desperation.'

Miles Gibson

The ghost of Charlie's mother came floating through the back of a chair. She had found her missing shoe. She skipped lightly across the room, smiling a secret smile, and embraced the ghost of the barber who had just emerged with his arms outstretched, through a bulge in the opposite wall; and together they vanished, hand in hand, dancing down through the garlands of roses in Charlie's threadbare carpet.

Einstein, suddenly maddened by the pressure of the barometer in his skull, began to bark and run in circles. The storm had returned to crush the city. The sky swept down like a boiling ocean, breaking in waves against the buildings, bending windows, squirting through keyholes, drenching attics and swamping cellars. Flagstones buckled and walls were collapsing. Asphalt and stone broke like icing sugar. The furniture, floating through basement windows, was shipwrecked in the foaming streets. Alarm bells clattered, sirens wailed, horns were blaring and men were shouting.

Beneath the city the sewers exploded, rattling all the manhole covers until at last with a deafening roar, they were borne aloft like dinner plates on spouts of sour brown gravy. Along parades and avenues, through every wretched street and alley, the underworld threw up jets of turds that jumped like ornamental fountains.

'I don't like the look of this weather,' the Mariner said, tearing at the ivy to peer through the shivering window.

After the flood came the fire. Gas pipes, loose in the oozing clay, began to rupture, fuel tanks fractured and started to burn, electrical circuits were snorting sparks. For a hundred miles the cars, trucks, buses and squads of emergency vehicles, trapped in a terminal gridlock, were promptly abandoned by their screaming drivers as fires broke out all around them.

A chemical warehouse caught alight and silently spread a blanket of poison over the northern suburbs. To the east and the west gas explosions ripped up streets and brought down terraces of houses.

Somewhere in the south of the city, in a painted house behind a tall security fence, the wife of Ambrose Pangloss burst into flames inside her life support machine. The conflagration triggered all the fire doors and sprinkler systems, trapping Ambrose in his study and drenching him with rusty water. When he broke down the door to reach his wife's bedroom, it was too late. The love of his life had turned to ashes inside her steel and glass coffin.

'Is it time?' Charlie cried, gazing down on the flooding world. The force of the storm had sucked out a row of shopfront windows. At the far corner of the street, two men were attempting to paddle a raft upstream towards a blown-out grocery shop. The raft had been made by lashing together some wooden packing crates. The sailors were stealing everything they could snatch, loading their boat with a random cargo of bottles and boxes. You had to admire their spirit. They had less than four minutes left of their lives and they were out there shopping for luxuries. They were fighting with a carton containing a hundred tubes of spearmint flavour Plaque-Buster™ toothpaste when the raft buckled and sank beneath them. They called out and waved their arms, swept away in a rushing torrent of rain and mud.

'Time?' the Deep Time Mariner growled, turning abruptly and knocking Charlie to the floor. 'Time? It's time I was gone!'

'Is this how it ends?' Charlie shouted.

'I've no idea,' the Mariner said impatiently. 'It's your planet. It's your funeral.'

'No!' Charlie shouted. 'You can't leave me here. I don't believe this is happening.'

'Another dream!' Einstein barked, creeping behind his master's legs. 'Tell me it's another dream.'

'The time for dreams is passed,' the Mariner said. 'This is the end of dreams.'

'It can't be too late,' Charlie said. 'It's never too late. There's always a chance.'

'It's too late for the Antarctic wolf and the Atlas bear,' the Deep Time Mariner shouted. 'It's too late for the Barbary lion and Arabian ostrich. There's no hope for the Caribbean monk seal and the Mauritian giant tortoise. No chance left for the Guadeloupe storm petrel and the Madagascar serpent eagle, the elephant bird and the passenger pigeon, the sea cow and the ocean mink, the Bali tiger and Eskimo curlew. So don't ask me for any favours, monkey-man!'

'There's nothing to be done?' Charlie said.

'Nothing,' the Mariner said mildly. 'Consider yourselves a vanishing species.' He pulled the pistol from his flying suit and carefully checked the compression chamber. He had instructions to employ whatever force he felt necessary to allow him to complete his mission. There was still enough power in his sedative gun to knock down a full-grown rhinoceros.

'There's one last word of advice,' he said, slapping his pockets and turning to Charlie as if he'd forgotten something.

'Yes,' Charlie said eagerly. 'Yes.'

'Be nice to each other,' the Deep Time Mariner said. 'Talk to your dog.'

'Is that it?' Charlie shrieked.

60.

At that moment the ghost of Fat Harry came plummeting through the ceiling. He had come straight from an air disaster in mid-Atlantic. He was baffled and confused by the interruption in his journey. He was wearing a pair of one-size airline slippers and holding a Super-Executive breakfast menu card in his hand.

'Am I dead, Charlie?' he wheezed as he hit the floor.

Charlie jumped back in surprise, peered up at the ceiling and nodded his head at the corpulent phantom.

'Bugger it!' Fat Harry said, staring mournfully at the menu. 'I was going to have the deluxe breakfast.'

He had been flying to New York for his latest, and most important, one-man exhibition at the Andy Warhol Museum of Everyday Life when the aircraft had hit a freak storm five hundred and forty miles across the Atlantic.

He should not have died. He should not have been locked in that doomed aircraft. He was booked to catch an earlier flight but once he had packed and was ready to ride to the airport, he'd had a vague, uneasy feeling that something was missing. He checked his tickets and passport, wallet and fly buttons. Nothing was out of place. But the feeling continued to trouble him until he'd realised what he'd forgotten. He hadn't told Charlie! He couldn't leave without calling him. He wanted Charlie to know all about the big exhibition and feel pleased and excited for him. He still thought of Charlie as his friend. So he put down his suitcase and pulled the phone from his jacket pocket.

The phone seemed to ring for a long time and, when it was finally answered, an unknown voice had challenged him.

'Who are you?' Patch Armstrong said suspiciously. His voice sounded familiar but then, she had known a great number of men and she couldn't tell one from another. 'If this is a dirty phone call, I'm warning you now, I'm holding a night-attack alarm. One false move and I'll burst your eardrums.'

'Harry!' Harry said. 'It's Harry. Can I speak to Charlie?'

There was a long pause, a brief scuffle, and then he heard Baxter's stinging voice.

'Do you know the time?' she shouted. 'It's five o'clock in the morning. There are little children in this house who need to sleep. What the hell is wrong with you? Do you want to stunt their growth? Are you sick in the head or what?'

'Hello, Baxter,' Harry said cheerfully. 'It's Harry. Harry Prampolini. You remember me.'

'I'm trying to forget!' Baxter snapped. Fat Harry the circus freak with his cheap jokes and swaggering walk and greasy grin and one-man shows at every important museum in Europe. Fat Harry the tattooed toad with his ridiculous pink silk suits and crocodile shoes and his big cigars and his work included in the Tate gallery's exhibition of Post-Nuclear Art. There seemed so much of him to forget.

'Can I speak to Charlie?'

'He's not here.'

'But it's five o'clock in the morning.'

'He's still not here.'

'Do you know where he's gone?' Harry said. 'It's important that I talk to him. Is he at the office or something? Has he gone away on a business trip?

'Search me,' Baxter said.

Fat Harry might have considered it if he hadn't been so pressed for time. 'But you're married to him,' he grumbled. Why did she always want to play games? There was something deeply disturbed about Baxter. 'Don't give me all this horseshit. I've got to catch a plane.'

'Don't let me stop you,' Baxter said.

'Will you give him a message?'

'Run your own errands!'

'What's that supposed to mean?'

'We threw him out!' Baxter exploded. 'I don't know and I really don't care where the bastard has gone. He's no longer my husband or the father of my child. He's finished. He's nothing. If you want to find him, try looking under a stone!'

And she slammed the phone and burst into tears.

Harry continued to hold the phone against his ear for a few moments, listening to nothing. His first thought, once he'd made sense of Baxter's bulletin, was to ring again and offer his own opinions about the marriage and her skills as a wife and mother. But there was no time for a shouting match. It was impossible.

He rode to the airport feeling bad, lost his coat and missed his flight. He sat in the Super-Executive lounge drinking endless cups of black coffee while they searched for the coat and found him a seat on another plane. Why did they build these airports to look like cheap hotels? A wasteland of self-service snackeries, industrial carpet and shopping arcades. There were plastic plants potted in concrete blocks and chairs bolted into the floor as if they feared madmen would steal them. The coffee began to turn sour in his stomach and the neon strips burned his eyes.

He didn't recover his spirits until he was soaring over the Atlantic and the smell of breakfast had started to drift from the galleys. He accepted a glass or two of champagne and felt his good humour return as he settled down to wait for his breakfast tray.

But breakfast would never be served.

Miles Gibson

The storm was a funnel of darkness, reaching up through the banks of cloud, like a cobra drawn from a basket. As they approached, the funnel became a violent whirlpool of smoke and soot and human debris that seemed to suck them into its throat. The big Boeing bucked and yawed as the pilot lost the controls and they descended, down through a maelstrom of lampshades, knitting needles, telephones, electric toasters, forks, spoons, frying pans, beer cans, bamboo chairs, spectacles, gloves and artificial limbs. The four engines stopped and in the silence everyone screamed.

The flight attendant who had been serving Harry with his third glass of champagne was suddenly called away and catapulted to the tail section where she became violently attached to the ceiling, crawling around on her hands and knees, sobbing and pleading with God to set her back on her feet again. But God couldn't hear her through the commotion.

The aircraft broke up before it hit the water. As it plunged through the clouds its tail broke away, tore a great hole in the tourist cabin and sprayed all the passengers into the sky.

Fat Harry was sucked from his seat and perched on a cushion of freezing air. All around him men and women were performing cartwheels and somersaults. A woman tumbled past him with her skirts blown over her head. She paddled at the air with her feet and stretched out her arms like wings. A long string of amber beads, spun from frozen droplets of urine, trailed from her legs like a spider's thread. A naked man hung upside down with a briefcase clasped against his chest. His false teeth had been knocked from his astonished mouth and he kept pecking at them with his nose as they floated before his face. Fat Harry laughed and closed his eyes and there was darkness and then silence and nothing more until he came melting through Charlie's ceiling.

61.

It was a fast and easy death compared to the fate of Baxter, who would die in the arms of Patch Armstrong as they lay together in the bottom of a Tesco freezer.

As the storm knocked down power lines and washed away the roads, the Mothers would find themselves increasingly isolated from the world. At first they were content to barricade the house against the rumours of rapists and raiders but gradually, with the passing of the days, they would forget their fear of bandits and hope for the sight of a search party armed with bales of emergency rations.

The TV and radio would be dead, the phones would no longer work and the heating system would fail. There would be no lights. There would be no refrigeration. The kitchen would be a museum of impotent machines without the strength between them to brew coffee or make toast. The water that oozed from the taps would be dark and as thick as blood.

'If they're not going to help defenceless women and children, we've got to go out there and help ourselves,' Patch Armstrong would announce one morning, as the Mothers huddled around a fire they'd make from the nursery furniture. 'We'll go out there and fetch back our own supplies. We need food and fuel and candles and soap and batteries for the radio and more blankets and pillows and God knows what else.' She would look excited and confident, as if she were planning a camping trip.

'The roads have been washed away,' Baxter would remind everyone, as she volunteered herself for the task.

'We'll walk,' Patch would reply boldly, clipping a rubber baby blanket over the straps of her dungarees. She would work the blanket into a hood to protect her head from the rain. 'We'll swim. We can't sit here and watch our children starve.'

So they would splash their way from the house, across the concrete perimeter that had once been a garden filled with food, to embark upon their dangerous mission. Only when they had reached the gates would they discover the full extent of the destruction. The roads would be rivers of mud, blocked by trees and the wreckage of cars and fallen buildings.

Three hundred yards from the house, exhausted, cold and drowning in mud, they would be rescued by the driver of an army truck who would promise to take them as far as the nearest Shoppers Paradise™. He would tell them about the curfews, the rationing and the problems in the military hospitals.

'They've evacuated London. Thousands and thousands killed in the flood. They say it's worse than a war. You shouldn't be here. You should be at one of the district camps. They're giving out identity cards and emergency ration books. No coupons – no food. Have you had your vaccinations?'

Patch and Baxter would shake their heads and glance at one another and wonder what he was talking about.

'You need your vaccinations. They reckon there's cholera in the camps. They're digging graves like there's no tomorrow.'

The women would listen but not believe him. He only half-believed it himself. It seemed impossible, even then, that the world was coming to an end. Something would happen to save them.

It would have to be a miracle.

The truck would dump them a little distance from a super-market set in a glistening lake of mud and screened by a collapsing wall of sandbags. A capsized train of supermarket trolleys lay half-submerged in the mud like the spine of a skeleton dragon.

'It's no good,' the driver would warn them. 'All the food

belongs to the army. You'll have to get yourselves ration books. It's a tin of fruit, an ounce of tea and kiss goodbye to the milk and sugar.'

'Are you kidding?' Patch Armstrong would ask him, as she splashed down from the truck. 'We've got little children to feed. That's more important than ration books. They'll have to make a special effort. We want orange juice and eggs and banana cake and SugarFrosties™ and peanut butter and chocolate pudding and all kinds of stuff.'

'Good luck!' the driver would laugh as he drove away through the gathering twilight.

The supermarket doors would be chained and guarded by dogs and soldiers. The building itself would be dark and its windows protected by massive iron shutters.

'We could bargain with the guards,' Patch would suggest to Baxter as they crouched in the shelter of the sandbags.

'We can't bargain with anyone unless they take Visa™ or American Express™,' Baxter would reply. 'I forgot to bring my cheque book.'

'Forget the plastic. They'll do anything for a knee-trembler,' Patch would declare, pulling at the rubber blanket and trying to squeeze the mud from her hair. 'They're soldiers.'

Baxter would have to persuade Patch that this was a bad idea. Despite her considerable size and strength, even Patch wasn't big enough to tackle six soldiers and their dogs.

'I'm not going out there alone,' Patch would snort when Baxter expressed this concern for her safety. 'We're doing this together. You can do that little guy and I'll do the one standing next to him.'

'I can't do anyone!' Baxter would be horrified. She'd peep at her miserable khaki rapists, huddled together beside an oil drum fire, and know that she was destined to starve.

'Think of Victor. You're making this sacrifice for him. It won't take long and they'll probably settle for hand relief.'

'The thought of it makes me want to be sick,' Baxter would say as she turned to leave and struggle for home.

'Do you have a better idea?'

Baxter would already have regrets about volunteering for this crazy campaign. Nothing had been planned. Nothing had been known about the hardships that might confront them. They had no idea how they would transport their supplies, even if they could find them. Finally she would convince Patch that they should, at least, search for a breach in the store's defences before they surrendered themselves to the soldiers.

It would be raining, a freezing black rain, as they crept past the guards towards the back of the building. And there, to Baxter's great relief, they would find an unlocked door that would lead them into a corridor and up a flight of concrete stairs. But they would follow the stairs into the roof of the building only to find themselves trapped among the girders and cables that supported the supermarket ceiling.

Beneath this ceiling they could imagine shelves still loaded with spinach and spuds, apples and grapefruits, fancy cakes and sliced loaves, pork chops and lamb cutlets. They wouldn't know they were wasting their time. The supermarkets would be empty. The soldiers would be guarding them because they'd have orders to protect any building that might be used as a mortuary.

'Where do we go from here?' Patch would ask in despair as she tried to stare through the darkness. She could have debauched a soldier and be stuffing the pockets of her dungarees with slabs of hazelnut chocolate.

'There must be a way down through one of the ventilators or something,' Baxter would reply as she started to crawl across the ceiling.

Einstein

And so their hunger would drive them out across the treacherous girders in search of a loose panel among the dead lights and ventilators. They would shuffle forward, inch by inch, like terrified tightrope walkers, until they found a spyhole in the brittle plasterboard.

'I can't do it,' Patch would whisper, as they knelt down to peer into the gloom of the ransacked store. 'If we jump from here we're going to break… '

These would be the last words she uttered because, at that moment, the ceiling would shatter and drop both women forty feet to their deaths in an empty ice cream freezer.

And this was a fast and easy death compared to the fate of the rest of the Mothers who would perish, with their dead children clasped in their arms, from cholera, typhoid and malnutrition.

And these were swift and simple deaths compared to the fate of Ambrose Pangloss who would suffocate, alone, in the absolute silence of the presidential lift, trapped between floors in the empty Pangloss Building. While he had the strength he would scream for help but no one would pay him any attention. He would scratch and claw at the stainless steel tomb. He would shrivel and shrink and, in the agony of dying, find himself gazing at the Gates of Heaven.

His final words would be: 'I can see God! He's a Rhode Island Red!'

62.

Fat Harry sat up and brushed at his sleeve. He was wearing a torn silk jacket with a carnation in the buttonhole. He tried to adjust the bent flower by poking it with his thumb.

'Who are you?' he said, cocking his head and staring at the Deep Time Mariner.

'He's a Mariner,' Einstein said, creeping forward to sniff at the ghost. He caught the smell of the cold Atlantic, Super Executive cologne and burning aviation fuel.

'Hello! A talking dog!' Fat Harry said. He beamed with pleasure. 'I hope he doesn't want breakfast.' And he raised his arm slightly, curling his fingers, searching for the call button in his phantom seat.

'Don't speak,' Charlie said, with his eyes blinded by tears. 'There's been a terrible...'

'It's a real tonic to see you again!' the ghost said, grinning at Charlie. 'I wanted to talk to you before I left. I'm flying to New York – all expenses paid. They're going to hang me in the Andy Warhol Museum of Whatsit. You've got to laugh. They think I'm a sodding genius.'

'You deserve it, Harry,' Charlie said gently. 'You worked hard for it.'

'Why don't you come with me?' Harry prattled. 'I heard about your troubles with Baxter. Bad business. Why don't you come aboard? They're just serving breakfast. I'm having the deluxe special...'

'Don't speak.'

'We could have some fun – it would be like the good old days. We had some fun, didn't we, Charlie?'

'We had some fun,' Charlie said.

Harry fell silent and frowned suspiciously at his shoes. 'That's funny,' he said. 'I can't feel my legs...'

Charlie reached out for him but Harry was peacefully fading away. It began with his hands and feet, spreading rapidly through his limbs until there was nothing left of him but his teeth and the buttonhole, hanging in the air for a moment, until they also disappeared.

Charlie knelt on the floor and pressed his hands against the carpet.

'Harry,' he whispered. 'Harry.'

The Deep Time Mariner grunted, turned on his heel and vanished through the door.

'He's gone!' Einstein whistled, tilting his ears.

Charlie stood up and looked around him. The room was empty. He was alone.

A moment later the Mariner burst back into the room and waved his pistol at Charlie. 'Blast your eyes!' he shouted. 'Bring the dog and I'll take you with me!'

Damn the paperwork! Damn his instructions! What could they do to him? They could send him on a frog hunt to Ursa Major – that's what they could do to him. He wasn't going to think about it. He didn't care about the risks. He'd grown fond of Charlie. He was a monkey-man, it was true, but he also had spirit and a love for the Ancient Gardeners. They could find him some work on the ark. What harm could there be in it? What danger was a single specimen without the prospect of a mate? They weren't criminals. The text books were wrong. They were clowns. That was their strength and their tragedy.

'There's no future for you!' he bellowed, above the roar of a gas explosion. The windows bulged and finally shattered, covering Einstein with fragments of glass and thick, wet cactus slices.

The curtains blew out to embrace the rain.

'I don't care,' Charlie said, wiping his eyes and scrambling to his feet. 'We'll take our chances.'

'You're such a fool!' Einstein growled scornfully, shaking the glass from his coat. 'Think what you're doing!'

'I'm trying to keep us alive.'

'Why?' Einstein demanded. 'Do you want us to finish our lives in a cage in some god-forsaken zoo?'

'We can't stay here!'

'We'll finish as prisoners in a freak show beyond the stars' Einstein grumbled.

'We'll be corpses in the rubble if we stay here arguing about it, you stupid stubborn animal!'

'Shut up and get moving!' the Mariner roared.

63.

They followed the Mariner from the apartment, along the narrow passage to a door marked Emergency Exit. A broken padlock hung from a chain. The Mariner kicked the door open, bowed his head against the storm and clambered onto the fire escape.

'Follow!' he shouted as Charlie and Einstein watched him ascend the spiral of iron stairs.

The little dog whimpered and looked at Charlie. The treacherous staircase was rocked by wind and slippery with rain.

'I can't do it!' he barked.

Charlie gathered him into his arms and staggered after the Mariner. The rain stung his face. His bare feet were chilled on the iron rungs.

As they climbed towards the roof they saw fires burning across the city, the cords of black smoke strung between heaven and earth like fantastic mooring ropes. The wind bore a mad cacophony of alarm bells, whistles and air raid sirens.

'Follow!' the Mariner bellowed, as Charlie sank beneath the dog's weight and he grasped at the railings for support.

When he reached the top of the fire escape he paused, fighting for breath, and stared out across the concrete roof towards the chimney stacks and the whipping television masts. There, partly sheltered by the stacks, was the Deep Time Mariner's spacecraft.

At a distance, the main body of the craft looked like a stranded submarine, some nine or ten metres in length and three metres high, with a strange, translucent blister, like a conning tower, amidships. The hull was wrapped in a sheath of polished blue scales that reflected the ship's surroundings as perfectly as mirrored glass.

As Charlie drew closer he saw that the ship was supported on eight hydraulic legs which had clawed themselves against the roof of the building and gave the machine the attitude of a crouching spider, preparing to pounce on her prey. Between her legs, protruding from the polished belly, was a pod of surveillance equipment and navigation lights.

She was a primitive vehicle, by the standards of the Deep Time Mariners, a Swordfish class freighter designed for coastal work among the moons of the Cyclops Cluster and refitted for the emergency evacuation of Earth. She had already completed fifteen missions and was responsible for the future survival of several species of antelope, two giant lizards, the elk and the polar bear.

When the Mariner approached the ship the cargo doors swung open and he beckoned Charlie and Einstein aboard.

The flight cabin was dark and stifling. At the back of the cabin, confirming Einstein's worst suspicions, was a large and heavily armoured cage equipped with harnesses and hammocks and still smelling strongly of polar bears.

The Mariner settled down in the pilot's seat, sighed and peeled off his gloves. He flexed his graceful green fingers and studied the instrument panels, murmuring to himself in a strange language and gently shaking his huge head.

'Is there something wrong?' Charlie whispered.

The silence was startling. The ship had locked out the noise of the storm, the screeching wind and rain. They were locked in an airtight cocoon. Buried in a vampire's coffin.

'Shut up!' Einstein snapped, as he tried to worm his way under a seat. 'It's bad enough without you looking for trouble.'

'It feels warm in here,' the Mariner replied, frowning at Charlie. 'Does it feel warm in here?'

'Yes,' Charlie said, through chattering teeth. The sudden change in temperature was making his wet hair steam.

'There must be a snag in the air conditioning lines,' the Mariner said. He shrugged. 'I suppose it will sort itself out.'

'Is there anything I should know?' Charlie said nervously. 'Do I have to strap myself down?'

'No,' the Mariner said. 'Just make yourselves comfortable, keep quiet and don't touch anything.'

'Right!' Charlie said. He sank deeper into his seat and sat motionless, clutching his knees.

'Are you ready?' the Mariner said.

Charlie nodded grimly, his face as white as starch. Einstein whimpered and folded his ears.

The Mariner tapped a tune on a keyboard and the flight deck computers stirred in their sleep, yawned and opened their beautiful eyes. At once the dark cabin was transformed into a dome of glittering lights. A monitor in the overhead switch panel shuffled through all the maps of the heavens, selected the relevant galaxy, found Charlie's little solar system and drew up a plan of the Earth.

'This is it,' the Mariner said, smiling softly to himself.

Charlie rolled into a ball, clenched his hands around his head and screwed up his eyes, waiting for the thrust of huge engines to thump him into the cabin floor. He expected a roll of thunder, a belch of dragons' fire, the crunching and grinding of metal bones. But nothing seemed to happen. They were already two hundred feet above the rooftops before Charlie knew they were launched into space. He glanced down at the city as it retreated beneath them. There was a slight shudder as the legs of the Swordfish retracted and locked themselves away. The ship pitched to starboard, hung motionless for a moment, and then catapulted into the eye of the storm.

64.

They broke through the darkness into a dazzling sunlit haze where millions of fragments of human wreckage were hanging suspended like flotsam in a crystal sea. They were flying through great drifts of handbags, walking sticks, saucepans, library books, lampshades and shoes. Beside them a twisted bicycle was performing a series of somersaults for an audience of spanners. Above them, thousands of empty hamburger boxes circled like flocks of scavenging gulls.

Charlie cupped his hands around his face, shielding his eyes from the sun and searched for the world that had disappeared beneath the poisonous layers of cloud.

'Can you see anything?' Einstein said, perching on Charlie's knees to gain a better view from the windows.

'Nothing,' Charlie said. The storms had buried Europe, from the Baltic to the Adriatic. He turned to the Mariner but found him absorbed in conversation with one of the ship's computers, planning the height of their orbit and the speed of their final ascent.

For a few minutes they continued to sail towards the sun, the Earth shrinking and curving beneath them, until they had passed beyond the storms and the clouds began to evaporate. Then Charlie looked down and saw the Nile, like a serpent glittering in the light, twisting towards the sulphurous smog that shrouded the city of Cairo. He was so excited that he cried out and hauled Einstein forward by his collar but the river had gone, they had crossed the Red Sea, and now they were looking down on the deserts of Arabia, set like splashes of molten silver in the folds of ancient mountains.

Einstein

As they watched, the Himalayas came into view on the port bow, that great wall of terror reduced to a shimmering bracelet of bronze, gilded with snowfields and glaciers. The ship tilted, turned south, south east, over the smoking plains of India towards the Bay of Bengal and Charlie, who had seen no greater natural wonder than the mudbanks of the Thames, was bent to the window, astonished.

London might have been lost in a whirlpool of fire and rain and, for all he knew, half of Europe was engulfed, but here was the rest of the planet drenched in sunlight, unfolding like a magic atlas of mountains, rivers and forests.

'It's beautiful,' Charlie whispered. 'I never imagined how beautiful!'

'You sound surprised,' the Mariner said.

'But I never saw it from here… ' Charlie said.

'It's not a very big planet,' the Mariner said. 'You could have walked around it in your time. You were never more than a visitor. You should have gone out and seen the sights.'

'I wanted to travel. I never had the opportunity,' Charlie said. 'I had to find work and earn a living and keep my house in order. I had to play my part.'

'Stuff and nonsense,' Einstein snorted. But he was a dog.

'I never knew a planet that didn't look good when you were waving it goodbye,' the Mariner said, to comfort him.

And then Charlie remembered one perfect summer morning, years before, when he'd woken early and gone down from the summerhouse into the stillness of the garden and walked, barefoot, through the prickling grass, with the air still sweet with the smell of night flowers and the sunlight gleaming through the trees like the first morning in the world and then the blackbirds had started singing as if they were trying to break his heart. He had felt himself tremble with laughter, with pleasure, with fear at the terrible beauty of life.

'I can't leave,' he said softly. 'I must have been mad. It's impossible. I don't belong on Mars.'

'We're not staying on Mars,' Einstein said impatiently. He felt sick and his ears were ringing. Space travel didn't agree with him. 'We're on a voyage beyond the stars.'

'It's too late,' the Mariner said, glancing at the rows of monitors on the overhead switch panel. 'I've programmed the master computer.'

'I need you to set me down!' Charlie cried. He was a fool to have thought that he could ever want to escape the Earth or not be a part of its ultimate fate. He would rather suffer the catastrophes that threatened to overwhelm the world than live with the knowledge that the world was gone.

Why should he alone survive to mourn the Earth? If he stayed with the Deep Time Mariner he would shrink away through the cold and lonely wastes of space until he was nothing more than a fragment of bone, a crystal of ice, an echo of an echo from a distant, dead planet. He knew he could not endure it.

'Think!' the Deep Time Mariner shouted. 'I'm offering you survival. I'm saving your life. You are the final paragraph on the last page of history. Imagine that. After you there is only darkness.'

'No!' Charlie shouted. 'I belong down there on Earth. I don't want to survive if it means nothing more than becoming a freak show attraction.'

'You won't be seen as a freak!' the Mariner said indignantly. 'We're a very superior civilisation. When we've sorted out the paperwork and squeezed you through quarantine regulations perhaps I'll take you home with me. My father once kept a monkey. I think it was a Yellow Cyclops Howler.'

'I want to go back to Earth!' Charlie insisted.

'You'll die if you return,' the Mariner warned.

Einstein

'I'll die if I leave.'

'That's true,' the Mariner said. 'But you'll finish your days in comfort and civilised company. We could even extend your life. You'd live for another two hundred years with a little corrective surgery. You'd have time to write an account of your species for the Cyclops Library of Natural Science. You'd be a celebrity.'

Charlie didn't hear him. He stared down from his armchair in the sky and he thought of those who were turned to ghosts and those who were ghosts to come: the few brief weeks of happiness in the attic over the barber's shop and all those long and dreary years of quiet desperation; and if he could have his time again he would have none of it, he would have none of its smothering ugliness and monstrous cruelties, but go out into the precious world, or what was left of it, and plant his feet against the earth and turn his face towards the sun and feel the cool rain against his skin and the wind pulling his hair and be glad, for one moment, to be alive.

'And you?' the Mariner said, turning to Einstein. 'Will you crawl back to your hole in the ground or will you come with me and fly to the stars?'

The sun was already behind them now and the night was stealing over the curve of the planet.

'I have to stay with Charlie,' Einstein said, slapping his nose with his tongue. 'I have to stay with him. I'm a dog.'

The Mariner sighed and then, without warning, began to take them down towards the jungles of Borneo, clipping the coast of Vietnam and gliding over the South China Sea towards the islands of the Pacific. It grew darker as they descended until the night was all around them and the ocean shone with a ghostly phosphorescence.

They flew over a string of islands that seemed at first no more than outcrops of coral breaking the surface of the deep until, as the Swordfish swooped, they began to assume the fantastic shapes of childhood maps of treasure islands. Here, behind their ship-wrecking reefs, were small lost worlds of beach and forest, water-falls and sleeping volcanoes.

As they circled the largest of the islands, Charlie caught a glimpse of a deep lagoon, canoes drawn under a cluster of palms, the flash of lights from a fishing village.

The spacecraft stretched out its legs and gently came to rest on the beach. The computers muttered to themselves and rolled their jewelled eyes. The monitors bickered as they ransacked themselves for charts of the planet's oceans.

The Mariner threw a switch to release the cargo doors and the cabin was filled with the perfumed warmth of a tropical night. The air was spiced with woodsmoke, incense and jungle flowers. They heard music and laughter from the village and the booming of breakers on the reef.

They clambered down from the ship and stood together on the moonlit sand and above their heads, in the vast darkness, swirled millions and millions of sparkling stars.

Einstein sneezed and ran in circles about the beach, barking for joy and snapping at all the crumpled beer cans and twisted polythene bottles and knots of coloured plastic rope that came tumbling at him through the surf.

Charlie looked at the Mariner and wanted to say what he felt in his heart but found that he could not speak for tears.

'How much time do you think you have left?' the Mariner asked him. He would not look at Charlie but turned his huge head and pretended to study the moon. 'Do you suppose even here, in this last acre of paradise, that the storms will not destroy you, that the parakeets will continue to fly, the dolphins to swim, that everything will continue?'

'I must believe it,' Charlie said.

'And what will you do here?'

'I'll plant a garden,' Charlie said gently. He sat down on an old tractor tyre, half-buried in the coral sand, and looked towards the lights of the village and the shadow of the forest beyond. 'I'll plant a garden if I have time.'

'Choose the high ground,' the Mariner said.

He turned then, without another word between them and walked quickly back to his ship. Charlie and Einstein stood on the shore and watched him take the Swordfish from the beach and over the luminous sea. They watched him sailing into the night, a fleeting shadow against the moon. They stood and watched until there was nothing left of him but a small bead of light that flickered briefly and was gone in the cold eternity of stars.

Down & Out in Shoreditch & Hoxton by Stewart Home

A slice-and-dice splatter novel in which time-travelling streetwalkers hump their way from the trendy east London of today back to the skid row mutilations of the Jack the Ripper era. Amid the psychological dislocations, warm blood isn't the only thing that gets sucked by the night creatures who haunt Home's anti-narrative. This is without doubt the weirdest book ever written, the illegitimate offspring of the Marquis de Sade balling a post-modern literary extremist at at ladies of gangster rap convention.

'A repellent, sick psychodrama that is sadistic, morally reprehensible and has no redeeming features whatsoever. I loved it.'
– Kathy Acker

Judas Pig by 'Horace Silver'

Billy Abrahams is a career criminal who makes a very good living from violence, armed robbery, operating sex shops and stealing from other criminals. But he becomes increasingly haunted by childhood ghosts and by the ever-growing influence of Danny, his psychopathic partner in crime.

Billy finds himself starting to look beyond the violence and the scams, slowly descending into a drug-fuelled netherworld that affects his judgment and his perceptions. He is finally tipped over the edge when Danny commits an act even Billy cannot stomach. And that's when things really start to go wrong...

Judas Pig is the real deal. This explosive first novel from a reformed career criminal comes with authenticity stamped all the way through. Dark and vivid, bleak yet often funny and beautifully written, this is a book that will stay with you long after you turn the final page.

Confessions of a Romantic Pornographer by Maxim Jakubowski

Following the death of a minor league writer, a mysterious woman whose own past is full of contradictions is called in to investigate his life and to discover the lost manuscript of his memoirs, lest they incriminate people in high places.

Her journey of discovery becomes a dazzling and confusing exploration of the nature of autobiography and the awfully grey zones between truth and fiction. With every new revelation come another series of questions.

279

Grief by John B Spencer

'*Grief* is a speed-freak's cocktail, one part Leonard and one part Ellroy,
that goes right to the head.' George P Pelecanos
When disparate individuals collide, it's Grief.
John B Spencer's final and greatest novel.
'Spencer writes the tightest dialogue this side of Elmore Leonard, so
bring on the blood, sweat and beers!' Ian Rankin

No One Gets Hurt by Russell James

'The best of Britain's darker crime writers' – *The Times*
After a friend's murder Kirsty Rice finds herself drawn into the
murky world of call-girls, porn and Internet sex.

Kiss It Away by Carol Anne Davis

'Reminiscent of Ruth Rendell at her darkest' – Booklist (USA)
Steroid dependent Nick arrives alone in Salisbury, rapes a stranger
and brutally murders a woman.
'A gripping tale of skewered psychology... a mighty chiller,'
The Guardian

A Man's Enemies by Bill James

'Bill James can write, and then some' *The Guardian*
The direct sequel to 'Split'. Simon Abelard, the section's 'token black',
has to dissuade Horton from publishing his memoirs.

End of the Line by K T McCaffrey

'KT McCaffrey is an Irish writer to watch' RTE
Emma is celebrating her Journalist of the Year Award when she hears
of the death of priest Father Jack O'Gorman in what appears to have
been a tragic road accident.

Vixen by Ken Bruen

'Ireland's version of Scotland's Ian Rankin' – *Publisher's Weekly*
BRANT IS BACK! If the Squad survives this incendiary installment,
they'll do so with barely a cop left standing.

The Justice Factory by Paul Charles

'If you like Morse you'll love Kennedy' – *Talking Music*, BBC Radio 2.
'Paul Charles is one of the hidden treasures of British crime
fiction.' – John Connolly

Miles Gibson

grew up in Christchurch, Dorset. He was educated at Somerford Junior School and Somerford Secondary Modern (now the Grange) where he failed to make an impression but finished a toast rack in woodwork.

When he left school he wanted to be a painter but joined a Bournemouth advertising agency on the advice of the careers' master who thought advertising was 'something artistic'.

He trained to be an art director by making tea and running errands until he entered a writing competition for university undergraduates organised by a large London agency. They seemed impressed by his qualifications – toast rack first class with honours – and a few months later he was offered a job as a junior copywriter at J Walter Thompson in Berkeley Square.

When he won a *Telegraph Magazine* Young Writer of the Year Award in 1969 he turned his attention to serious writing. For a time he wrote features for the *Telegraph Sunday Magazine*. His first novel *The Sandman* was published in 1984 and since that time he's written a small shelf of books, including works for children. His novel *Kingdom Swann* was adapted for BBC Television as Gentlemen's Relish starring Billy Connolly and Sarah Lancashire.

Miles Gibson is married and lives in London.

The Do-Not Press
Fiercely Independent Publishing

www.thedonotpress.com

All our books are available in good bookshops or –
in the event of difficulty – direct from us:
The Do-Not Press Ltd, Dept EINSTEIN,
16 The Woodlands
London
SE13 6TY
(UK)

If you do not have Internet access you can write to
us at the above address in order to join our mailing
list and receive fairly regular news on new books
and offers. Please mark your card 'No Internet' or
'Luddite'.